Captain Patty

and the

Nameless Navigator

Joan,

Enjoy the story!!

Erin Curry

CAPTAIN PATTY
AND THE
NAMELESS NAVIGATOR

The Adventures of Captain Patty,

Book One

Erin Cruey

Thank You...

To God, the true author of adventure.

To my great-grandma, Ethel: the writer who inspired me. Your love of words and story has been a source of joy in my heart and I hope that this book will reflect the love of adventure and mystery that you had in writing.

Main Characters

The Guests

Charles Wellington, a captain in the British Royal Navy and father to Samantha.

Samantha Wellington, a twelve-year-old colonial girl and only child of Charles.

The Crew of The Smooching Sally

Patrick "Patty" Peterson, captain of *The Smooching Sally* and pirate.

Reuben Gayle, an eleven-year-old pirate and cabin boy.

Hamilton "Hammy" Pye, carpenter of *The Smooching Sally.*

Redmond "Red" Cade, quartermaster of *The Smooching Sally.*

The Trading Post

Louis Guyon, owner of *Louis's Trading Post.*

Ines Guyon, wife to Louis.

The Crew of Revolution's Wrath

Rudiger Bartleby, wanted pirate and captain of *Revolution's Wrath* and admiral of his own fleet.

Bartholomew Severn, first mate to Rudiger Bartleby.

Le Bateau, janitor aboard *Revolution's Wrath.*

Chapter Index

Chapter One:
At the Port of Nassau

Have you ever longed for adventure? The kind that makes your heart beat fast and the blood soar through your veins? The kind that makes you stare danger in the face and gives you such a story to tell afterwards that no matter how many times you tell it, people want to hear it again?

I had an adventure like that, and it changed my life forever.

My name is Samantha, and it all began when it was still summer, in the latter part of August, 1751, during the reign of King George II. I was twelve years of age, moving away from the islands of the Caribbean with my father, Charles Wellington. My father is a captain in His Majesty's Royal Navy and had recently been ordered to the city of Boston in Massachusetts Bay. It was the seventh time we moved in my lifetime, yet it was to be expected as my father was an officer and had to go where the crown ordered him to go. I can't say I was sorry leaving Nassau. Though I loved the beauty of the Caribbean, it was a bit warm for my taste and I was never fond of the annual hurricanes that threatened to blow our house away.

Our things were sold and whatever trinkets we wanted to keep were packed. We were saying farewell to my uncle, Silas, a government official in Nassau, and getting ready to board our ship to Boston. I was walking alongside my governess down one of the city streets following my father and uncle, and it was so hot that I thought the bonnet I wore upon my head would melt. As I tried to get more shade from the palm trees I walked beside of, I complained to my governess, Mrs. Lewisham.

"When are we going to be in Boston?" I asked while panting, the sweat dripping from my face.

"Soon. Very soon, dear," she said sweetly in her thick country accent. I don't know how my governess handled it. She was pregnant, she and her husband George (my father's friend in the navy) had told us some months before, and if I could barely handle the humidity, I could only imagine how she felt.

"Soon isn't soon enough," I said as I wiped my brow with a handkerchief. "I am glad we're leaving now."

"Aye," her husband beside her said with a grin. "And I think your father is glad as well."

If my governess and I had trouble with the heat, my father must have been at war with it. There were three things he always said he hated - slavery, bad character, and having to wear a British officer's wool uniform in the summer. Everywhere he went he always had to wear the blue and white suit of a naval officer. It was wonderful in the winter, but in the summer one felt terribly itchy, sweaty, and overly warm. But I never saw him complain too much about it, for he always said there were things in the world much worse than an uncomfortable coat, and wearing it was a matter of pride for mother England.

We finally stopped at the port we were to board our ship at and said good-bye to my uncle. For me, it was the happiest moment of my life, and I sported a wide grin as I made my farewells.

"Are you sure you can't stay longer, Charles?" my uncle asked my father as he shook his hand. "I don't like you and your family traveling the seas at this time of year, what with the weather and all...and of course, there's the pirates..."

My father gave Uncle Silas a look of disapproval for mentioning pirates. He did not wish to frighten my governess or me. "No, Brother, I'm afraid not." He sighed. "I have much to do in Boston, and I'm afraid my daughter is longing for the cooler temperatures of our new home."

My uncle laughed heartily. "Well, I can't say I blame her for that. The islands are a bit warm for my taste as well, but I suppose if you live here long enough you eventually get used to it."

"I suppose so." My father laughed back.

"Are you sure I can't persuade you to stay longer?" Uncle Silas continued, and I stopped and looked at my father with a begging horror to decline. "After all, my secretary has an amiable sister you should meet. Lovely lady, recently widowed…"

My father's grin faded and he pressed his lips together in a frown. "Silas, we already talked…"

I looked at my uncle, secretly shaking my head. If there was one thing my father didn't want to talk about, it was courting. You see, my mother died on the voyage from London to Philadelphia. I was but a baby, and I think my father never got over her death. He rarely spoke of it, a past too easily haunting for a man so devoted to those he loved.

Any lady our family and friends introduced us to simply remained an acquaintance, and I suppose, like him, I preferred it that way, too. My father deserved someone decent and likable, full of charity and virtue, which is nothing like the ones we had already met. Those ladies were too prim and boring, and to me they always seemed a tad snobby.

"Say no more," Uncle Silas interrupted, waving his hand. "Very well then. Good-bye, Charles!"

I sighed in relief as I continued towards the ship. The brothers embraced warmly, for they expected not to see each other for a while. "Farewell, Silas. I wish I could stay and help you more than I've been able to." My father smiled, tipping his tricorn hat.

"'Tis alright. I shall manage here without you. I admit I will miss you, though, and my darling little niece." My uncle tipped his hat, which lifted his wig, making me giggle.

My governess, her husband, and I curtseyed, and before I knew it we were upon our boat that was to sail for our new home. We entered *The London Mussel* and I sighed at the sight of it.

Our ship was big, but not near as big as some of the ships my father had sailed on. It was a pleasant boat nonetheless, and when I looked upon the deck and sails, I thought of a thousand different ways to explore my surroundings. While my governess and her husband went below deck, my father led me to the front as it began to sail from the port.

"Look at the water, Sam," he said, pointing towards the blue, glass-like sea. "Do you see how clear it is?"

"You can even see the fish swim around," I said, smiling. "They are beautiful."

"You won't see fish like that in Charles Town or Boston for that matter." He laughed. "This colony is a wonder, is it not? It's a shame we have to leave so soon."

"'Tis," I said, staring at the sea in awe. "But at least we get to see new places."

"Very true. It's never a dull moment in a sailor's life."

"Is that why you joined the Royal Navy?"

"One of the reasons," he said, leaning against the rail. "I wanted to see worlds like this."

"I want to be an officer just like you," I said, leaning against the rail like him. "I want to sail and see the places you've seen and more!"

"Well, I don't know if you'd want to be an officer," he said, eyeing me carefully and making sure I wasn't going too far off the rail that would make me fall overboard. "After all, the uniforms are quite uncomfortable in the summer. But if you want to sail and see the world, then you should do it. It would be the adventure of a lifetime."

Little did I realize that my adventure was just about to begin. Days had passed and we were still nowhere near Boston, but Nassau was out of sight. We were surrounded by sea - gallons and gallons of it. But the somewhat calm waters that began our voyage began to disappear. Larger and longer ups and downs filled our minutes and hours and the waves began to pick up. Even I knew to see that much white foam on the waters was not a good sign.

My father, when he took a look at the sea, became quiet, and he told my governess and me to remain in the cabin and stay away from the edges of the ship. My governess became worried and asked him what was the matter, but he reassured her that everything was fine and that he was going to go talk to the captain of our ship. The rest of the passengers shared our concern, and we would soon find out what caused the sea to act so strangely.

The boat began to rock back and forth once again, and my poor governess became seasick. My father was still on deck with the captain doing who knows what, and I knew not when he would be back. It was dark outside, I could tell, and I began to hear a few rumbles that I thought could be thunder. My governess pulled me close and whispered, "Perhaps we should've stayed in the islands a bit longer."

A few minutes passed until my father and George came to the cabin where we were at. "A storm is moving in," George said as he took a cloth and wiped a few drops of rain away from his brow. "Looks like a big one. I declare I haven't seen such clouds in my life!"

"It's nothing to worry about," my father said as he looked at my concerned face. "I've been in plenty of storms before. There have been worse."

"Hmph!" George snorted. "Then you should get a mutiny started, Charles. I think you would know more about navigating this chopped tree better than the imbecile we have now!"

"Your language, George!" my governess scolded. "You're in the presence of children."

"Aurora, what?" George asked in defense. "I'm sure the lass is thinking it too!"

"I have said my peace," my father interrupted, changing the subject. "And I'm sure the captain will listen to my advice. A galleon ship is like any other ship. If he sticks to the basics, we should all be fine."

Suddenly a loud thunder clap was heard. I jumped at the sound of it, running to my father and burying my face into his chest. He held me tight as the boat suddenly gave a violent jerk, tossing a few people from their hammocks and making a few of the younger children cry.

"Sticking to the basics!" George huffed. "That man is sailing us right along with it! I'm going up. Someone ought to make sure he doesn't sink us all!"

"I'm sure the captain knows what he's doing," my father said, but it was too late. George was already stomping up the steps towards the deck and captain, his face red with frustration.

My governess sunk herself back into the bed bunk, too sick to move now that the boat rocked even further. As I held on to my father, he gently took me by the shoulders and faced me to him.

"I need to get Mr. Lewisham," he said, looking towards the deck. "He does no good talking to people who don't have the time for lectures. I need you to stay below deck, Sam. Stay with your governess. Can you do that for me?"

I nodded with a frown, not wanting my father to leave for I was already scared enough.

"That's my brave girl," he said with a smile. "I'll be quick. Don't leave the cabin."

I nodded as I watched him run to the deck and out of my sight. I sighed heavily as I returned to my governess, my face sunken with loneliness as I wished my father was with me.

"Don't worry, my dear," Mrs. Lewisham said as she patted my hand. "We're all in the Lord's hands. We'll be fine. Don't you worry."

I nodded and smiled as she looked up at me.

"Now hand me that chamber pot..." she said, turning green again. "I think I feel dinner coming up."

I fumbled for the pewter bowl and handed it to her before she could get any throw-up on my dress.

A stretch of time had passed and the storm worsened after each minute. Louder and louder the thunder roared and the boat began rocking so much that I expected the ship to turn over any minute. Our cabin brightened from the flashes of lightning as if night had turned into a bright summer day.

I was scared and my governess was of little comfort as she tried to lie down as best she could, a half-full chamber pot clutched in her arms. I heard shouts from the sailors above, yelling something about "port" and "sails." I heard a deckhand mention repairs and lifeboats, and as I was about to start praying for the good Lord to save us like the apostles on that fishing boat, a great crash was felt.

I was knocked from my feet, tumbling to the floor and rolling down the cabin with a dozen food kegs and luggage. What few candles for light flickered out, and as I lifted my head to look for my governess, I found that I was immersed in darkness.

I heard cries coming from all around me, yet I knew not who they were from. Trickles of cold water ran past my hands and legs and soon I heard a man yell beside of me that we had sprung a leak. Within seconds I heard more cries as another loud bang on the ship was felt and then I found myself being pushed and shoved by an unseen crowd making their way above deck.

I called for my governess, nearly screaming at the top of my lungs. Amidst all the voices, I could barely make hers out. I heard her call my name and she sounded scared, but no matter how hard I looked for her, the darkness of the cabin still blinded me. As I struggled to get up and make my way to her calls, the crowd suddenly moved again, taking me with it. Before I knew it, I was stumbling out of the cabin and onto the deck.

The color of the sky was the first thing I noticed as rain whipped my face. Clouds swirled above me as if being stirred in a pot and their color was of a pale green mixed with gray. As I stood to my feet, eager to get out of the way of all the sailors and passengers running to and fro, I felt a terrible wind hit me from both sides, threatening to knock me down again. Giant waves crashed into the sea and onto the ship, and as a splattering of white foam and salt water threw me against a rail, I thought for sure the end would come in a matter of minutes.

Then I saw him. My father, once busy helping the deckhands keep the ship from falling apart, now noticed me fallen and clawing the deck to get back up. "Samantha!" he shouted as he dropped the ropes in his hand. "Don't move! I'm coming!"

"Daddy!" I shouted, my voice being drowned out by the storm as another giant wave headed towards the ship. "Daddy, help me!"

He ran as fast as he could from the other side of the deck, dodging people this way and that to get to me. I never saw him with so much fear in his eyes, and it made me feel that much worse. Before, he was good at least trying to hide his concern, but now it was all in the open. I couldn't help but think I was doomed.

And then I saw the wave. It was massive, like the rogue waves you hear sailors tell children at the docks about, and it was headed right for me. I struggled up and grabbed onto the rail, holding on for dear life as I heard my father scream my name.

He was too late.

The wave came down, mostly missing the ship but hitting me with a side slash. I felt a great icy weight suddenly rip me from the rail, my sight and air being stripped from me all at once.

I was in the water, being churned amongst some debris from the rail, drowning.

A thousand thoughts ran through my mind as I struggled to swim up. I was scared. I was cold. I didn't want to die. I wondered what had happened to my father and whether I would see him again. I prayed to God for help, my arms and legs kicking wildly as I continued to sink down. And then, as soon the world started to dim and I thought I would join my mother in Heaven, I felt a strong arm pull me up and towards the surface.

I coughed and choked as the stormy sky greeted my vision once more. My eyes focused as I noticed someone was holding on to me, leaning against a large piece of debris. The person's coat was of a deep blue color, and instantly I recognized who had saved me.

"Daddy?" I shouted to be heard over the storm.

"Are you alright, Sam?" he asked as he panted, trying to catch his breath. I looked around and noticed he and I were both in the water while the ship, with a chunk out of its side and deck, slowly floated alongside.

I nodded as my body shook, still recovering from the shock in entering such cold waters. "What happened?"

"The wave knocked you off the ship," my father said as he noticed a few others splashing about in the water, swimming towards ropes being lowered from what remained of the deck.

"And you jumped in?" I asked, in awe.

"Of course," my father said as he held me tight. "But now's not the time to talk about what happened. We need to get back to the ship. Here, grab this board and hold onto it. Don't worry; I won't let you go. Now paddle!"

He and I both started paddling towards the ship, riding and dodging the waves up and down, nearly being toppled over during each turn. But no matter how much we paddled, the ship seemed further and further away, and pretty soon it seemed as if the ship was being moved away from us altogether.

"No..." my father moaned as he paddled even harder. "No...come back!"

I looked in horror as I saw the tide pick up, taking our ship away from us. No matter how hard we paddled and how fast we swam, the waves still hindered us and kept us at bay. Within minutes the ship looked dimmer, and before we could do anything more, it disappeared from our sight.

We were fortunate the storm began to still, moving northwest and away from us and calming the once thrashing waves, but we paid little attention to any of it as we struggled to think of what to do next.

"We're stranded…" I panted as tears streamed down my face. "There's sharks and fish and who knows what else that could eat us…"

My father tried to remain composed, but I knew he was thinking the same thing. "We'll be alright, Sam," he stuttered quietly as he pushed me on top of the board. Then he swam a few feet into the distance, gathering up another larger board for him and me both. "We'll just stay atop this and float. Hopefully that'll keep whatever creatures are here away."

"But how will we get out of here?" I whined, clinging onto the bigger board as my father set me on it.

"We'll have to wait." He sighed as he got onto the board himself. "I'm sure the ship will turn around and come looking for us. They'll have to."

"But what if it's damaged? Or worse?" I said as I wiped more tears from my eyes, thinking of my governess and her husband.

"Then someone else will rescue us," my father said as he wrapped his arms around me in a warming embrace. "But for now, I'm simply thankful. Thank the Lord you're alright. I should've never left you below that deck. I'm so sorry, Samantha. I'm so sorry…"

I heard a quiver in his voice then, and I hugged him back, for I knew what was going through his mind. Of all the stories I heard from my father and the docks, many of them were about people falling overboard and becoming lost at sea. But out of those same stories, I could remember none where anyone had survived.

As my father and I bobbed up and down on our damaged debris boards, I looked up to the sky and prayed, knowing full well I might not live to see the end of the day.

Chapter Two:
Adrift at Sea

My father and I had been adrift at sea for what seemed like months. All I saw was water, and never had I loathed it so much in my life. I wanted adventure, yes, but not this kind. Lying on a piece of wood, bobbing up and down in the ocean with the Caribbean morning sun beating down upon me was not an adventure. It was torture.

By the time it reached noon (for the sun was directly over us), I began to get a terrible pain in my stomach and a dry, parched feeling in my throat. I was hungry and thirsty all at the same time, and I turned to my father for help. Poor man; he was still drifting along with me, and I had a feeling he wouldn't be able to do anything, but I had to ask.

"I'm so hungry and thirsty," I said weakly, barely above a whisper. "Do you have anything?"

"I have no food," he said sadly. "But no fear, Sam - a man can go some days without food. The blessed Lord went on a fast for a month, remember?"

"But I'm still thirsty," I whined. "Can't I drink the ocean water?"

"No!" He was firm with me this time, and I looked at him strangely. "Whatever you do, don't drink the water!"

"But why not?" I asked, dumbfounded. "It's not that dirty."

"It's salt water," he continued. "People can't drink salt water without getting sick. If you drink it, you'll die. Do you understand?"

I nodded, but I wasn't at all happy. I was angrier and more frustrated than ever, floating on top of the one thing I wanted most and couldn't have. "What are we to do, then?"

"Be patient," he encouraged. Then taking my hand in his, he smiled. "Another ship will come along. Don't worry. We'll be back on board in a little while."

We said nothing for the next few hours. Pretty soon it became so hot that we both became sleepier instead of sick. My father (though he tried to fight it) began to doze off, but I was eager to stay awake. I prayed the same prayer over and over, that God in His mercy would give us help. I wanted to find a ship that would bring us aboard and save us.

In all my determination I was able to stay alert, and pretty soon a sight that made me scream in delight came upon my eyes. My prayers had been answered! It was a ship, tall and beautiful like the churches of London, coming towards us. Eagerly I pulled on my father's shoulder to rouse him, all the while splashing and saying, "A ship! A ship! We're saved!"

My father was equally delighted, though he didn't go into hysterics like I did. He quickly put his arms around me and embraced me with a fatherly warmth that made me smile, and I knew at that moment our patience and hope and prayer paid off.

My father took a piece from the wreckage and put his British naval jacket upon it, waiving it in the air like a flag. It apparently got the ship's attention, for soon the behemoth of a boat was sailing towards us. This delighted us even more, but our smiles would soon be replaced by fear once the ship came close enough for us to see what flew upon its main mast.

"Daddy, what's wrong?" I asked, seeing a look of concern on my father's face. "It's a ship! We're saved! Shouldn't you be happy?"

"I am happy, Sam," he whispered. "But then again, it might be better if we stayed here in the water."

"What do you mean?"

"Look at the flag," he said, his eyes squinting. "What does it look like to you?"

"It looks black," I replied. "But I can't tell what's on it."

My father grabbed my hand and held it tight. I noticed a small boat being lowered away from the ship, and in the boat were two muscular looking sailors rowing towards us. They were not dressed like British officers, but looked like dock workers. I turned to my father, but he neither said anything nor looked at me. His eyes stayed on the men rowing towards us.

The men came and lifted us on board. They asked us if we were alright, and my father replied that we were.

"Only I'm hungry and thirsty," I chimed in, but after a sharp glance from my father, I decided to keep my mouth shut.

"Well, we have food and drink on our ship," laughed the first rower. He was a large man with bright red hair and freckles, and he wore a blue scarf on his head. His clothes were a little worn and tattered, but otherwise he looked fine.

"You'll see our captain," said the other rower. "He'll get you taken care of." He was a smaller man with black hair and a thin beard. His eyes were the darkest of brown, and I daresay his gaze could pierce any onlooker.

"I thank you for rescuing my daughter and I," my father said carefully. "We were thrown overboard while traveling from New Providence. We were caught in the storm."

"Yes, we saw the storm from afar off," the red-haired mate said. "It looked rather dreary. Whoever you traveled with should have been more careful in choosing his routes."

"Pray, tell me, sir; who is your employer?" my father asked as we approached the ship, ready to be hoisted up on deck.

"We are privately employed," the black-haired man said.

"By a company?" my father asked.

"No…" The red-haired man shook his head. "He means we are employed by our captain."

I looked upon the ship I was about to board and read its name upon the front side. It said *The Smooching Sally* and my brow went up in trying to figure out why a ship would bear such a strange name.

We were brought on deck and I was introduced to a completely different scene than what I was used to. I saw no women or girls and very few children (the youngest one being a blonde-haired boy my age who was busy polishing the back rail.) I did see, however, many men - tall, short, large, small, plain, and fancy - all working about the ship in what seemed the commonest of clothes, which was very strange, at least for officers.

I suppose I had been used to seeing the sailors who worked with my father. Officers wore the uniform of the crown. Not one of them would ever be caught in common clothing while on duty for fear of punishment.

"You'll be seen by our captain now." The black-haired man bowed his head and went towards the back of the ship where the captain's quarters were held. My father and I stood in the middle of the boat and waited, not only observing our surroundings but also cautiously watching our benefactors. Though I felt no uneasiness with these men and boys, I could sense my father was worried. I looked at his face, and he seemed to have his eye fixed upon the captain's quarters. Once or twice he surveyed his surroundings, but I think he knew them well enough. The ship was like any other ship he had sailed on, anyways.

I couldn't help but wonder why my father was so quiet and why he kept me so close until I decided to look around myself. I looked at the people again, but only a few looked back. Most were still working busily. The ship looked normal enough, too. There was plenty of wood and buckets and mops and cloth. My eyes drew upward and glanced upon the flag. It was black, as I remembered it, but when the wind blew east and the black fabric unfolded, I beheld a white skull with crossing bones. I gasped and grabbed my father's arm, for the flag was familiar to me from terrible stories. It was the flag of a pirate, the Jolly Roger, and we were aboard their ship.

Now I understood my father's fear.

The door to the captain's quarters opened with a slight creek, and out stepped the black-haired man with another of equal height behind him. I looked upon the stranger and was taken aback, not only with fear but with a perplexing impulse to laugh. The fellow looked funnier than any other I had ever seen.

He had a tricorn hat like most men, but instead of it being plain, it held a giant peacock feather that rose high from the back. He wore a white shirt with a full cravat at the front with a long purple rider's jacket to cover it. The sleeves of the shirt puffed out of the jacket and his trousers and boots, both black, were smooth and perfect. His jacket had large gold buttons with colorful fabric around them and he wore a large red sash for a belt around his waist. The man seemed to jingle as he walked, and I noticed as he came nearer to us, the red sash had tiny metal circles dangling from the sides so that every time he walked, the metal would hit together and sound.

"Presenting the captain of *The Smooching Sally*!" the black-haired man called out, and the fanciful man stood before us. I curtseyed as a young lady should when being addressed to a captain, and my father slightly tilted his head. It was the most disrespectful I had ever seen him behave.

"Good afternoon, young sir and young lady," the captain began, bowing his head, causing the peacock feather to nearly tickle my nose. "My quartermaster tells me he found you adrift at sea following the great storm."

"Aye," my father answered. "We are grateful for your rescue."

"'Tis no need for thanks," the captain said with a smile. He twirled his brown mustache, which wasn't very long but certainly matched the curly brown locks he sported underneath the hat. Poor fellow; he looked terribly like a Cavalier from the previous century.

"May I ask who you are and where you are headed?" the captain continued, now smiling at me.

My father cleared his throat and I sensed a hint of anger. "My name is Charles Wellington, and this is my daughter, Samantha. We were on our way to Boston in His Majesty's colony of Massachusetts Bay. We departed from the port of Nassau not long ago." He paused, his brow lowering in a serious pose. "I must request that my daughter and I be given safe passage to New Providence where we will be allowed to board the next boat to Boston. If you would be so kind as to drop us off there, I assure you, you shall be paid a handsome sum for our safe passage by my family's purse."

"I'm sorry, but I'm afraid I can't do that," the captain said, remorseful. "We are already past New Providence a great deal, not to mention the tides tell me there may be another storm system near that way. I assure you the next piece of land we cross will be a stopping point where you and your daughter may get off."

"May I have your word on that, Captain?" my father asked.

'You may," he said. He turned to his quartermaster. "My dear Mr. Cade, will you show these two gentlepeople to the guest room? Also, give them food and drink, plus something to dry off with. Perhaps we have some extra clothes to spare."

"Aye, Captain," he said, and we followed him below deck.

Chapter Three:
Chocolate for Rum

mmediately my father and I were given a splendid meal in our quarters for dinner. We ate salted pork and potatoes along with the most delicious pineapple you had ever tasted. My father requested that we only be given fresh water instead of fermented drink for my sake, and we were. The captain had ordered we stay in our cabins to rest from being adrift for a day, and I must admit the room we were in was quite comfortable. It wasn't at all cramped or musty, and the sheets and linens for the bunk were very fine - even finer than the bed I laid in at home in Nassau (or at least I thought so.)

My father said little as we ate, only asking me how I was now and then and making sure I was feeling better after being adrift since the previous day. After dinner and some rest, night finally fell upon the ship, and being tucked well into bed I expected to get the best sleep I ever had, until my father (who was supposed to be sleeping in the long chair near to me) shook my shoulder and shushed me to keep silent.

"Are you well, Sam?" he asked.

"I am," I said.

"Are you well enough to abandon this ship?"

My eyes widened at my father's madness. Surely the man was joking. We had spent nearly a day adrift at sea with no hope of a rescue, and by the grace of Almighty God a ship (albeit a pirate one) pulled us aboard and treated us as royalty. Never had we been threatened and never had we been hurt. Why my father would want to leave all of this special treatment was beyond me.

"I don't understand," I whispered bluntly. "Why must we leave?"

"Do you not know what we are on?"

"A pirate ship," I answered, crossing my arms. "But they don't act like pirates. Maybe they're privateers."

"These men are no privateers," my father said. "Not with a flag like that. Besides, the king has little use for them. It's not safe here, Sam. We must leave."

"They've done nothing to us…"

"Nothing yet. They're not to be trusted."

"What shall we do then?" I huffed, frustrated. "Jump overboard, perhaps?"

My father shook his head, unaware of my sarcasm. "There are a few smaller boats on the side of the deck that we can lower to the sea. We can sail to the nearest island and get help."

"But that would be stealing!" I exclaimed, astonished. "We can't take one of their boats!"

"I don't want to, my dearest. Thievery is a vile practice and I am ashamed to even think of it. But I am willing to stoop to the lowest level as long as it keeps you safe."

I could see an honest fear in his eyes. He was the bravest man I ever knew, able to face any danger that would muster against him, but when it came to his family, he trembled at the slightest scratch.

"They haven't done anything, Daddy," I said with a sad face. "They've been quite nice to us, actually."

"I fought pirates before, Sam. I know what they are capable of. The stories you hear on the docks don't do them any justice. They can't be trusted."

For my father's sake, and due to my own fear now, I jumped out of bed and readied to leave at once. We quietly left our room and snuck up to the deck. The moon lit up the sky, and at first I stopped to stare at the stars and their sheer beauty. The sea was calm and a slight breeze blew. I felt as if I were in a dark Heaven for that tiny moment.

My father surveyed the scene and was surprised to find that not a sailor was on deck. "'Tis strange," he muttered to himself. "At least a watch boy should be out."

"Perhaps he is on the other side," I whispered.

But there was no time to talk or speculate with my father. He tugged me along towards where the boats were and we tip-toed silently. I looked around, and the main stairs that led below deck (across from our guest room) were lit up. Laughter could be heard sporadically here or there, and I turned to my father in question.

"I think they're all below deck," I said in surprise.

"Engaging in revelry," my father muttered, disgusted. "These pirates are bound to the drink. At night, many a times, they dance with a bottle of rum until the sun rises."

"Rum?" I asked, sticking my tongue out. "I bet they smell in the morning."

"All day, in my opinion." My father smirked.

We made our way to the first boat on the left side of the deck. It was small with a few pieces of rope and two horizontal boards for seats. It wasn't as nice as *The Smooching Sally*, but it was good enough to row to an island nearby. My father began to untie the rope that fastened it to the ship and fixed it to where he could lower the boat to the sea.

"Get in, Sam," he said gently as he helped me up and into the craft. "Careful now. Don't slip."

"Thank you," I said, sitting on the back board and waiting for my father to join me. I eyed the deck and the crew's revelry continued. Rum, thought of as a drink of the degraded man. Their voices and cheers could be heard well.

"Are you in, Sam?" my father asked, his hands on the boat, ready to climb aboard.

I nodded. "I'm ready when you are."

My father smiled. He grabbed the rope that would pull us down and he was about to get in, until a giant hand grabbed his arm and turned him around.

"Where do you think you're going?" It was the black-haired man, Hammy. Though his name was silly, he still seemed frightening in the night.

My father said nothing, and I looked at them both with trembling. Pretty soon the red-haired man who picked us up from the sea joined him. "I told you, Hammy! I thought I heard something!"

"You're right, Red!" Hammy said. "These two were caught disobeying the captain's orders!"

"Now why are you going off and leaving?" Red asked, his brow going up. He turned to Hammy. "I guess we'll just have to take them back to the captain."

"Or so you think!" My father turned quickly, grabbing the cutlass from Red's side and pointing the blade towards our finders. Both Red and Hammy (who had neglected to carry a sword at his side) threw their hands high in the air and stared at my father strangely.

"You will let my daughter and I leave this ship, sirs, under penalty of death!" my father barked. "We will not be held prisoner by your vile hand!"

Red looked over to Hammy and only shook his head in confusion. It was as if they didn't know why my father was pointing a sword in their faces.

My father's demands and the disappearance of the quartermaster and his friend must have stirred a commotion, for now a few more men of the crew approached us out of nowhere. I gasped in fright and looked at my father in anxiety. How we were to escape now was anyone's guess.

I suddenly felt a cold hand on my shoulder and another set of them pulling me out of the boat. I found myself on the deck across from my father, being held by unknown assailants against my free will. My father looked at me, terrified yet as brave as I'd ever seen him, and threatened the men who held me.

"Let her go!" my father demanded, his voice loud and clear.

"We do not want any needless violence," the man behind me said. I dared not turn around to look at my captor. I kept my eyes only on my father - my only comfort, my only friend for the past few days.

"Lower your sword, sir." I recognized the voice that spoke those words. This time I turned to my right side and beheld the captain of the ship. He looked as calm and as cool as ever, and I suspected that because the man was so composed, he wasn't one bound to the bottle. "We are men of peace, I and the crew. We mean you no harm."

"You're pirates!" My father didn't trust any of them. He knew their kind very well; much better and more than I could ever dream of knowing. He fought them off the shores of Florida and South Carolina as a British officer, and now he was fighting them again; only instead of defending the colonies, he was defending me.

"We are pirates, in most eyes I suppose." The captain nodded solemnly. "But just because we carry the name does not mean we act like them."

"A name is everything," my father retorted. "If you bear the name, you bear the traits. I've never seen a friendly pirate, or a merciful one."

"You must get out more." The captain smiled. He turned to a few more of his crew and nodded to them. They went to my father from behind, and though he put up a good struggle, they overpowered him. Soon Red had his sword back at his side, and three men held my father at bay. The captain paced back and forth, muttering something to himself, but I didn't know what. I suppose he was thinking aloud, figuring out what to do with a young lady as myself with a rabid father.

Finally he stopped and turned to Quartermaster Red. "My dear sir, might I ask that you return our Mr. Wellington to the guest room?" Red nodded, but my father refused to go, and firmly planted his feet to the ground.

"I will not leave without my daughter!" my father shouted.

"No harm will come to her, I assure you," the captain said, straightening his coat. He turned to me. "Miss Wellington, I should like to speak with you in my office for a moment."

My father's eyes went wide and his face flushed red as he struggled even harder to get to me. I turned to the captain, who waited in expectation. I suppose I had no choice in the matter, as the man who held me nudged me forward. I let out a deep breath of defeat, nodding in agreement. The three men who held my father were literally dragging him below deck as I was escorted to the captain's office and quarters.

The captain went ahead of me, opening the door so that I could enter the room first. Two other members of the crew followed and the captain shut the door and sat in a leather seat behind an oak desk. His room was exquisite! Exotic decorations - fabric, artwork, and craft - were assembled richly throughout the place. I felt as if I were in the presence of the king himself! But I shook my head, ignoring my awe. Though the man had lovely taste, I felt I should remain alert for my father's sake.

The captain offered me a seat, which I took rather cautiously, and I sat facing him at the desk while the two crew members stood in attention near the door. The captain folded his delicate hands and set them on the desk, beginning the conversation.

"Miss Wellington, I apologize for the disturbance that was displayed," he began. I gulped and swallowed my fear.

"'Tis alright, Captain," I said as brave as I could. "I admit I do not like being held against my will, though."

"You are a brave young girl to speak so freely." The captain laughed. He began to tap his fingers on the desk. "Many girls, or women for that matter, never speak their opinions, especially to a man with a high ranking like myself."

"Well I'm not like those girls," I said sharply.

"You're quite right," he said, tapping his fingers faster.

"Captain, I demand that you release my father and I. We have done you no harm and have given you no ill will. Why will you not release us?"

The captain was taken aback. "What makes you think we are holding you captive?"

"You're pirates! That's what you do," I said, dumbfounded. "You kidnap innocent people, hold them for ransom, and then kill them if you are not paid!"

"You judge like your father, young one," the captain said, tapping his fingers still. "Not all pirates are wicked, just as not all girls are quiet."

"Well if you're not wicked, then why do you call yourselves pirates?"

"We don't call ourselves pirates. It's what everyone else calls us." He tapped his fingers even faster, and by this time the habit began to annoy me.

"I say, Captain," I said, tightening the grip on my seat. "Do stop that tapping!"

"I'm sorry," he said, looking at his hand. "I am...in need of it...excuse me!" He quickly got up from his chair and went to an armoire and fumbled for the handle. My brow went up as I watched him with the armoire. I thought for a moment. Perhaps he was getting into his stash of rum. After all, pirates could never do without it.

The wooden doors opened wide, but instead of finding filthy jugs of rum, I found something stranger. My eyes widened at the sight of it.

"Captain, what is that you are getting into?"

The captain turned to me with a smile and said, "Every pirate has their obsession - most make it gold, some make it power, and even more make it rum. But then there comes a time when something mightier than gold, power, and even rum arrives, and no man, no matter how strong he is, can resist it."

He pulled out the delight of his eyes and held it before me. There were a dozen others like it stashed in his armoire, all lined up like dominoes in a game.

"A pie?" I asked, eyeing the thing he held. "You mean to tell me your obsession as a pirate is a pie?"

"Oh, but not just any pie," he replied passionately. "'Tis a chocolate pie!"

"Chocolate?" I shook my head. Surely I had met a lunatic. "But what about all those things you mentioned - gold, power, and rum? Do you care nothing for those things?"

"Gold can only drive a man mad, Miss Wellington," the captain began, taking a bite out of the pie. "Power can make a man corrupt. Rum can make a man degrade himself. But chocolate can do no harm! Well, except when you eat too much of it. Then you might want a chamber pot on hand..."

"You're the strangest pirate I've ever met," I said, shaking my head with my brow up.

"I'm probably the only pirate you've ever met," the captain said with his mouth full. "Aside from everyone else on this ship."

"But your crew - weren't they drinking rum below deck?"

He shook his head and laughed. "We don't keep rum on board. You see, we did some years ago when the previous captain, Willy Whalebone, sailed this ship, but the rum caused us to become mad and crazy. We couldn't get a thing done, and we were doing more harm than good not only to others, but to ourselves as well. When Willy died, I became captain, and one of my first orders was to have all the rum dumped overboard. But the men still craved the drink, so as a substitute, I introduced them to chocolate, and since then they have been hooked!"

"But what about gold? And why are you sailing? Did you hide your gold on an island and you're off to fetch it?"

"A treasure hunt, you mean?"

"Aye."

"'Tis a misconception about any pirate, good or bad," the captain said. "I mean, why on earth would a pirate (or any man for that example) give up his gold to bury it in the sand and never see it again only for others to find? 'Tis only a rumor amongst the colonists. I think they got it from Admiral Bartelby - he's the only pirate who ever buried anything, and he didn't bury his treasure. He buried his dirty laundry."

"You mean his secrets?" I asked, thinking I had come across some great mystery of Rudiger Bartelby, wanted pirate of New York.

"No, I mean literally his dirty laundry," the captain said, eating another piece of pie. "He didn't like to wash clothes and he was too cheap to have them done professionally."

I only sat there with my brow still up. My mouth was open but no words came out, for I didn't know what to say. The captain only smirked as he went and sat back down in his seat. "'Tis a surprise for you, I'm sure," he said. "We're God-fearing men, Miss Wellington. You need not fear us. Though I must ask you, before you retire, do let your father know that if he intends to lower a tiny boat like the one he chose earlier into the sea, he must be informed that we are far from any island at the moment and we're in shark-infested waters."

The two men from the door came up and helped me to my feet. I turned back to the captain before heading out.

"Sir, may I ask your name?" I asked.

"Captain Patrick Peterson," he answered with a smile. "But you may call me Captain Patty."

Chapter Four:
Captain Patty's Story

When I had returned below deck to my quarters I found my father in a mad state. Apparently he had taken his fists and banged on the door for quite some time, and the poor man's hands were red as a summer apple when I walked through the door. He embraced me, asked me if I was treated well, and then demanded to know what all had happened in the captain's office. He told me to hold nothing back.

Before I said anything about what had happened, I told my father the captain's name. "Patrick Peterson," I repeated. "He said he used to sail under Willy Whalebone. Do any of the names sound familiar?"

My father nodded. "Aye, they do," he began. "Or at least the latter. I've never heard of this Patrick Peterson, so he must be a new captain. But the name of Willy Whalebone, or William Welds as he was originally known, is synonymous with treachery. A common thief he was, and good at it, too. He traveled all over the world, from the Americas to India and back. A vile man, he was...vile..."

"So you know the former captain?" I asked.

"Only by name," he continued. "I was young when he sailed the seas. Captain Whalebone died about twelve years ago."

We left it at that, and I didn't press my father for further information. I could tell he was tired of waiting for my story. I told him everything. I told him about my demands I made to the captain and how the captain answered me. I told him about the mysterious armoire and the pies therein. At first my father thought I was joking, but after I swore that I was telling the truth, he was taken aback.

"Surely these vermin are up to something," he muttered to himself. "The late night parties, the chocolate pies…it doesn't make much sense." He set himself upon a chair and stroked his chin. "We must be on our guard, Sam. These pirates are quite clever and crafty, so as long as we stay aware and keep our eyes open, we can be a step ahead of them and then plan our escape."

"But the captain said we are in shark-infested waters and we're not near any islands at the moment," I chimed in.

"That, I'm afraid, makes sense," my father said sadly. "We've been at sea for a while now."

"So what do we do?" I asked.

"Every pirate eventually stops sailing to plunder," my father said. "We wait until they dock."

I hated to wait for anything but I couldn't disobey my father. He was a professional sailor and he always knew what he was doing. I relented and sighed, wobbling tiredly to my cot where I would sleep, and after my father tucked me in and sat in his chair near the door so he could watch over the room, I quickly fell into a deep sleep.

The next morning I awoke to the most wonderful feeling. I felt rested and full of energy, ready to begin my day. I put my hand to my eyes and rubbed the sleep away, but because I was so comfortable in my bed, I decided to turn over on my side and lay there for a few extra minutes. When I turned, I kept my eyes closed, for I was too lazy to open them, and when my other cheek hit the pillow, I felt something furry upon my face. It tickled my nose at first, but it didn't faze me. I only thought of it as possibly a fur blanket to keep me warm at night. But when I then felt the same fur tickling my chin, my attention was grabbed. Could the blanket have possibly moved?

I opened my eyes to see who the culprit was ruining my perfect morning. When I glanced upon my pillow and saw it, I jumped out of bed, screaming in terror at the horrid thing I saw. A giant orange pile of fur moved around in circles on my bed, and the only thing I could think of was a rat on the ship giving me some sort of strange and incurable disease like the rats that came to Europe and brought the plague.

My father was jolted from his slumber and fell out of the chair as he scrambled to my side, trying to calm me down from my hysterics.

When my father saw the thing, he bade me to get away from it. We slowly backed up towards the door, him standing guard in front of me, and stopped to watch the animal run around in my bed.

"What is it, Daddy?" I asked, my teeth chattering as if I were covered with ice. "Is it a rat?"

"If it is a rat, it's the strangest one I've ever seen," he said, staring at the thing with a peculiar type of curiosity. "Are there such things as orange rats?"

"Maybe it has a disease," I added, remembering the terrible stories of the plague and the smallpox from back home. My eyes widened at the thought of something worse.

"Then wash your hands! Wash your hands!" Something squawked in the strangest type of voice from the ceiling. It wasn't very bright in our room yet, so when we both looked up, we saw nothing.

"Who is making that racket?" I asked.

"You never listen to me! You never listen to me!" the voice squawked again.

"But I am listening to you," I said, now annoyed.

"Tell the truth. Tell the truth." Silence soon followed.

I turned to my father. "Do you think it's one of the pirates trying to scare us?" I whispered.

He nodded. "Perhaps," he whispered back. "We mustn't fall for it, then."

Flapping was heard, and as I and my father ducked to miss being hit by a flying blue thing, we knew a pirate had to be in our room. The parrot landed on the bed next to the furry thing still going around in the sheets and just stared at us.

"I knew it!" I exclaimed quietly. "There is a pirate here watching for us. There's his parrot!" I smiled at it, his blue and green and yellow colors vibrantly bringing light into the room.

"Hello, he is a pretty thing, isn't he?" I said, talking to the parrot sweetly. The bird tilted his head upward and squawked.

"I am a woman. I have a mind of my own!" it said as loudly as it could.

My eyes widened. Was that the parrot?

"Do parrots talk on their own?" I asked my father.

He shook his head, his face full of perplexity. "I don't think so."

The parrot squawked again. "Would you like some food?"

I looked at the parrot and screamed at the top of my voice. "EVIL PARROT!" I ran to the door and flung the piece of wood open, my father trailing behind and trying to catch me. I didn't care where I went or who I went to. I leapt over and began to run across the deck of the ship, yelling and screaming and ignoring the now confused shipmates who were busy cleaning the deck. In my ignorance and blind fear I found myself running into an old acquaintance - Captain Patty himself, his spyglass in hand, glancing over the sea.

"Captain Patty! Captain Patty!" I began to talk as if my mouth were run by a horse. "In my cabin there's an evil parrot who won't stop talking and then there's a bright orange rat that has the plague and smallpox and every other disease and they're all out to get me!" At the sound of the orange rat, many of the crew began to shout and holler as well, taking their buckets of soap and suds and dumping it on themselves. Apparently they were afraid of disease.

"Calm down, all of you!" Captain Patty ordered. He shook his head and put his fingers to his lips and whistled. By this time my father had joined me, he too wanting some answers, but he would have no time to ask anything, for that parrot came flying out from my cabin and landed straight on Captain Patty's outstretched arm.

"Is this your evil parrot?" he asked me.

I nodded, afraid to even look at it. Surely it had red eyes.

"This parrot is not evil, I assure you. We even bought him from a priest. He was my wife's parrot, and he has a tendency of repeating the words she has said to me over the past few years."

The parrot squawked. "You need to go on a diet. You need to go on a diet."

"My wife called him Ralph." The captain rolled his eyes and shuddered at the parrot. The parrot only cocked its head and said, "Your pants have ripped. Your butt is too big."

"And the rat?" my father chimed in, eager to get a word.

"He's right here." Everyone stepped aside as the furry orange thing wobbled to the captain. He bent down, picked the thing up, and rubbed its furry head. "This is Franky, and he is not a rat. He is a hamster."

"A what?" I asked, relieved it wasn't a rat.

"A hamster. We traded for him from the Spaniards. They said hamsters were all the rage in Spain."

"And you bought them because they were popular?"

"A modern pirate needs to keep up with the times." The captain nodded, flickering the giant peacock feather in his hat proudly.

"So they're just normal animals?" I asked, putting my hands on my hips.

"That's correct."

I shrugged. I had went mad for a nagging parrot and a hamster from Spain. Embarrassed, and yet annoyed at the same time, I turned around and huffed, stomping back to my quarters (my father following me) and going back to sleep. I wanted to forget that morning.

That evening on the ship, the captain had invited us to the dining hall for dinner. "You can't stay cooped up in the cabin forever," his courier had said. "It gets so dark and damp; it surely would make you sick." My father, though he hated to admit it, said that I could use the fresh air, but told the courier to relay to the captain that at the first sign of drunkenness or debauchery, we were heading back to our quarters. My father would not stand for having me in such a terrible predicament, but secretly I think he was afraid to refuse their request, thinking that they were going to make us dine with them tonight anyways.

The captain sent us some more fresh clothes to wear, and since I was the only woman on board, I was given boy's clothes this time. (I had already worn the only girl's dress they had, but it was too big and uncomfortable to wear anymore.) I admit that it was the first time I had ever worn a pair of pants, and though they felt strange to have on in the beginning, I began to prefer them over the rigid corsets and heavy dresses that I normally wore.

"I say, Daddy! These trousers the pirates wear are quite comfortable," I said as we walked towards the dining hall, following the courier.

"They may be comfortable, but they're wear for the vile man," he said with a bit of disdain. "Besides, it isn't proper for a lady. You're lucky I allow you to wear those."

"But why do we women have to walk around with bone and metal cutting off our breathing along with a ton of fabric hanging off our shoulders? I think women should wear pants. They're much more comfortable."

I don't think my father heard any of my complaints. I was determined, however, that if I ever got home again in one piece, I was going to have my governess sew me a pair of pants at least for free time.

"I still can't believe you kept your officer's coat, though." I changed the subject, holding my nose. "I love you dearly, but I'm not looking forward to sitting next to you at the table. You smell like fish and seaweed!"

"Honor is more important than aroma," my father added, though when he wasn't looking, I caught him sniffing his jacket and sticking his tongue out in disgust.

When we entered the dining hall, I found myself surrounded by long wooden tables filled with every kind of delicious food you could think of. Giant pewter mugs of drink sat near every plate, and setting and benches were aligned so well that one would think you were in a school.

My eyes widened to see the crew members, both young and old, busy walking about and talking amongst themselves, deciding what to eat first. But they didn't grab anything from the serving dishes in the middle of the tables. I figured they were waiting for Captain Patty to allow them to eat.

The courier sat me and my father near the door and away from the main group of sailors (for my father requested it), and I sat with my hands folded in my lap, twiddling my thumbs. I dared not touch any food so as to seem impolite, and if the sailors were to wait for the captain, I was going to wait too. I don't know why I wanted to show respect to a pirate captain, but Patty was different - almost like my father, in a way - and he seemed nice; nice enough for me to show at least some manners and decency.

My father waited along with me (not out of respect, but out of fear of disturbing their peace, I presumed.) When the captain finally entered the front of the room with two men following behind, the sailors stood to their feet, and my father and I followed.

"Gentlemen..." the captain began. He turned to me. "And lady..." I smiled for his acknowledgement. "We are about to eat the bounty for which we have toiled for. I have requested Mr. O'Leary to prepare the benediction of the meal."

Mr. O'Leary (who I presumed was the dark-haired Irish man who went up to the front first) nodded his head in greeting. "Let us pray," he began. Every man on the ship bowed their head, removing their hats and putting them to their lap in reverence. The man prayed the prayer over the meal, and though I prayed along, I couldn't help but listen with confusion – and excitement – over a simple prayer I'd heard many times before.

I found it strange that an entire pirate ship would be praying before a meal. I spoke to my father about it afterwards, and he told me that he wasn't surprised - he had heard of a few religious pirates who, even though they acknowledged God and even went to church, still went on with their vile deeds. "You'd be surprised how many call on His name yet don't bear it in their hearts," he said.

I sadly agreed, as hypocrisy was an unfortunate commonality amongst many a man. But Captain Patty was a wonder! He not only acknowledged God in his words, but in his actions as well.

We ate in silence while the rest of the men laughed and talked and cheered. My father only looked around and ate slowly, keeping watch on everyone in the room. I, on the other hand, didn't care what happened as I was curious about Patty. He was a strange captain and I wanted to know more about him.

After dinner, a few of the men got up and cleaned the rest of the plates and dishes, for it was part of their chores for the night, and the quartermaster stood to his feet and shouted, "A song! A song! A song from the captain!" Every man in that room cheered except for my father, who still sat in silence.

The captain stood up and blushed in humility, bowing his head in agreement. "My viola!" he called out to a young lad about my age. "Thank you, Reuben." The boy handed him the instrument and string, which he got from who knows where, and the captain put it to his shoulder and played. The song was at first soft and gentle, and I admit that the captain played a beautiful note. He was as good as Mr. Lewisham's second cousin back in England who had made his profession as a musician to the queen. After about a minute or so the music sped up, and instead of a fancy tune, the captain switched tempos to a faster beat, tapping his boots to the floor on rhythm. I felt as if I were in the English countryside or Scotland even, for the music there is divine to me. Men began to clap, some began to dance, and I eventually found myself doing both. But my father scolded me and bade me to sit back down in my chair, for it wasn't proper for an English lady to be dancing on a pirate ship.

The dancing and "revelry" (as my father called it) continued on for about an hour until the men's feet had tired. I don't think that the captain ever tired with his viola, for he seemed like he wanted to keep playing. But something else started gleaming in the men's eyes and the captain returned his viola to the boy.

"Bring it out!" the men cheered. "The last of the feast that shall end the day!"

My father's brow went down, his foot stamping on the floor, and throwing himself into the air, he shouted, "My daughter and I shall not remain here any longer to watch you get drunk. I insist that we be excused to our quarters!"

Poor Daddy. He thought they were bringing out some rum.

The blank stares that my father gained through his brave attempt at negotiation caused me to laugh. I admit that I couldn't help it, but seeing my father confused, I tugged his smelly coat and whispered to him, "They're getting chocolate. I told you they don't drink rum."

After a few seconds of embarrassing silence, my father sat down, not really knowing what to think. Hammy, who had been so patient while waiting for chocolate, called out, "Can we have the chocolate now?"

The captain nodded and out it came. Bricks and bricks of it, mugs of it melted and mixed with water. I could only imagine how expensive it was, but I don't think it mattered to the pirates, who were drooling like dogs when it came into their hands. Never had I seen such a deep love for desserts and never had I felt such a deep relief that these men didn't drink rum.

The servers had come around to our little corner table and with a plate set before us, asked if we would like to try it. I looked to my father for permission, and he nodded and said that I could have it. Perhaps it was the lure of the chocolate that clouded his thinking, or perhaps it was that he could only sit there, dumbfounded at the fact that I was telling the truth.

I grabbed a piece and thanked the server. It was a wonderful thing, this sweetness called chocolate. Even my father mumbled that it was good. I got up from my seat and told my father I was going to thank the captain for the chocolate, and he nodded. "Alright. Just don't stay long." Again I was surprised, but I thought I'd make the best of it.

I trotted up to the captain, who was busy eating some chocolate on his own, and also saw Franky the hamster sniffing little bits on the floor.

"I say, Captain," I began, holding my breath as I picked up the furry thing and put him on the table. "Do even the animals eat this delicacy?"

Captain Patty's brow went up and he took a tiny piece of chocolate from Franky and waved his finger at him. "Franky!" he scolded. "You know eating this can make you ill." He whistled and Ralph the parrot came flying to him. Patty bent down to the hamster again. "The chocolate belongs to the parrot."

He held out his hand and offered it to Ralph. "To my favorite parrot." He smiled, and in reply the parrot squawked and took it and flew away.

"Oh Captain, why did you give the chocolate to the parrot if the hamster couldn't have it?" I asked, consoling poor Franky.

"I don't like the parrot," he said with a guilty expression. "I like the hamster."

"I see," I said, shaking my head like my father would.

"Ah well." The captain laughed, putting another morsel to his lips. "He doesn't eat it anyways. Don't worry; he only takes it to throw at the crew."

"And I'm sure the crew enjoys being pelted by chocolate." I chuckled.

The captain smiled. "So, how are you enjoying yourself, Miss Wellington?" he asked, reclining in his chair. "Was the food good?"

"It was all delicious, thank you! The chocolate was divine. It was the first time I ever tried it and I hope it shall not be the last."

"I'm glad to hear it."

"And I enjoyed your turn at the viola, sir," I said. "I've never heard of a musical pirate."

"I thank you, and I'm sure my father would thank you as well. 'Twas he who taught me when I was a lad."

I pulled up a stool and sat on it, eager to hear what the captain was saying. "If you don't mind me asking, Captain Patty, but was your father a pirate?"

The captain smirked and shook his head. "No, he was never a pirate. He never even got on a boat. He was a baker on the coast of Scotland."

"Then how did you become a pirate? Aren't pirates born into this lifestyle?"

"Some are, like Hammy, whom you've met, but most aren't. Many choose to become pirates because they want to, and the rest choose because they have to."

"Which one were you?" I asked, hoping I wasn't being too nosy.

"The latter, as it is with many on *The Smooching Sally*," he answered, and I noticed a sadness entered his expression.

"What happened?"

The captain leaned forward and sighed. "I was eight years old and walking home near the port in Leith. I had just left the shore and I was with my younger sister, who was five at the time. We walked by the docks as we did every afternoon, and some sailors stopped us and asked if we could help them load supplies onto their ship. Our parents had taught us to always lend a helping hand to those who need it, so we set down our fishing rods and buckets and resolved to help them. They gave us boxes, small ones so that we could carry them, and told us to load them on the ship. I should've known then that it was a trap. As soon as we got on board we were grabbed, and even though we kicked and screamed for help, no one heard us. You see, the sailors were actually pirates, and their captain was a young Willy Whalebone. This ship was their ship. They bade me and my sister to board it, for they needed extra crew. But when the captain saw my sister, he told the men to let her go back, for it wasn't proper piracy to bring women aboard. I, being a young boy, was kept, so they dragged my sister back to the docks, freeing her, and they set sail. I never saw my family again."

"You were kidnapped?" I said, feeling pity for the poor man.

"Aye."

"How awful! Did you ever find out what happened to your family?"

"Alas, I did not." Patty frowned. "I returned to Leith many years later after Captain Whalebone perished and I was free to sail on my own. They were not there. My father's bakery had become a cobbler's shop, and what used to be our house was now an abandoned shack. I don't know what happened to them."

"But what about the young lads on your ship? How did they get here? Weren't they kidnapped too?"

Patty shook his head firmly. "No. The few young lads we have here are either relatives of the crew or orphans. I'd never bring the pain of separating any child from his family, for I know that pain all too well. The children on this ship are on it because they chose to be."

"You aren't like a normal pirate, are you?" I asked.

"Nay." The captain smiled. "Indeed, I am not a normal pirate at all."

"Then how did you become so abnormal when you were surrounded by such thievery?"

"Three things, Miss Wellington, that I remembered every day: my faith, where I came from, and where I was determined to go. And I pray that those are things you remember as well."

"I shall," I said, but before I could say any more, the ship rocked violently and some loud crashes were heard. Everyone was thrown into a panic, and before I knew it, the pounds of chocolate that were still available were gobbled down in a nervous gorge. Some men ran to the deck, others shook in their stools, and still others ran around in circles trying to figure out what to do. More crashes came and the boat felt as if it were about to tip over. I grabbed the beam next to me and looked to Captain Patty. His face was firm and I saw no fear in his eyes. As my father ran to me, the captain shouted at the top of his lungs, "Man your posts! Brace the ship! 'Tis Jonah's whale that is trying to break us!"

Chapter Five:
Jonah's Whale

"Man the decks! Man the decks! Keep this ship afloat!" The captain barked out orders like I had never seen. The men scrambled this way and that as if they were in a state of panic, but they held it together thanks to their captain. Patty ran up the stairs and into the darkness of the night, determined to face whatever monster we were up against. My father wasted no time taking me with him, ordering me like a sailor to stay away from the rails and edges and to watch out for water and debris. I dared not disobey, for the last time I did, I found myself stranded in the middle of the ocean. I didn't want to be stranded with whatever was attacking us.

Like a good sailor, my father put aside his judgments of the pirates and offered his services to Patty. The captain gratefully obliged and said that he needed men to arm the canons. My father agreed and ran to his post, for he had experience in battle at sea.

I stayed put as the men began to load the canons with large iron balls that I knew would hurt the monster. So much water was splashing back and forth onto the ship that one thought we were caught in another hurricane, but we weren't. A giant thing kept knocking us, trying to break the ship. The boat rocked back and forth, and I saw Franky the hamster rocking back and forth along with it, until I caught him and put him in my pocket. A young boy my age came running up to me and held as tightly as he could to the wooden post as I did.

"Are we safe here?" I asked, my voice shaky with fright.

"I think so," he said. I recognized him as the same boy who handed the captain the viola a moment earlier. "This has happened before. The captain says we're okay to be here, away from the rails."

"My father said that too," I answered. "What's your name?" A bit later I found it odd that I was asking a boy's name at such a stressful time.

"Reuben," he answered. "Reuben Gayle."

"I'm Samantha Wellington."

"Nice to meet you," he said warmly. "We don't have a lot of girls on board. Well…none besides you, I mean. I hope the men are treating you well."

"They are," I said, and after I finished talking, a huge bang was heard. It was the first round of canons. I looked around, the captain's sword in the air, and he looked mighty powerful. Again the men loaded the canons and dreadful sounds - almost groans - from the monster were heard. Patty brought down his sword, yelling, "Fire!" The canons blasted with light, and one would think we were in a true battle. I turned to glance at my father, and he was busy at work. He looked like the most courageous man there, and I was so proud at that moment.

The monster gave a yell and the boat finally stopped shaking. I looked over to Reuben, who looked at the captain, and the men began to cheer. The monster had been defeated and was swimming away. I ran to my father, embracing him, and looked to the sea. I couldn't see much, for it was still dark outside, but I could see the shadow of a very large creature on the water glistening from the moonlight, and I could see a hump of sorts sticking above the sea. I gasped when I saw it, for never before had I seen anything like it.

When the men had settled down, the captain had sent a few men to check on damages done to the ship. He then turned to my father and, offering his hand, thanked him for his help.

"You manned the canons well, my friend, like a true and brave sailor. Perhaps we can now lay aside our differences and be equals?" I looked to my father and expected him to answer as nobly as the captain had said, but my father only looked at Patty and said, "I helped to save lives, but we are not equals."

I was shocked at the horridness displayed by my father, and I could only expect Patty to take his glove off, slap the man in the face, and challenge him to a duel to defend his honor, but the captain did no such thing. He gently put his hand back to his side and said, "I can only offer." He turned around and walked away, eager to check the status of the ship.

My father and I stayed there near the rail for a few moments or so, waiting for the damage report to see if we could return to our cabins. I said nothing to him, for I was ashamed of his behavior. He said nothing as well, and I sensed he knew what he had said was wrong. He just didn't want to admit it.

Reuben, the young lad with golden hair and brown eyes, came running down the deck repeating what the men had found on the ship. I called him aside, eager to hear the news. "Reuben, is it safe for us to return to our cabins?"

"It is," he said, carefully keeping his distance from my father. "But we have to make a stop. We've lost a nose and an arm, and we have a few holes in our ship that need to be plugged."

"A nose and arm?" I wanted to cry. "What poor soul was hurt?"

"Oh, no one special." Reuben shrugged his shoulders. "Just Sally, at the front of the ship. Her nose got chipped and her arms fell off somewhere. We need to get them replaced."

I felt a little silly wanting to cry over the ship's decoration at the front. Reuben laughed and said it was alright, and then started to run off to tell the others. Before he could leave, my father called out to him and asked where we were stopping. "Louis's," he replied, and off he went.

I asked my father if he knew what Louis's was, and he shook his head. He had never heard of it.

The next morning, after getting a not-so-wonderful night's sleep, we went up to the deck, eager to find out what Louis's was. I hoped it wouldn't take us long to get there, but only the captain knew how long it would take. I decided to ask him while we all sat down for breakfast.

My father gave me permission to ask the captain, as long as I didn't talk too long. I agreed and skipped to Patty as he ate some chocolate pie and ham.

I approached Patty and was surprised to see Reuben eating with him, and I smiled at my new friend and he smiled back, his mouth too full to talk. I pulled up a stool next to the captain, and before talking about what I wanted to talk about, I thought I had better apologize.

"I'm terribly sorry for the way my father talked to you, sir," I said. "I don't think he meant it. I think he's starting to take a liking to everyone."

"I'm sure he didn't mean it," Patty said kindly. "These officers, professional sailors as they call themselves...they think they know everything and for the most part they do. Pirates really shouldn't be trusted. But the one thing they can't do that a pirate can is think outside of the box. Pirates can never change, they think, but pirates know that an officer can change very easily. And I think your father is starting to change. I think he's seeing that not all pirates are what he thought they would be."

"Well you've definitely changed my thinking," I said with a grin. "Pirates are so much fun!"

"Don't think that they all are," Patty cautioned. "Your father is right; most of them can't be trusted. Use your judgment, and use godly wisdom in figuring out whether a person is wrong or right. Pray about it and watch what they do. It will define their character. Then you'll know if they're good or not."

I nodded, not expecting Patty to be that wise. I was wrong yet again.

"I must ask, sir - what is Louis's?" I asked, changing the subject. "Reuben told me we were going there yesterday." I smiled at Reuben, happy to mention his name. Reuben smiled back, but I think I embarrassed him, for he blushed.

"Louis's is a trading post near here," the captain answered, taking another bite of chocolate. "Whenever we need repairs we go there, for officers don't use it. Pirates sometimes use it, but only for information or the occasional fill up of food and rum."

"Then who uses it?" I asked, confused.

"Merchants. Other sailors. Some privateers," Reuben chimed in.

"And us," the captain said. "I've known Monsieur Louis for quite some time. He, too, was kidnapped by Willy Whalebone as a lad from Calais, but when Willy died, he decided to open up his own trading business. He didn't like life on the sea, but he loved the new world. And he is an engineer, so he'll help us fix the damages on our ship caused by Jonah's whale."

"Jonah's whale?" I asked. "Is that what attacked us last night?"

"Aye," Reuben said. "'Tis rumored to be the very whale that swallowed the prophet Jonah!"

"I would think he'd be a nice whale," I said.

"We all thought." Patty shook his head. "And he was, until Willy Whalebone came along. He came across the whale one day, and eager to kill it for the hunt, he began to shoot canons at it. He nearly destroyed the poor creature, but the whale was smart enough to outmaneuver him. The whale escaped, and now every time he sees a ship he attacks it, for he's afraid that it is Whalebone out to get him."

"Is that how Willy Whalebone got his name?" I asked.

"Aye," Patty replied. "The whale nearly killed him twice, but couldn't. His bones were as strong as the whale's."

"I see," I said. "I certainly hope not to run into that whale again, then. He was dreadfully frightening."

"Well, hopefully Louis's post will help you get your mind off the whale." Patty smiled. "The man sells the best chocolate around!"

Chapter Six:
Louis's Trading Post

It was late in the afternoon, about dinner time I suppose, when a great wailing was heard. At first I thought that Jonah's whale had returned, and I ran to the nearest post to grab it, but after a short conversation with Reuben (who I could now call my friend), I learned that the reason the men had been weeping was that they had gone down below deck to retrieve some chocolate to have with their dinner. To their severe disappointment, the attack from Jonah's whale had put some holes in the ship, and even though they were quickly taken care of, the damage had already been done. The chocolate was ruined.

Because the ship had no more chocolate, the captain bade the ship to go even faster than before. Poor souls; they were dreadfully irritable without their chocolate, so the ship flew like a bird to Louis's Trading Post, wherever that was.

I told my father about our trip to the trading post, and after the words had left my mouth, he smiled. I asked him what his cause of sudden joy was, and he answered, "Don't you see, Sam? We have our ticket out of here. Where there's a trading post, there's bound to be other ships which we can board."

"But the captain and Reuben said that the Royal Navy doesn't use this post," I said. "I think they think it's beneath them."

"Ah, but you're wrong," my father replied. "Your young friend said that privateers use it, right?"

"Aye," I said.

"Privateers are employed by the crown. We can just board one of their ships."

"I don't think Captain Patty will like it," I said with a frown. "I don't think I'd like it, either."

Days later we were roused to the navigator's cry. "Land!" he warned. I was up early that morning, eager to get the first glimpse of a Caribbean sunrise at sea, and I was ecstatic to know that not only did I see my sunrise, but the sights of the trading post as well. My father smiled and nodded as I jumped around happily, and I think I made poor Hammy nervous with my hysterics, for he nearly dropped his tools. Captain Patty was busy with sea charts in his office, and Reuben was there too, but soon the entire ship was astir as the post drew nearer and nearer.

I was surprised when I saw the location of the post when it came into view. It wasn't located on an island, but on long, unending land. The mainland, according to Reuben. I had also overheard from one of the pirates swabbing the deck that the post was in a land called Florida, but I had never been there before. It wasn't a British colony.

The post was also much smaller than I expected. For such a large clientele, this Louis character didn't have much of a business. There were a few cottages here and there, and smoke could be seen rising amidst the palm trees from a few chimneys. Little areas carrying fruits of all kinds stood near the docks and fish stands, and some vendors could be seen beckoning the couple of people that were there in the village.

One thing I did relish was the smell of the air. There is nothing clearer than sea air. It was so easy to breathe! And the plants were so green - just like my favorite dress back in Nassau. I could only imagine what kind of animals lived on the land. It would certainly be a fun exploration!

Captain Patty had the ship anchored in a matter of minutes. When we prepared to leave, I saw my father look around and lower his brow. He told the captain, "I thought you said this was a trading post."

The captain nodded as he lifted his hat and fanned his delicate face in the heat. "It is," he answered. "But this isn't exactly your normal trading post."

My father wrinkled his lip at that and took my hand, helping me and Franky, who I kept in my other hand, down the bridge to the land. I couldn't help but wonder if he was planning yet another escape from the pirates, but after looking around the docks, I changed my mind. Even if we ran, there was no place to go. There wasn't even another boat besides *The Sally*, save a few tiny ones for fishing. And since we weren't in a British colony, my father's naval coat would only harm us because of British enemies. We had to be careful we weren't spotted by the townspeople.

And so my father and I, Reuben, the captain, Hammy, Red, and a host of other pirates went ashore. A number of the ship's crew stayed on board to manage things and make sure the damage sustained through Jonah's whale was controlled. To the captain's dismay, Ralph the parrot (who wasn't much liked by anyone I think) flew by, and it seemed that he was determined to follow us and nag us all the way to Louis's. "Wash your hands!" the bird would squawk. "Don't step in that!" he repeated over and over. I could see even my father wanted to strangle the thing and eat it for dinner, but he kept his composure, for he was a gentleman.

It wasn't long until we were walking into a large shack covered with palm branches and sticks. It had a sign at the front that was written in a strange language. I didn't know what the letters spelled, for they certainly weren't English, but I did recognize one word on it: Louis. I knew we were at the post.

The captain went in first while the rest of us followed. I stayed close to my father and held Franky tightly. The store was dark with a bit of light shining through the windows. The floors were squeaky because of the old wood. There was a lot of dust in the place, but the exotic things that stood on the shelves and against the walls made up for any negative thing. Plants, art work, food, clothing, fabrics, and even small animals in large cages were on display. I couldn't help but think this store would be a merchant's gold mine.

The captain stood near the counter and called for the master of the house. "*Monsieur Louis?*"

"*Oui!*" a cheerful voice from the back called out. Suddenly a tall, well-built man came forth, entering through the lines of beads he used as a door to the other room. The tall man twirled his black moustache and his black hair was thick and greasy. His skin was rather pale, and he grinned widely, exposing a few missing teeth. "*Monsieur Pattee!*" The man standing before us was the famous Louis, friend of the captain's, and they happily embraced as they had not seen each other in a while.

"*Comment ça va, mon ami?*" Louis asked the captain in French, but before Patty could answer, Louis gave out a yelp as he set his eyes on my father and I.

"*Les Britanniques!*" he yelled as he eyed my father in his smelly British coat.

"*Les Français,*" my father huffed underneath his breath.

"Gentlemen, gentlemen, may we save politics for later?" Captain Patty held his gloved hands up. "After all, much more important business is at hand. Monsieur Louis, I am in need of your services. You see, my ship was damaged..."

"Another spat with Jonah's whale, say no more!" Louis said, finally speaking in English. "Or was it a run in with the English navy?" The man turned and eyed my father again, but my father only turned his head in disgust.

"The first one," Patty explained, putting his hand on Louis's shoulder. "But an even greater tragedy has struck us, my friend. Whilst the whale attacked us, our entire supply of chocolate was damaged by leaking salt water."

"*Non! Le chocolat?*" Louis's face paled further and it looked as if the entire world was coming to an end. "Say no more. I have exactly what you will need. Please come in, and whatever you need you can buy. Your ship shall be repaired as soon as my men can get on board."

"*Merci, Louis! Merci.*" Patty bowed his head in thanks. "And whatever you do, do not forget to store our food supplies with chocolate!"

Chapter Seven:
The Real Treasure of the Pirates

Monsieur Guyon led us through the large trading post that he called home. I'll admit that it was the most different trading post I had ever seen in my life. There were many exotic items, like plants and caged animals and spices and fruits, but also many fancy items that I had only seen in manors of the wealthy. The rest of his shop (past the first main room) was decorated heavily in the French style, which wasn't surprising since the man was French anyways, and there were colorful tapestries hanging from the windows and hand-painted portraits of various events hanging on the walls.

I held Franky in my hand, oohing and aahing at all the different items I saw for sale. In one bowl, I saw a bright yellow fish, and he swam around in circles, blowing bubbles at me as if saying hello. He was certainly a tiny thing, and I tugged my father's smelly coat and asked if he had any money on him.

"What for?" he whispered to me as we walked towards the back of the home.

"May I buy the fish? I could call him Harold!" I smiled a big grin.

"You don't know where it's from."

"I do too! He's from the water."

"I don't think that counts." My father smirked. "Besides, I don't have any money. And if I did, I wouldn't be giving it to this Louis chap."

I frowned as I waved good-bye to Harold, but was comforted in the fact that at least I still had Franky for the moment.

Louis led us to the back of the store past a magnificent French door set and into the handful of rooms he called home. On the right were two small bedrooms with a few beds (the guest rooms were what Louis called them) and on the left was presumably his room, for there was a canopy bed with rich tapestries and an armoire in there. In the center (which was the largest room) was part of a kitchen and dining room, and there stood a young woman, very beautiful, busy mixing some sort of batch to take it to cook on the outdoor stove. Her eyes widened and her mouth dropped, and in a second she ran to us and looked angrily at Louis.

"*Louis, eres muy estúpido!*" she began yelling in the language of Florida, Spanish. What all she was saying I did not know, but her passion and fury over the matter turned her face a bright tomato red and I knew she meant business. She spoke over and over about "*el pollo.*" What *el pollo* was, I had no clue, and I turned to my father as he had dealt with the Spanish in his travels.

"What's she going on about?" I asked.

"It's hard to say," he answered. "She's arguing so fast I can't tell what she's saying."

"Oh it's rather simple," Captain Patty interrupted. "The young lady had a set of chickens ready to kill and prepare for this week's meal. Unfortunately Monsieur Louis was in need of some feathered pillows to match his new bedding set. Having the fabric, he needed the feathers, and so plucked the little birds and sold what remained of the chickens to a local farmer who needed much more poultry for the celebration of his daughter's wedding feast. Señora Ines is not a happy woman at the moment."

"Señora Ines?" I asked again.

"Monsieur Louis's wife," Patty answered.

"The woman complaining about the chicken," Reuben clarified.

I slowly nodded, somewhat beginning to understand. I turned my attention to the couple and watched them go at it. Ines continued on in her native tongue while Louis started arguing back in what was a mixture of English and French. The two clearly had no idea what they were saying to each other, but something must have worked, for before I could say "chicken pot pie", they were instantly very sorry for having hurt the other's feelings and there was hugging and kissing in both parties.

"How on earth did they clear all of that up without understanding each other?" I asked in wonder.

"'Tis the language of love, little one," Captain Patty said as he sighed a heavy sigh. "It is the universal language that everyone understands, no matter where they are from."

Louis ushered Ines back into the kitchen and off she happily went. Louis returned to us and apologized for the commotion but added, "Ah, *ma femme est jolie!*"

Captain Patty smiled. "A thousand couples shall never equal the happiness you and Ines share, my friend. But pray, I do not wish to seem in a rush, but my ship is in dire need of repair, and I am in need of a fill up."

"Relax, Pattee," Louis shook his head. "You have plenty of time. Come, stay a while! Like I said, I will sell you more, so wipe the worries from your mind. I can't, after all, forget my favorite customer! With your business I can live like a king in a castle!"

"*Merci, mon ami.*" Patty tilted his head in respect. "I shall have the money to you as promised as soon as I get back on board. It seems I have forgotten to take a coin purse with me…"

My father chuckled to himself, and I, the captain, and Louis looked over to him in surprise. Louis was the first to speak. "Do you find something amusing, Englishman?"

My father shook his head with a smirk, and I took a deep breath, knowing where this conversation was heading. He had the sort of look in his eye that hinted trouble and a smart attitude. I picked up Franky out of my pocket and rubbed his little ears, trying to get my mind on something else.

"I find it…odd…to say the least that you have the money to pay for such services, Captain," my father began. "You live not the life of a pirate and do not raid or plunder, yet you always have a gold coin or two to spare. Don't tell me you inherited Willy Whalebone's wealth and have been able to live off of it all these years."

Patty shook his head. "Alas, I haven't. Captain Whalebone wasn't the wisest of stewards when it came to the monetary throne."

"Monsieur Pattee has something more valuable than money, Englishman," Louis said in an almost arrogant tone. "You officers think pirates only plunder for money. You are wrong. The coin or drink is not our most valued possession."

"Then why plunder and raid? Unless your hearts and souls are so tarnished that only the most vile of professions satisfy them." I shuddered at my father's harsh response.

Louis, eager to set my father straight, nodded with a curled lower lip and walked over to a cupboard and began rummaging through some things. I looked at Patty, feeling very sorry for him at my father's consistent distrust, but Patty said nothing and did not seem fazed by it. Perhaps my father's bickering became expected and the captain was getting used to it.

Louis finally stopped rummaging, and with a quick "Aha!" he walked back to my father with a confident air. He took the item in his hand and slapped it into my father's empty one and said, "You see the real treasure of the pirates? This is how Pattee gets his money."

My father's eyes were widened in surprise and I could tell he didn't expect such a silly thing to be handed to him. My curiosity peaked at that moment, and I nudged up against him to look at the mysterious paper that was so highly prized.

"Is this a treasure map?" I asked, trying to find the X.

"Not a treasure map, Miss Wellington," Captain Patty explained. "'Tis a navigator's map, showing all the routes of the seven seas."

"And a very detailed one at that…" my father said, and to my surprise my father seemed in awe of what he held. Obviously the map in front of him was rare. I'll admit that it was heavily detailed and showed even parts of the seas that I had never known to exist (and I had spent many hours studying my father's maps of New Providence when trying to skip my embroidery lessons.)

"I don't understand," I piped up, looking at Captain Patty with a confused brow. "How can a piece of paper give you so much money to live on?"

"'Tis simple, Miss Wellington," the captain replied. "I have the largest and most detailed collection of navigation maps amongst any pirate. I let others have a peek at my maps for a small price. Mostly merchants and privateers, anyways. I have even sold a few to people like Monsieur Louis, but only the maps I am comfortable parting with."

"I still don't understand why maps are worth more than money, though," I said, scratching my head.

"Knowing the seas can guide a man to find safe ports and escape the watchful eyes of pirates or pirate hunters," Louis declared. "And more! There is still land to be colonized and riches to be discovered. And knowing all the routes can make sailing much easier. Travel will go faster, bad weather can be navigated around, safe trade routes can be established, enemies can be avoided. There is no downside to having such a wealth of knowledge!"

"Who made these maps?" my father asked, and I swear that he almost sounded like he was admiring them.

"Well, I did," the captain answered simply. "That's what I was on Captain Whalebone's ship. I was his navigator and cartographer."

"This, Englishman, is what the real treasure of the pirates is," Louis continued, snatching the map from my father and rolling it up quickly. "Why do you think the captain sails around everywhere, huh? He updates his collection constantly."

And with that, Louis stuffed the maps back into the cupboard, never letting them come out again.

"Well..." my father began after a long sigh. "I see."

"You see nothing, Englishman," Louis sneered. "For if you tell anyone of Monsieur Pattee's maps, we will all be ruined! Pattee has had a bounty on his head for years. Bartleby will stop at nothing to get them!"

"Bartleby?" I asked. "Wait, he's..."

"The one with the dirty laundry?" Patty chimed in. "Indeed he is."

My eyes widened in excitement. The captain was wanted by another pirate, something that clearly showed him to be more privateer than my father wanted to admit.

"Bartleby?" my father repeated, as if confused. "*The* Rudiger Bartleby?"

Patty nodded. "Aye. The one and the same."

A strange look came upon my father's face, one I hadn't seen in a long time. He looked hurt, sorrowful, and yet I could see a hint of anger in him. Though I was sure Captain Patty had nothing to do with it, I was certain Rudiger Bartleby was a name my father knew more about than he let on.

My father nodded to the captain. "You must have done something terrible for him to put a price on you. He has only done that to his greatest enemies."

"Evading him has never been easy." Patty sighed. "I have had…many…close calls. Too many, in fact."

"Well," my father said with a comforting look. "It seems we have found something in common after all, Captain."

I looked at my father, more confused than ever, yet also with excitement. The way my father talked, it seemed he not only knew who Bartleby was, but had met him. "Daddy, have you fought Bartleby in the navy?"

My father looked at me, saying nothing, like he didn't want to discuss the matter.

Apparently Captain Patty knew something as well, for he did not wish to press the matter like I did. "Well!" he chimed, "I daresay after all this excitement with the whale and loss of chocolate, I am in need of a rest, as I'm sure my guests are. And of course, I shall retrieve money for your services."

"Say no more, Pattee," Louis said. "I will have Ines prepare us a meal, although I hope you do not mind fish. It seems that is all we have at the moment. Come, at least stay on the beach tonight. Your ship will be finished within two, three days."

"*Merci, Louis.*" Patty smiled. "*Merci.*"

I approached the captain, tugging on his sleeve. "Shall my father and I return to our cabin on the ship?"

At first Patty said nothing, glancing at Louis with a pouty look as if secretly communicating something. Then, after a shrug, Louis turned to my father and I and said, "Of course, you can stay too." He sighed, but then added, "The Englishman sleeps on the couch!"

My father narrowed his eyes, but thanked him nonetheless.

Chapter Eight:
One Night in Florida

My father was in a quiet mood. Whether it was because he was still upset we weren't able to escape the pirates yet or because he had failed to expose some deep, dark mischief from Captain Patty, I wasn't sure, but he said little at dinner that night. I admit his quietness was a comfort, though. It gave me a chance to hear more of Ines speak her Spanish (which I thought a delightful language to listen to) and Louis answer in his French. How they seemed to communicate so naturally was still a mystery to me, but I think I will take Captain Patty's word in that everyone understands love, no matter what language they speak.

While my father remained uneventful, the captain was as cheerful as ever. On and on he went about how excited he was to receive his chocolate, and when Ines offered us all some for dessert, the smile on the captain's face became even bigger. Whatever trouble there was with Jonah's whale and *The Smooching Sally* losing an arm and a nose seemed to disappear with every bite. Such was the power of the chocolate, and I daresay I wish my father took some so he wouldn't have looked like such a grump.

Although at the end of dinner, there was a moment when his grumpiness turned to befuddled amusement.

We were just finishing dessert when my father caught Señora Ines glancing at him from across the table. At first he and I thought nothing of it as we were clearly strangers and Ines was probably trying to figure out where we'd come from. But after a few wiggles of her brows and stifled laughs trying to be hid behind her hand, my father turned to me and whispered, "Why is she giggling at me? Am I doing something funny?"

I took a sniff of his coat and looked at him. "Maybe she thinks you stink. I know I think you do."

My father rolled his eyes. "Hilarious. Really."

"What? I'm only being honest. All I can smell is seaweed."

My father glanced back at Ines as she began nudging Captain Patty next to her. The captain looked to Ines in concern as the woman wiggled her brows and grinned.

It made me want to laugh. "I think Ines fancies you, Daddy."

My father's face turned pale and he looked mortified as he met eyes with Louis, who only glared back. I could only imagine what was going on in his head, and doubtless the thought of Louis challenging my father to a duel was not out of the question.

I shook my head, taking a drink of orange juice. Poor Daddy – always the ladies' man, even when he didn't want to be!

Ines turned back to us and began to speak. What she said, I wasn't sure (as I don't speak Spanish), but the captain quickly translated.

"Señora Ines wishes to know why your wife is not with you."

My father paused from his eating and frowned. I admit even my spirits sank as my mother was a topic my father wished to avoid. He rarely spoke of her, even to me, and most of the time when he did talk, he became so choked up in sorrow he'd have to change the topic.

He gathered his composure, offering a polite smile that was terribly weak, and said, "My wife died just after Samantha was born. We were crossing the Atlantic, heading to Philadelphia when she became ill. She died on board."

Captain Patty matched my father's troubled look as he relayed the news to Ines. Ines only frowned, but before she could say anything, the captain continued. "I am sorry to hear that, Charlie. It is a terrible feeling to lose one's other half. I understand your pain all too well."

"Thank you for your concern," my father answered quietly.

"I take it you never remarried?"

My father shook his head. "No."

The captain met his gaze with a look of understanding. "It is difficult to replace the ones we love, is it not?"

"Indeed."

The captain took a bite of chocolate and leaned forward at the table. "I think finding a good woman is like finding a pearl in the Pacific. Difficult, but certainly worth the wait."

"I should like to think so," my father said.

"And yet when that pearl is found, all the difficulties in finding it is forgotten. Tell me, Charlie – if you found a pearl, would you keep it?"

"I would treasure it always," my father replied as he looked to me. "As long as Samantha approves, that is." He smiled as he kissed the top of my head.

The captain gave a snicker as he nodded in agreement, soon giving an "oof" as Ines once again nudged him in the ribs. She was wiggling her brows again, glancing at my father as he took a drink of tea. She giggled as she said to the captain, "*Él es muy guapo!*"

I wasn't sure what that meant, but whatever it was, it made my father nearly spit out his drink and start coughing.

Captain Patty smacked himself in the forehead as my father tried to hide his cough, his face turning red in embarrassment. "I take it you speak Spanish?" he asked as I patted my father's back.

My father nodded. "Not fluently, but I understood that!"

"Understood what, Englishman?" Louis sneered as he sat up, alert.

Captain Patty cleared his throat after pursing his lips together. "Nothing of note, Louis. Only that our dear Charlie here speaks both French and Spanish. I'm afraid we will be unable to insult him because he'll understand it."

My father frowned as Patty only smirked back.

I turned to Reuben, perplexed as to what was really being said. "I don't understand. I thought Ines liked my father. Was she really insulting him?"

Reuben chuckled as he shook his head. "On the contrary. She's going on and on about how handsome he is." He paused, looking over to the Frenchman. "I wouldn't let Louis know that, though."

I could only laugh along with Reuben and Captain Patty.

When evening came, my father and I were led to the first guest room in Louis's home. It held a tiny bed, small enough for me to fit in, and a lop-sided couch was next to the wall with a tattered blanket draped over it. Feeling rather sorry, I offered my father one of my fancier blankets, but he declined, saying that he would be fine and found the Florida weather too hot for a blanket anyways.

The night was peaceful, filled with the sound of crickets and the sea wind gently blowing, making me feel more relaxed than sleepy. I admit it had been a pleasant evening, what with seeing Louis's trading post and learning about Captain Patty's skills as a navigator, and his being wanted by Rudiger Bartleby.

Bartleby! I wondered why the name resonated with my father so strangely. Rarely did he talk of his adventures as a sailor, and when he did, it was always about something happy or how he helped people. He rarely spoke of his enemies, except how they were vile and evil and deserved the noose they hung upon. He never mentioned meeting Bartleby before tonight, and I daresay the look he gave when speaking about it made me wonder all the more about his knowledge of New York's most infamous pirate.

I sat up, the blanket I slept with sticking to me in the humid weather, and looked across the room, noticing my father gazing out the window, the moonlight shining upon his face. He looked sad, like he was thinking about something he didn't want to think about, and I was eager to see what was wrong.

"Daddy?" I whispered, and immediately he sat up and looked at me in concern.

"Yes, Sam?" he answered back. "Is everything alright?"

I nodded, lying on my side as he got on his knees and knelt beside me. "I was just making sure you were well," I answered. "You looked sad just now."

He smiled as he looked down, taking my hand in his. "I was just remembering your mother, that's all. Sometimes I think about her at night before I fall asleep."

I nodded, feeling sorrier for him more than ever. I didn't remember my mother - I was a baby when she died while crossing the Atlantic - but my father spoke of her every once in a while. She had light brown hair like me, but green eyes and a fair face. She was a lovely woman both in form and virtue, my father always adding that he thought her to be likened to an angel. My father never thought of remarrying, though many people we knew encouraged it. He said he would never find anyone as good as my mother.

"I'm sorry, Daddy." I frowned. "If it makes you feel any better, I miss her too."

"I know," he said, the sadness still in his face. "But it's late, Sam. You need your rest. Go to sleep and think of her while you dream."

I nodded, but as my father got up to return to bed, I pulled his hand back. The question of Bartleby lingered in my mind, and for some reason, as strange as it was, I couldn't help but wonder if my father and Bartleby were connected.

"Daddy?" I asked. "You looked sad earlier today like you do now when Louis and Captain Patty mentioned Bartleby. Why?"

My father frowned, returning to his melancholy. "Go to sleep, Samantha," he said quietly, touching my forehead and kissing it. "Now get some rest."

Then he returned to the couch, laying his head on the arm rest and shutting his eyes. I was snug in my bed, pulling the blanket close to my heart, but soon sighed. My father knew something dire about Bartleby, and whatever it was, it made him think of my mother. Before the week was ended, I was determined to find out why.

Chapter Nine:
I Learn of Captain Bartleby

don't think I slept one minute that night at Louis's Trading Post - not even a wink. Whether it was from the steaming Florida heat or a busy mind trying to figure out my father, or both, I don't know, but regardless I woke up irritable and cranky. I couldn't help but wonder if my father slept much. Perhaps a lack of sleep was what caused his foul mood with the pirates the day before.

Breakfast cheered me up a little, however, as Louis and Ines served us the most delightful of fruits and breads and pork, all freshly prepared before sunrise. Señora Ines was a wonderful cook, and had she been a single woman, I would've begged my father to take her to Boston with us to be my governess. My real governess could barely fry an egg, let alone cook breakfast.

Despite my mood, my father seemed to be in better spirits, though I doubt he slept much the night before. At breakfast, he asked Captain Patty about the maps he made as Willy Whalebone's navigator. My father had always been fascinated by maps and their making, so he was all ears as Patty explained the instruments he used, the stars he recorded, and the routes he liked best. It was a strange, yet welcome, sight to see - both my father and Captain Patty carrying on a decent conversation that both of them seemed to enjoy. Even after breakfast they continued to talk, and as Ines returned to her duties and Louis to running the post, Patty even pulled out a few of his maps from the leather satchel at his side to show at no charge. My father seemed delighted to see them, and he looked them up and down, admitting quietly that the maps were fine work indeed.

While my father busied himself with the maps, Patty looking alongside, I decided to find out more about Bartleby. I wished to speak to Patty about the infamous pirate captain, but with my father beside of him, I guessed I would be scolded. My father didn't want me to know about Bartleby, that much I understood, but it only fueled my curiosity more. I looked around, wondering if I should go to Louis to ask him, until I saw Reuben playing with a wooden chess set across the room. Deciding quickly, I headed over to Reuben, sitting across from him and asking to join the game.

After a few sentences of small talk, I got straight to the point. "Reuben," I whispered. "May I ask you something?"

"Sure," he said, moving his pawn forward.

"I asked my father about Bartleby last night," I said, making my move. "But he wouldn't say much. What do you know about him?"

"He buries his dirty laundry," Reuben said matter-of-factly, almost with a chuckle. "Can't say I know why, though. Doesn't know how to use soap, I guess..."

"I know about the dirty laundry," I said, smirking. "I mean what else can you tell me?"

"Well..." Reuben said, pausing. "I don't know too much, seeing as I haven't met him."

"Has Captain Patty?" I interrupted, forgetting my manners for a moment.

Reuben shook his head. "Maybe. I don't know much about what he did with Captain Whalebone. I just know Bartleby by name. We try to stay away from him, what with the bounty and all."

"Of course," I said. "But what have you heard?"

"His ship's called *Revolution's Wrath*," Reuben answered. "He's mean and brutal, too. He puts the 'irate' in pirate."

"How awful."

"'Tis true." Reuben sighed. "He's sent many a Royal Navy ship to Davy Jones' locker. Other pirate ships, too, if they got in his way. He's even raided port cities in the colonies as far south as the Caribbean and as far north as Canada."

"It sounds like he travels everywhere," I said. "Why, though? He mustn't be a very good navigator to want Captain Patty's maps, and that's an awful lot of sailing to do for only a few raids."

"Rumor has it that he's looking for someone," Reuben said, stopping the game for a moment and looking at me with a serious face. "A nameless navigator."

"How can he know who he's looking for if he doesn't know the name?" I asked, perplexed.

"Bartleby's smart," Reuben said. "Brilliant, in fact. He can remember a face for decades after seeing it for a second. And once he makes an enemy, he never forgets. Only once has he lost a battle or raid - that's why he's so feared and so sought after by the navy. Some time back, he raided this one poor vessel, taking the captain and some officers hostage. The whole ship was searched and robbed, everyone on board facing death by the sword. And then the ship's navigator staged a revolt. He and some of the crew members managed to escape their bindings and freed the other hostages, fighting Bartleby head on. Before the night was over, the rebels won back their ship and crippled *Revolution's Wrath*, Bartleby barely escaping with his life as his own ship was bombarded by what few canons the rebels had. His ship started to fall apart and was left to sink in the sea, so he returned to *Revolution's Wrath* to save what was left of it while the rebels fled. Before he left, however, he vowed to seek vengeance upon the navigator who outwitted him, saying he would find him because he knew his face. Bartleby's been looking for him ever since."

My mouth stood agape, intrigued by all the information I just heard. "Do you know who the navigator is?"

"Like I said, a *nameless* navigator." Reuben shrugged his shoulders. "Some say the whole story's a myth anyways. That's the one thing about sea life - you never know what to believe."

But I thought there was more to Reuben's tale than what he was letting on. He was loyal to Captain Patty, the man who took care of him like a son. He knew Patty was once a navigator on Captain Whalebone's ship, and there was a time when he wasn't on *The Smooching Sally* when he returned to Scotland to search for his family. It was rare for a navigator to also be skilled as a captain, but Patty fit the bill perfectly. If I was to make a guess, Captain Patty was the Nameless Navigator, and it explained why Bartleby had a bounty on his head. The maps had to be some sort of cover story or connection.

I decided to say nothing more of the matter to Reuben or to anyone else for the moment, especially since I had no proof of my theory. If there was anyone I wanted to talk to now, it was Captain Patty, but I had to earn more of his trust, not to mention learn more of his mystery with Bartleby before I spoke. I needed history, reasons, more information as to what he did to make Bartleby never forget him. I needed to know more of the mystery of the Nameless Navigator, but how I was going to find out without talking to the captain was anyone's guess.

Chapter Ten:
Louis's Letter

I won't pretend that the first two days I had spent with Monsieur Louis were adventurous. Aside from my conversation with Reuben, which I could have easily learned on the ship, there was really nothing much to talk about. My father continued to be his usual self, grumbling this way and that about not finding any suitable merchant vessels docking so he and I could sneak off. When he wasn't complaining, he was working, either assisting the captain in whatever needed to be done or helping Hammy with ship repairs.

Captain Patty remained pleasant. He set himself with helping the crew when he could and choosing which chocolates to take aboard for our next journey. He also pulled out a few maps of the Florida peninsula he had been working on, and made a few marks here and there so as to seem busy. Louis and Ines, of course, continued on with their work at the trading post and cooking and being good hosts to us.

And so that left Reuben and I. We were bored not being able to do much grown-up work, so that left us to explore our surroundings. I was fortunate my father allowed me to run along with my new pirate friend, but I was not without limits. I could not leave Louis's house for any reason, unless my father accompanied me, and he demanded to be twenty feet or so away in case I needed any help. And so, while he went about helping wherever he could, Reuben and I went off on our own little adventure.

Reuben and I set off to explore more of the post and Louis's home. I liked this idea immediately, searching every nook and cranny to see if I could not only learn more of Spanish and French culture but also something related to the mystery of the

Nameless Navigator. You see, I had learned nothing more about Bartleby and the mystery surrounding the Nameless Navigator during the past two days, and I hadn't plucked up enough courage to ask Captain Patty about any of it in fear of being told the same thing my father told me. "Don't worry about it, Samantha," I constantly heard. "Get it off your mind."

But that didn't mean I couldn't *look* for something related to Bartleby with Reuben. And it didn't mean I couldn't ask more questions. Reuben, after all, was one of the few who would talk of the dreaded pirate and the myth surrounding him.

We were walking along, exploring and searching for anything of interest, and we entered a cluttered up room that was supposed to be Louis's study. I can't say much learning was done here, even though books were scattered this way and that. None of the items looked like they had been touched in ages. There was dust caked on every table and a musty smell lingered about the room. Parchments, art work, furniture pieces, old shipping instruments, and used rope were all strewn about in what appeared to be a junk pile.

"I say!" I gasped as Reuben and I entered the doorway. "Where on earth did Monsieur Louis get all this?"

"Travel and trade." Reuben whistled as he looked around the room. "Which, I might add, he must've done more of since I've been here last. At least before I could see the flooring."

"And my governess says I'm a mess," I mumbled.

"He's quite the collector." Reuben snickered, stifling a laugh.

I would've never known.

"Well," Reuben said, throwing his shoulders back, "I can't say we can get much exploring done here, seeing as we can't move. I can show you the formal dining room again, though."

"Oh nonsense!" I said, getting the strange feeling I could find something of interest in the piles set before me. "There's bound to be something fun here. Maybe some old maps!"

"I'm not sure," Reuben said. "But I wouldn't try it. I think if your father finds that you've fallen and broken your neck, he wouldn't be too happy with me."

"I won't fall and break my neck," I reassured as I took my first step onto a pile of old fabric. "I've balanced on plenty of brick fences back in Nassau when my governess wasn't looking and haven't fallen yet."

"Don't go without me, then!" Reuben called, holding his hand out so I could grab it and help balance him. "After all, you can't go off on your own. Your father worries enough."

"I think you worry enough!"

Off we went into the study, carefully stepping over boxes and crates, searching for something of interest. I don't think Reuben was too keen on this type of exploring, though, for I felt his palms get sweaty and saw his eyes dart back towards the door.

"Isn't this being nosy?" Reuben asked as he looked back at me. "I mean, I don't want to sound like your father, but it doesn't seem too proper going through someone else's things."

"We're not going through anything," I said with a chuckle. "We're simply walking through a room. It's not our fault Monsieur Louis has left everything on the floor."

"I don't think that's what I meant." Reuben huffed. "Maybe we should go back. I think I'd rather..."

And then suddenly, as quick as lightning, I felt my hand go down. I heard Reuben give a gasp as he toppled forward, myself toppling back, and before we could stop ourselves, we tumbled to the ground, knocking a bunch of letters off the top of a crate nearby.

"Oh, bless it all!" Reuben muttered as he sat up, looking towards the door. "Now we'll get it. See what you made me do!"

"What did I do?" I whined back. "You're the one who fell!"

"You went too fast!" Reuben looked at me vividly. "I'm sorry, but I can't balance on a rolling pin."

"Is that what you tripped over?"

Reuben nodded with a pout. "It had old dough on it. Crusty, green dough."

"Don't let it bother you. You're a pirate lad. I'm sure you've seen worse." I looked to the door. To my surprise, no one came. "Look..." I turned and poked Reuben, pointing. "I don't think they heard us."

"Probably because we only knocked over paper," Reuben said. "We were fortunate it wasn't one of Ines' vases. She'd be furious if one of those broke."

"Well?" I said, getting a mischievous gleam in my eye. "Let's look at them!"

"At what?" Reuben asked.

"The papers!"

"Now that *is* being nosy."

"It's not. We're just picking up what we knocked over," I lied, knowing my father would scold me if he saw me doing what I was about to do. But my curiosity was too deep, my longing for knowing the mystery of the Nameless Navigator plotting my every decision. Then, giving Reuben a nose in the air, I picked up the first paper and began to read.

The first letter was difficult to understand. Of course it was all in French, and there was no way I could read it. I handed it over to Reuben, asking to interpret.

"What does it say?" I asked, looking over his shoulder.

Reuben squinted his eyes, unsure if he wanted to look or not. Then, after a moment of self-debating, he shrugged. "I can't say. It's rather sloppily written. I can only make out a few words, something about fish and supplies and the boat being very smelly."

"Well that's no good." I frowned, picking up another letter. "Try this one."

Reuben picked it up, reading the French. "This is a letter of thanks to the local priest. Apparently Ines baked a rather nice pie for the parish picnic. I think Louis forgot to send it…"

I sighed, wanting something more exciting than letters about smelly boats and a picnic. I fumbled through, handing some letters to Reuben and taking some for myself.

"Go through these," I said as I gave him his pile. "Find something of interest."

"Like what?" Reuben asked.

"Like something about Rudiger Bartleby and the Nameless Navigator."

"That again?" Reuben scoffed, and I think by now he got tired of hearing of it like the rest. "Sam, I've told you all I know."

"I know," I replied, tossing a few letters in French aside. "But I can't help it. I'm curious as a cat."

"And you know what curiosity did to the cat, right?" Reuben shook his head.

"Yes, well cats have nine lives supposedly," I replied. "So let's just leave it at that. Now read."

He did as he was told as I read what was in my pile - mostly letters in French that I knew I could not read and frankly wouldn't care to. A couple of them were in Spanish from Ines, and they were perfumed so I could only assume they were love letters from when she and Louis were courting. I couldn't read those, either, so I tossed them aside with the rest.

And then, after sifting through almost my entire pile, I found it. Something I could finally read in English. But this wasn't just an ordinary letter. It was a once-sealed letter to Louis, and the words were slightly faded to show a secret type of ink was used to write it.

I read it quickly to myself, not sure of whether Reuben would want to hear it or not. This is what it said:

My dear mon ami, Louis,

Salut. I am sorry, my friend, that this letter must come to you in the most secretive of ways, but I am desperate and have to remain hidden. I'm afraid your years of warning have been right, for word has reached me that Rudiger Bartleby is making his way to South Carolina. I dare not take the chance of letting him find the maps, so I am sending my wife and son to you for safekeeping. I do not wish for anything to happen to them, so I ask you, beg you, to hide them in Florida amongst the Spaniards. I will join them once I have alerted the Royal Navy of Bartleby's arrival. His obsession with finding the Nameless Navigator will be the death of us until I do something about it, and I am tired of running.

My wife knows nothing of my deal with the Royal Navy to trap Bartleby, and I prefer to keep it a secret. She worries enough as it is. Make sure that she stays busy so as not to be concerned over what I am doing. And please make sure my little Reuben wears a pudding cap. He is just learning to walk and if he falls, I do not wish for him to hurt his head.

I am sorry, my friend, for this favor I ask of you, but thank you a hundred times for your aid and devotion. Once Bartleby is taken care of, I shall come to Florida. It shouldn't take long.

Sincerely,
Patrick A. Peterson

My eyes widened until they felt as if they could be stuck. It didn't take much intelligence to figure out this Patrick Peterson was the one and only Captain Patty, but to hear that Reuben was his *actual* son, not adopted or pretend, was simply breathtaking. Did Reuben know? Of course he would have, or at least I would think, especially since Captain Patty stayed with him. But why the last name difference? Captain Patty was a Peterson. Reuben's last name was Gayle.

And then there was the issue of Bartleby. It sounded from the letter that he was after more than just the maps. Now, more than ever, I believed that Captain Patty was the Nameless Navigator.

But then what about Reuben's mother? There was no woman on board the ship, though I heard Captain Patty mention he had a wife.

That was it, then. He *had* a wife. Poor Reuben must be like me. Motherless.

I suppose Reuben noticed my change in face as I was reading the letter, for at once he turned to me and said, "You must've found something interesting! You look like you've found the crown jewels in a wagon!"

I looked up, unsure whether to say anything at first, but my curiosity overwhelmed me. "Reuben," I asked very carefully, "this letter was written by Captain Patty. It talks about you."

Reuben's face became stern as he peeked over to look at it. "What's it say?"

"It says Bartleby was after you and that Captain Patty was going to send you and your mother to Florida to hide," I said, noticing Reuben's brow lowering. "Do you...do you know anything about this?"

Reuben looked up, a frown now on his face. "Of course I do. I've seen this letter before, you know."

"So is Captain Patty your real father?" I asked.

Reuben turned away, unsure of whether to tell me anything. "You aren't supposed to know. No one is. But yes, Captain Patty is my father. What of it?"

"Well why haven't you said anything?" I asked. "Why can't you talk about it?"

"Because," Reuben snapped, "it's what's keeping me safe! I told you, no one's supposed to know about it! Why do you think I use a different last name?"

"Keeping you safe from what?" I asked.

"From Bartleby!"

"Is Captain Patty the Nameless Navigator?"

"Bless it, why are you so nosy?" Reuben scowled, anger now clear. "Can't you see I don't want to tell you anything more?"

I frowned. "Oh Reuben, I'm sorry. Really. I can't help it. All this talk of mystery and Bartleby and maps has gotten me curious. I didn't mean to pry where I wasn't supposed to."

"Well, now you've done it already." Reuben huffed as he crossed his arms. "But you must swear not to tell a soul, not even to your father or mine!"

"I swear," I said as I crossed my heart. "But…if I may be so bold again…does this mean you have met Bartleby before?"

"Stop this obsession with Bartleby!" Reuben's voice neared a shout, and I feared we would be heard by the others. "He's a bad man, I tell you! Very bad! And if you want to know the truth, yes - I have met him before, though I don't remember it much since I was just a baby. And so did my parents."

"Oh dear," I said, frowning again. The letter was beginning to make sense now, as was Reuben's harsh feelings. "Then, your mother…"

"We never made it to Florida." Reuben sighed. "Someone in the Royal Navy tipped Bartleby off and he arrived the night before we were supposed to leave. He attacked our town, hacking and raiding until morning, searching for us. If it wasn't for my father's cunning, I would have never made it out of that mess alive. But my mother, well…she didn't. And that's all I'm going to tell you, because you aren't supposed to know the story anyways."

I felt more rotten than the garbage piled in Louis's junk room. There I was, excited over mystery and thinking I would find out about the Nameless Navigator, only to upset my new friend and learn how his mother died. Feeling rather guilty, I did the only thing I could do. I put my hand on his shoulder, the tears forming in my eyes, and said I was sorry.

"It's alright," he said in a friendlier tone. "You didn't mean it. And I'm sorry for getting so wound up. I've just never talked about it before except with the captain."

"I know how you feel," I said, trying to cheer him up. "I lost my mother, too. She died on the voyage to America and I was only a baby. My father says a great sickness hit the ship we were on and many people died on the voyage, my mother included. She had to be buried at sea."

"I'm sorry about your mother," Reuben said. "But it makes me feel better that you've told me that. It's nice to know I'm not by myself."

"Me too." I smiled.

He smiled back.

"So," he began, standing back up and helping me to my feet. "Can we continue our tour?"

I nodded. "Absolutely! I can't wait to see the dining room. But Reuben? Are we still friends?"

Reuben chuckled. "Of course we are. That's what friends do, you know. They forgive."

"Thank you," I said.

"Any time."

I smiled again as we walked side by side towards the door, only to find a frantic-looking Louis and my father standing before us.

"Agh!" Louis croaked, putting his hands over his mouth and staring. "My office! *Non!* It was so organized! What have you done? YOU HAVE MESSED UP MY OFFICE!"

My father crossed his arms and gave me a look that told me I was in trouble.

Reuben and I gulped at each other, a guilty look coming upon both our faces. Perhaps seeing the dining room would have to wait.

Chapter Eleven:
Francisco's Tavern

It was a dreadful punishment that awaited Reuben and I. Not only were we bade to clean the mess we made in Louis's office (which…to be honest, didn't take long since there wasn't much room to put things), but we were also denied the chocolate that came as dessert with dinner. Captain Patty felt awful denying Reuben and I the greatest of delicacies to finish our baked fish, tortilla bread, and fruits, but he agreed with my father that we should learn our lesson that being nosy wasn't a polite thing at all.

After being lectured and sent to bed early, the next day at Louis's greeted us with warmth and sunshine with a cool breeze. It was a beautiful day, much like a spring morning in Nassau. But something strange happened that morning when I awoke from my sleep. I had a feeling - a deep one - that something was wrong. I couldn't explain what was wrong, per se, but that the feeling hung around like a weight on my stomach. And even though the morning greeted me that today was going to be like any other day, I felt in my heart that trouble was ahead.

But being the brave soul that I was, I ignored the thought. Fear was for babies, and it had been a long time since I slept in a cradle.

As the feeling pushed to the back of my mind, I groggily got up and went to the washbowl to splash my face. My father, always up and early, was already dressed (albeit in his smelly coat still, the blasted thing…) and ready to go. He stepped outside the room to give me privacy, and I changed from my nightclothes to my regular shirt and trousers I had gotten from the ship. I stepped out, stifling a yawn as I am not a morning person like my father, and was greeted by Captain Patty and Reuben who stood chatting away in the hall awaiting for me to finish.

"Good morning, Captain! Good morning, Reuben!" I said, trying to be cheery. "Is the ship repaired or are we to have a land-lubber's adventure today?"

The captain gave a small laugh and covered his mouth with his hand. The poor fellow was still stifling a yawn like me. He was not a morning person, either. "The ship is almost finished," he replied as he finished his yawn. "About another day or so and she should be ready to sail!"

"So soon?" my father asked, and we all looked at him with the most perplexed look on our faces. My father cleared his throat, aware that all eyes were on him, and looked towards the floor in silence for a moment before looking back up. "I just meant I'm a little surprised such damage to a ship could be fixed so quickly. Are we sure this Louis chap knows what he's doing?"

"He's one of the best handymen I know," Patty replied. "Besides Hammy. That man could build a ship with just some paper and string."

"Actually, he did build a model of one," Reuben piped up. "Sailed for a little while before that blasted goldfish came and ate it…"

"Oh I remember that fish. Had half a fin," Patty mumbled, rubbing his chin. "Didn't we name him Herman?"

"I thought we named him Whalebert."

Patty nodded slowly. "That's it…"

"So," I interrupted, crossing my arms. "What's for breakfast? Is Señora Ines fixing something special? Or can I request pancakes?"

"You won't find much maple syrup here, my dear," Patty replied. "But when we stop in New York, I'll be sure to get you some."

"So what are we having then?" Reuben asked.

"Well…" Patty paused, and I instantly recognized the smirk as him having an idea we didn't know about. "I was thinking we'd go out to eat this morning. See some of the town. Have you ever heard of Francisco's Tavern?"

My father and I shook our heads. It's not like we went to Florida often.

Chapter Eleven: Francisco's Tavern

"Well you're in for a treat!" Patty exclaimed. "Best seafood in the area and scrambled eggs like you've never tasted before."

"Not to mention tea and toast for you, Englishman," Louis replied as he joined our conversation. "Or is that too plain for you gentlemanly type?"

My father rolled his eyes. "That will be fine. Thank you."

"Well, come along then!" Patty said, waving his hand. "Off we go to break our fast."

We followed Patty out of the room, Louis returning to repair the ship and Señora Ines quickly following as she saw us head towards the door. But before any of us walked out, my father was pulled to a halt by the captain.

"A bit of advice, Charlie," Patty said with a chuckle. He lifted the collar on my father's smelly coat. "When in the Spanish colonies, don't dress like the English navy."

My father nodded, albeit slowly. He didn't like parting with his officer's coat. It was like his identity, his character, and his livelihood all rolled into one. But even I knew Patty was right. If we were to go out into town, the last thing we needed was to draw attention to ourselves. After all, English officers weren't always liked in other parts of the world.

"Of course," my father muttered, and I could tell he was annoyed, but he took the coat off and handed it over. Patty then tossed it to Ines, who in turn tossed it into a bucket, muttering something in Spanish and pinching her nose.

"Thank heavens." Reuben exhaled in relief as Patty put a commoner's coat into my father's hands. "Señora Ines said she's going to wash the coat when she gets finished baking her pastries."

I smiled at the thought as I trotted up to my father, taking his arm in mine. It was nice to have him not smell like seaweed.

"The coat itches."

My father's voice was nearly drowned out by the revelry of the tavern as people ate and drank merrily around us.

"It's made of linen. It shouldn't itch as much," Captain Patty replied. I groaned. I knew the short-lived pleasantries between them would be even shorter-lived once we left the post.

"Well it does, Captain. It itches a lot."

"Says the man who wore a wool coat in summer for how long?"

"That was for king and country."

"I'm sure they'll forgive you for not roasting and smelling up the place for a day."

A pause came, and I felt like smacking myself on the forehead. My father lowered his brow. "I didn't smell."

"Of course you did," Patty replied. "You smelled like rotten fish boiled in garbage."

"What? How do you even know what that smells like?"

"Ever made a stink pot?"

"No, but I'm sure you have lots of experience with it."

"Not on the receiving end, unlike someone I smell. Didn't wash the coat after your last battle, huh?"

"I'll have you know it was washed, thank you very much."

"By a skunk?"

"By myself! I do my own laundry...sometimes...."

At first I thought my father and Patty's bickering to be like what was found on the ship when my father and I first arrived on *The Sally*. Pointless, arrogant, and rude (at least on my father's part). But after seeing the two of them chuckle after a few banters, I wasn't sure what to think anymore. Surely my father was having his usual "pirates are all evil and Patty is a pirate, so Patty must be evil" sort of conversations. But as I glanced back and forth, watching them come at each other with clever and somewhat insulting analogies, it almost seemed as if they were having fun.

"I don't get it," I said as Reuben looked at me and chuckled. "They're being so mean to each other saying such things, and yet they're laughing. *You're* laughing!"

"I just think it's funny, that's all," Reuben replied. "Oh bless it, don't give me that look! You just need to understand boys a little better."

"What do you mean?" I asked. "Are you saying they're just being boys?"

"I'm saying they're finally getting along."

"By insulting each other?" My brow went up but my brain was surely hurting. I didn't understand any of it. "Louis and Daddy insult each other all the time and yet I know they still don't like each other."

"It's different with them," Reuben said.

"It looks the same to me."

"But it's not," Reuben continued. "Our parents are laughing as they're saying it. They're being friendly with each other, you know? It's what boys sometimes do. Being sarcastic and insulting is like saying 'hello, how are you'."

I frowned, still not getting it. "Boys are odd."

"As if girls aren't, too." Reuben smirked, and I shook my head. Girls were much easier to understand. You could tell what a girl was thinking just by looking at her and seeing how she talked.

"All I'm saying is I think they've finally gotten some common ground. Ever since your dad saw those maps, it's like he changed or something."

"Daddy uses maps, but not often," I replied. "He does like to collect them, but I don't think that'd make him suddenly be friendly with the captain."

"Well, if it's not the maps, something must've clicked. And I'm not going to complain about it. It's about time your father calmed down and knew we didn't mean you any harm."

I smiled, giving a sigh. "It is nice, isn't it?"

"Very," Reuben replied. "I was starting to think he'd never trust us."

I was starting to think that too. But after seeing the smiles come from my father's lips, I couldn't help but wonder what made him let his guard down. Maybe it was the maps and the understanding that Patty really was more of a businessman instead of a pirate. Maybe it was because being a wanted man by Bartleby proved the pirates didn't consider Patty as one of their own. Or maybe it was just time. We had, after all, spent almost a few weeks with the captain and his crew. Perhaps my father began to realize that his judgments were wrong.

As I was pondering the thought, however, I soon heard a noise that would make me alert. And little did I realize it would be the first step to the most frightening experience in my life.

The door to the tavern swung open and in walked seven men, casually dressed like sailors and large and burly as if they could lift a table with a finger. They eyed the room when they walked in, and everyone – including my father and Patty – suddenly went silent.

I was unsure of why everyone had quieted, but one look from my father's eyes and the way he inched closer to me in a protective gesture told me whatever it was, it wasn't going to be good.

"Quaint little place, isn't it?" one of the men said as he picked up a guest's pint of drink and chugged it.

Patty lowered his brow. "Speaks English. Odd in the Spanish colonies," he whispered.

My father cocked his head to the side. "Not local and dressed like he's been at sea. Pressing for service?"

Patty nodded carefully, his hand moving to the pistol clipped to his side.

I gulped. It was the first time I'd ever seen Patty reach for his gun.

"Don't look at the men. Stay quiet. Be still," my father ordered me through a whisper.

I obliged, knowing what my father was warning me about. I'd heard stories of ships kidnapping innocent men and dragging them back, forcing them into service. My father once served under a captain who had kidnapped fifteen men from the town of Williamsburg just because he needed more sailors to run his ship. No volunteers had come when asked so the captain found his own help. After seeing the men plead for their lives and the chance to return to their families, my father vowed then and there that if he were to get his own ship, he would never do such a horrible thing.

But now I just hoped that horrible thing wouldn't be done to him.

The leader of the men pointed to a few young lads sitting at a table. The sailors grabbed them by the shoulders and pulled them to their feet, dragging them to the door.

The youngest of them begged. "*Por favor! No quiero...*"

"Shut yer trap!" the leader yelled as the poor man was dragged out the door with his friend. "You'll be deckhands for the *Malina Serus* now. Be thankful we've found you a nice paying job!"

The tavern remained still with fear until I heard Captain Patty whisper.

"*Malina Serus...*" he muttered under his breath. "I know that name..."

My father turned to him, his face pale. "I know it too."

"Bartleby's fleet."

My eyes widened with fear. I hadn't known Bartleby had a fleet to command, let alone he was near port! Whatever rotten luck we could've had suddenly grabbed hold of us that morn. I couldn't help but curse it.

"When they leave the tavern, we'll make a run for it," Patty whispered.

"Do you think the entire fleet is here?" my father asked.

"I don't know. I'd rather not chance to find out, though."

"Neither would I."

Before they could finish their conversation, however, the leader of Bartleby's kidnappers suddenly eyed our table. "Hello there! What have we in this lot? Looks like two little rats squeaking away."

Both Patty and my father suddenly silenced, looking towards the ground. I gulped, praying that somehow, someway the men would ignore us.

"You both look like strong lots," the man said as he began to circle our table. "Young. Healthy. And I think you're from out of town by the language you speak. Visiting the Spanish colonies, are we?"

"On our way to conduct business, my friend, if you catch my meaning," Patty answered.

"Business, eh?" the man said as his fellows began to surround our table. I started to shiver in fear.

"Yes," Patty answered, looking up and meeting the man's glare with his own. "And my business is my own, unless you want trouble with the brotherhood."

I knew nothing about the brotherhood or what that meant, but I could only assume that Patty was letting them know he was a fellow pirate and was someone not to be trifled with.

"I see," Bartleby's man said as he turned to my father. "And what of you? You on your own business as well?"

"Following the orders of my captain," he replied, changing his accent as he looked to Patty. "The crew and I are spending coin and time with the wenches before we sail off." He gave a laugh, his play-acting near perfect.

The man laughed alongside as he stepped closer. "And where you off to?"

"Tortuga," Patty replied as he leaned back, his hand still close to the pistol. "I hear rumors of merchant ships making their way to the Caribbean and am tempted by the plunder."

"You don't say."

"'Tis true. You can ask the waiter at the counter."

The man walked around and looked to me and Reuben. I froze, unsure of what to do as I held onto my father's coat. The pirate noticed it quickly and glared me in the eye. "Bit of a scared cabin boy, you have."

"Recently picked 'im up from a shipwreck," my father said quickly. "Bit shocked, he is."

"I'm sure," the man said as he turned his eyes to Reuben and the rest of the table. "So tell me, my brothers — where is the rest of your crew?"

Patty looked to my father and he pursed his lips. "Out on the ship doing chores," my father replied.

The man turned to my father. "I thought you said they were out spending coin."

Patty let out a sigh, knowing they were caught, and before Bartleby's man could pull out his own pistol and aim it at the captain, Patty whipped his arm around and took the man's pistol from his belt, pulling out his own and aiming them at Bartleby's men. The man yelled for his friends to attack, and suddenly I felt my father push both me and Reuben under the table, telling us to hide.

I didn't have time to agree as Reuben and I were forced under the shelter.

My father quickly spun and took two cutlasses in his hand — one from Patty's side and the other from one of Bartleby's men — fighting the seven men who now attacked with whatever weapons they had. Shots were fired and swords clashed with a loud metal *cling*, and within seconds I saw a few of Bartleby's men fall to the floor injured or unconscious.

I peeked up from the table and watched as my father and Patty stood back to back, Patty firing his pistols and my father swinging the cutlasses, felling his foes. It was a sight I never thought I'd see – a naval officer and a pirate fighting side by side, and doing it well. It was fascinating to see how coordinated they were, able to work with each other just by looking or saying a few words. They were natural partners, balancing out each other's strengths and weaknesses when fighting.

I was so proud of them both...until they started bickering again. And this time I knew it was for anything but fun.

"I thought you said merchants used this port!" my father barked as he parried a blow from another cutlass.

"If you had listened properly, I said it was *mostly* used by merchants!" Patty grunted as he dodged a shot.

"That's still no excuse for this! I don't want my daughter endangered by these pirates!"

"Well I don't want *anyone* endangered by them!"

My father grumbled as he kicked one of the men away from Patty's side. "If you knew Bartleby would be here, why did you stop?"

Patty looked offended, and for the first time I could see he wanted to punch my father. Luckily one of Bartleby's men tried to hit him first. Patty knocked the man across the teeth with the butt of his pistol, saving my father from being stabbed with a knife. "You think I knew Bartleby would be here? Why on earth would I stop and say hello to the one man on this planet who wants to capture me?"

My father only huffed as he took out another opponent. "I only mean I find it *convenient* that Bartleby just so happens to show up at the one port you stop at!"

Patty lowered his brow. "Are you saying I'm in league with Bartleby?"

My father took out his last man and glared at Patty. "Don't think I don't know of the pirate brotherhood. I know your kind sticks together."

Patty lowered his pistols and glared back. "And don't think I don't know what a paranoid, judgmental know-it-all you are! I'm not in the brotherhood – I only told them that so they'd leave us alone and we'd be able to escape."

"And a lot of good it did you!" my father scoffed. "We should've never come here. My daughter could've been hurt!"

Patty holstered the guns back to his side. "I didn't know we'd be attacked! My word! Do you honestly think I'm so cruel that I'd put Reuben, a boy under my protection, and Samantha at risk?"

"I'm a parent! What else am I supposed to think of besides the safety of Samantha? It's not like you'd understand."

Patty got up in my father's face and lowered his voice. "I understand much more than you think I do. Did you really think you were the only parent on my ship? Or are you too daft to see that Reuben is not just a cabin boy to me?"

I gulped, looking to Reuben. My father didn't know of their family connection, but I did. He stared at the captain blankly, almost confused. "I don't understand," he muttered.

"Reuben is my son," Patty said with a sneer. "And he's all that's left of the family that Bartleby tore from me. You have much to lose, Mr. Wellington. I understand that full well. But don't presume to think I know nothing of your concerns. I've already lost the love of my life to that wretched pirate and I refuse to lose my son to him!"

Before my father could answer, Patty stormed off, clipping my father's shoulder and then reaching under the table to help Reuben and me out from under it. I ran to my father and he embraced me back, kissing the top of my head. Reuben embraced his own father and our parents were silent for a moment as they met each other's sorry gaze.

I think that was when my father realized just how judgmental he had been. He watched them for a moment, seeing Patty's arm around the young pirate boy in a protective gesture, their bond just as strong as the one between my father and I, if not stronger. They had seen much together and I could only imagine the years of hurt and loneliness they had to endure. My father could only look away, his eyes meeting mine. I don't think he knew what to say.

Patty was the first to speak, interrupting the silence. "We need to get back to *The Sally* and leave. It's no longer safe to be here."

My father frowned. "What if the ship isn't fixed yet?"

"Then we leave anyways," Patty replied. "Unless you want to fight an entire fleet."

My father let out a heavy sigh, agreeing, and we rushed out of the tavern and back to the post.

Chapter Twelve:
To Open Sea

We arrived at Louis's within minutes, our breath coming out in scarce pants and our brows beaded with sweat. At first Louis laughed when he saw us, saying he "warned about not trying the chili pepper omelet that Francisco's always brags about," but after telling him we had spent our breakfast fighting pirates instead of eating, his face paled.

"Since when does Bartleby sail these waters in the summer?" Louis asked as we rushed through his home and gathered our things. Ines handed my father's British naval jacket back to him, unfortunately unwashed, and he hurried it on.

"He typically spends his summers near Canada and New England," Patty replied as he picked up his bag of maps and slung it onto his shoulders. "Something must've drawn him here."

"Did you let anyone know you were sailing south?"

Patty shook his head. "No. I've kept things quiet. Aside from three stops to Port Royal and a few on Nevis, I've been at open sea this season."

"It makes no sense," Louis muttered as he stroked his chin. "How would Bartleby know you're here?"

"I don't know." Patty sighed. "Unless one of the crew's talked. But I don't think…"

"What of you, Englishman?" Louis set his eyes on my father, who had been rather quiet since we left the tavern, and approached him. My father looked up but said nothing, and I stood by his side in silence. I think my father was still feeling guilty about what he had said to Patty and didn't wish to further their argument.

But Louis was going to pull him into one whether he liked it or not. "You're in the Royal Navy. Where were you stationed?"

"Nassau," my father said, eyeing him back. "But I was being sent to Boston for a new command post."

"Well you should be aware of who is traveling the seas at this time," Louis continued. "What have you heard of Bartleby? Was he spotted in Caribbean waters?"

My father looked away, not wanting to say anything.

"Well?" Louis pressed further as he got in front of my father's face. "Your silence is telling me you know something, Englishman. What is it?"

My father looked up as Patty and Reuben now watched for his answer.

"I'd heard rumors...speculations, really..." my father began, rubbing the back of his neck, "that Bartleby had been spotted moving south. We doubled our forces in Nassau and..."

"And you said nothing?" Louis's eyes lit up with rage.

"We were heading north to Boston," my father explained, "*away* from the Caribbean. How was I supposed to know we'd cross paths?"

"You could have at least warned us of the possibility," Patty replied, perturbed.

"I didn't know he'd be at the mainland," my father explained. "The admiralty had told me that Bartleby was expected to be arriving at the Caribbean islands to plunder. Obviously they were misinformed."

"Obviously," Louis spat. "So is there anything else you want to tell us before we all are caught?"

My father beaded his eyes and was about to say something before Patty interrupted him.

"There's no time for arguments, gentlemen. For now, all we can do is flee. Is the ship able to sail, Louis?"

He sighed, shrugging his shoulders. "I've yet to fix Sally's nose and arms, but the holes should be patched up. Hammy was checking the left side of the ship, though, just in case."

"We'll make do with what we have, then. And the chocolate?"

Louis shook his head, making Patty cringe. "I haven't been able to load yet. I was going to fill your cargo when you were ready to set sail."

Patty puts his hands on his hips and sighed. "This day can't possibly get worse."

Louis looked as if he felt terrible. To deny Patty his chocolate was the most terrible of news. He was about to say something in consolation, but Red – Patty's quartermaster on *The Sally* – came running up.

"Two galleons coming from the east!" he panted, his eyes wide in fear. "They fly the Jolly Roger with Bartleby's colors and are moving fast!"

Patty calmed him by putting a hand on his shoulder. "What two ships did you see?"

"The *Malina Serus* and the *Carolina Gust.*"

Patty paused, heading out of the house and looking towards the eastern sea. There were two ships in the distance, fast approaching and flying black and white Jolly Roger flags at the top of their masts. Patty bit his lip as he turned back to Red. "Lift the anchor and prepare to sail. We cannot tarry and must be swift! Where the *Serus* and the *Gust* are, *Revolution's Wrath* isn't far behind."

"Aye, Captain!" Red ran back towards the ship.

"I'm sorry, my friend," Patty said softly as he clasped Louis's hand. "I wished to stay longer but I don't want to endanger you and Ines."

"Say no more," Louis said with a choke. He clasped Patty's hand back. "Godspeed, Captain. Be safe!"

"Hide in the glades until Bartleby leaves. I'll return when I can!" Patty called out as we ran away towards the ship.

I sped behind the captain and Reuben, rushing towards our ship as fast as my legs could carry me. I was hungry, my legs ached, and my heart thundered inside my chest. As my father took my hand and we ran up the bridge to the deck, my eyes met the third ship suddenly coming into view on the sea.

A great ship – larger than any galleon my father had sailed on – began to sail towards us. And though I couldn't see the name upon the side, I could guess what ship had arrived.

Revolution's Wrath.

Bartleby was coming.

The ship was astir as the crew ran here and there to get us moving. The sails were raised and I prayed for a fast wind. With no rows and an inability to move on our own, we were at the mercy of the elements. The faster the wind blew, the faster we could get away from Bartleby.

I stuck my hand out and felt the breeze that brushed through my fingers. It was weak, barely moving the hair upon my head.

If our luck was bad leaving Nassau, our luck became worse leaving Florida. If I could run on the water, I think I could be faster than the ship.

Patty was busy ordering his crew about, calling for cargo to be dumped overboard if it meant us speeding up. I asked Reuben if they had been this close to Bartleby before and he nodded, but his paling face told me that this was a rare occurrence.

"I don't know how he found us," Reuben muttered as if in a daze. "We were so careful and quiet. I don't understand…"

"We still can get away," I reassured him, trying to be confident. "My father and I survived being thrown overboard, didn't we? If we could survive that, we can survive Bartleby being behind us!"

"But the chance of it all…it makes no sense…" Reuben paused, his lip starting to quiver. "What if we get caught?"

It was best not to think of it. "Don't worry, Reuben. We'll be fine. God will take care of us."

Reuben nodded, wiping his eyes.

We were ordered to help throw more cargo overboard. Rueben and I lifted small crates full of who-knows-what, tossing them into the sea and hoping that the ship would speed away from the port. Louis's post was slowly fading away from view, but the three ships of Bartleby remained in sight. Doubtless the men sent to Francisco's Tavern were late in reporting back to their captain or they somehow got word to him that there was trouble, and Bartleby was not one to let a ship escape him.

I began to fear we were doomed.

My father busied himself with the captain, maintaining the sails and making sure they were getting the most wind. As I was taking another crate to the railing to be dumped, however, I heard my father speaking to Patty.

"Captain," he began, and I noticed his look of guilt had not disappeared. "I wish to apologize..."

"Don't worry about it, Charlie," Patty interrupted. "Now isn't the best time to have a chat about being sorry."

"I only meant..."

"I get it. You're just not the trusting type. That's fine with me."

"But it's not just that..."

"We'll have a talk later, Charlie. For now, help me with the sails!"

"Captain, please!"

Patty stopped, looking at my father with the same look I gave him. Confusion, a wonder of why my father found it so urgent to speak his mind at a moment there clearly wasn't time to. Patty crossed his arms, almost perturbed, but cocked his head to the side as if willing to listen.

"Captain, I know it is uncouth of me to interrupt you at a time like this, but..." My father paused, looking away and pursing his lips. "I...I feel as if I'm putting your crew in danger with my being here. I'm sorry...I think this is my fault, and..."

Patty's look softened as he eyed my father's Royal Navy uniform. It dawned on me then that Patty having an officer on board his ship endangered the crew even more. If Bartleby discovered my father and his status within the navy, he might suspect Patty as a privateer employed by the crown. Perhaps even a spy.

And whatever mercy Bartleby would have had on Patty with him being a fellow pirate would have been gone. A pirate was more likely to destroy his enemy if he thought he was going to betray him.

"It's alright," Patty reassured him. "If we are caught, I won't reveal who you are or your connection to your daughter."

My father nodded, but his look of worry remained. "Thank you, but..."

Before my father could finish, however, Hammy stormed the deck from below. His face was ruddy, sweaty...and he was panicked.

"We're leaking," he said, bending down and putting his hands on his knees to catch his breath.

Patty's eyes widened. "We're *what?*"

"Leaking!" Hammy repeated with a scoff. "We were finishing putting tar on the holes this morning. Some were still drying and some didn't get the chance to be repaired! My men are fixing what they can, but I don't think it'll be enough."

"I thought Louis said the leaks were repaired."

"There were others we missed. I didn't get a chance to look on all of the other side before we left port." Hammy rubbed his brow in frustration. "I can fix the leaks but with a lack of wind and extra water weight, we won't be able to outrun Bartleby's fleet. With two galleons and a man-of-war behind us, one of them is bound to catch up."

I froze, this time alongside Reuben who had stopped to hear the conversation. A look of horror came upon the lad's face, matching my father's, and I knew what they were thinking.

We were going to be caught.

The captain said nothing at first, but after Hammy asked, "What are we going to do?" Patty lowered his brow and clenched his fists.

"Bartleby may have the speed and strength, but we have the intellect. Even if he captures us, we can still win the day." Patty pulled Hammy to him and spoke quietly. "I'm initiating Plan 47. Hide your tools and stay alongside the cook and his mates. Bartleby will doubtless take us aboard the *Wrath*. When we are gone, fix the ship as best you can and return. Tell Red to give the signal when it is night. Stay your distance until you see it. We will meet on the other galleon. I will spread the word above and you will spread it below. Understood?"

Hammy looked shocked, and at first he shook his head. "Are you sure you want to do that? It's awfully risky. Not to mention the ship..."

"Will already be on its way down and there is nothing we can do about it," Patty interrupted with a smirk. "This is our best chance of survival, Mr. Pye. A pirate with much power also has much to lose, and it is time that Mr. Bartleby is humbled. Fate has chosen today to be the day I confront my enemy for the last time. I am tired of running and shall not run again. Besides -

I've yet to have a plan that's failed and I do not plan on failing today!"

Hammy nodded, wanting to hesitate, but after a final order from the captain, he sped below deck to spread the word.

My father looked to Patty and asked the question I was wondering about. "What's Plan 47?"

"On your ship, do you have a plan for every foreseeable circumstance?"

"Yes," my father replied.

"So do I," Patty continued. "I've learned long ago that the best way to handle an emergency is to plan for one. Forty-seven is one of many I have prepared my crew to face."

"And what does it entail?

Patty's face looked grim. "If all goes well, it means I'll be getting a newer ship."

My father's eyes widened. "A what?"

"You needn't know all of the details," Patty replied. "It will take too long to explain, and I don't wish you or your daughter involved in it. You are my passengers and therefore are in my care. I will not endanger your lives any more than I have already done."

"But Captain…"

"No, Charlie. Not this time," Patty said, clasping his shoulder. "I know we have our differences and I am willing to overlook them. You are a British officer and are bound by oath to fight the pirates who abuse the privilege of the seas. I will not deny your honor and I will not scold you for duty. But I ask you, *beg you*, to put aside your judgments and trust the kind you have sworn to hunt and hang, as it can save you. Will you trust a pirate with your life, and will you trust a fellow parent with your daughter's life?"

My father looked to me, unsure.

I nodded to him, hoping he would agree. Patty had never let us down before. He was honorable, a man of his word, and I could only imagine his determination in wanting to protect not only the crew, but his beloved son as well. Patty had much to lose, but he would not give up his treasures without a fight!

But whether my father would agree to trust was unknowing to me. He fought pirates, hated them. It was the greatest of hypocrisies to put faith in the very people he had loathed with all his soul.

And yet they stood. Side by side, facing each other. Pirate to officer, officer to pirate. Man to man. Father to father.

As an officer, my father would never budge, but as a parent? Trust would be his only option to keep me safe.

My father gave a sigh, almost as if it pained him, but faced the captain, sticking out his hand. "I trust you," he said quietly, his voice low. "But I ask that you protect Samantha above myself. My life is unimportant, but hers is irreplaceable. I have already lost my wife and cannot bear to lose my daughter."

"I understand, Charlie," Patty replied as he took my father's hand with a firm grip. "Fear not. I will protect her."

"Thank you."

Patty let go of his hand and gathered Reuben and I to the circle of conversation. "Charlie, I'll need you to go with Hammy. Throw your officer's coat overboard and let the sea take it. Without your coat, you are just another sailor. Samantha, you will go with Reuben and be with the cabin boys. Bartleby will not take you aboard his ship and you should be safe with them."

My eyes filled with tears as I ran to my father, hugging him tight. "We'll be separated?"

"Only for a little while until Bartleby leaves," Patty replied in comfort. "I know you're scared, Samantha, but you must be brave. Pretend to be a part of the crew. It will save you in the long run."

I looked to my father as he put his hand to my cheek, stroking it. "It's alright, Sam. I won't let anything happen to you. I promise."

He kissed the top of my head and held me close as the captain turned to his crew. "Plan 47!" he shouted at the top of his voice. "Man your posts! We are about to be boarded!"

I watched in fear as Bartleby's ships edged closer, praying I would live to see tomorrow.

Chapter Thirteen:
Bartleby

I t had been a few hours since Hammy first told us of the leak. We were moving slowly with a lack of wind and a ship filling with water, and the majority of cargo was dumped overboard, making the ship lighter than a sloop. Hammy had been busy draining as much water as he could, but with Bartleby's fleet within cannon shot distance, the captain bade everyone to drop what they were doing and ready for Plan 47. Red took a few of Hammy's tools while the others were hid. Hammy joined the cooks below deck. Reuben and Patty gave each other one last embrace before parting ways.

And lastly, my father and I spoke with each other, hoping it was not a good-bye.

My father stood at the edge of the railing on the back side of the ship, his blue officer's coat in his hands. He fingered it carefully, sadly, and looked upon it one last time before he was to cast it out to the sea.

I stood beside him, resting my head on his arm. "I'm sure the navy will give you another one once we get to Boston."

It was my thought that he didn't wish to part with the coat, but after he looked at me with sad, gray eyes, I think the coat was the last thing on his mind.

"I should've never left Nassau," he said softly.

"You couldn't help it. Uncle Silas said the navy requested you in Boston," I reminded.

"I could have turned them down." He sighed, rubbing his brow. "You would've been kept away from this mess if I had."

"It's not like you knew we were going to be thrown overboard, rescued by pirates, and chased by other pirates. I mean, even I know that only our rotten luck could've caused all of that."

He lowered his head, shaking it. "I'm sorry, Samantha. I tried to protect you from all of this."

"But you have. As long as we listen to Patty, everything will be alright."

He faced me once more. "Are you sure about that?"

I frowned, giving a huff. "Daddy, you said you trusted Patty!"

"I trust him, Samantha, as much as it pains me to trust a pirate," he said. "But even that may not be enough to save us."

"The captain is clever, Daddy. If anyone can outsmart Bartleby, it's him."

"Perhaps," my father replied. "But sometimes even cleverness cannot save everyone."

He took the coat, tossing it into the sea, and then turned to me, hugging me tight. "I love you, Samantha. Never forget that."

It was strange hearing the fear shaking his voice. Was he afraid something terrible was about to happen? Did he fear that Patty's plan would not work? His doubt made me anxious. "I love you too, Daddy," was all I could say in return.

He pulled away from me and held me straight by my arms, getting on his knees to face me eye to eye. "Whatever happens, you must be brave. Do you understand? Even if something happens to me, you must still be brave and not look back. Your survival is everything."

"What are you talking about?" I asked, my lip starting to quiver. From the way he talked, he spoke as if he didn't believe Bartleby would spare us. Or that he was planning something. "Do you think something bad is going to happen?"

"No, my darling," he said with a comforting smile. He put his hand to my cheek and caressed it. "Whatever happens, you mustn't worry."

I wanted to say more to him, but my worries bested me. Had he somehow figured Patty was the Nameless Navigator? Though I wasn't sure he overheard Reuben and I speak, he doubtless had heard of Bartleby's obsession of finding the maps. As an officer, he knew of Bartleby much more than I could ever dream of.

And maybe that's why he told me to forget about Bartleby. He knew Patty was the Nameless Navigator. He knew that sailing with Patty was a danger and that it put me at risk because Bartleby would have no mercy on the man that bested him.

No wonder he wanted to escape Patty's ship so badly.

Fear grabbed my heart, and suddenly Patty's confidence in facing Bartleby seemed like the plan of a man who was desperate and had nothing to lose.

I opened my mouth to speak, to tell my father what I was thinking, but the captain's call silenced me.

"Man your posts! Plan 47 begins now!"

My father kissed my cheek and hugged me once more before standing straight. "I love you," he said through muffled voice.

I held onto him, not wanting to let go but knowing I must. I repeated that I loved him and that he was the best father in the world.

He smiled at me one last time before ushering me towards Reuben at the center of the ship. Bartleby's fleet approached, and as they took their positions to aim their cannons, Patty ordered the white flag to be raised in surrender.

I watched as my father took his position below deck with Hammy and the other kitchen staff. My heart was pounding and my eyes wanted to do nothing but cry, but after a small smile of confidence from him before he left, I gulped down whatever fear threatened to overtake me and stood firmly beside Reuben.

Plan 47 had begun, and I was going to face Bartleby not as a girl, but a sailor.

When I first saw *Revolution's Wrath* up close, I couldn't help but hold my breath.

Rows and rows of cannons faced us, one shot threatening to turn us to dust upon the waters. Had it not been for the flag of surrender flying high on our mast, I was certain Bartleby would've taken little time to win the battle. The other two galleons from his fleet circled us from behind, making sure no trickery or escape could be planned.

Chapter Thirteen: Bartleby

Revolution's Wrath and *The Smooching Sally* now faced each other, and before a minute passed, a wooden plank was brought forth to allow Bartleby's crew to board our ship.

Reuben and I remained still as we watched, Patty approaching the plank with his hands held in the air. A group of ten men from Bartleby's ship appeared and crossed over, greeting us with their typical pirate charm.

Was it Bartleby at their front? The leader of the group, a blonde-haired and freckled man who looked to be the same age as my father, crossed his arms and laughed as he beheld the deck. He turned to Patty with a scoff. "In Florida, you ran away from us rather quickly, Captain. Now that we've caught you, you surrender without a shot. You must be cowardly indeed to not even bother defending your ship."

"Cowardly, no," Patty began as he faced the man. "Wise, yes. I know that my galleon cannot withstand a fleet's attack, especially since it is on its way down."

The leader snickered. "Heavens, don't tell me you sabotaged your own ship in thinking you could escape us."

Patty frowned. "No."

"I was going to say," the leader said, "you certainly saved us the trouble of sinking it for you."

Patty said nothing as his eyes beaded.

The leader was unimpressed. "Why were you running from us?"

"We weren't running."

"Do not think you can deceive me, sea filth. I know what transpired at Francisco's Tavern. My men at the docks saw their brethren injured on the floor when they returned from delivering us the Spaniards. Why did you attack my men?"

"I was only defending myself from being pressed into your service," Patty replied. "But I would also like to ask why a fellow pirate, such as yourself, would dare attack one of your own! Is there no honor amongst you?"

"There is honor and respect amongst the brotherhood, which you have not shown. Now tell me your name, sir."

"Patrick Peterson, captain of *The Smooching Sally*."

"A foolish captain for a foolish ship. How quaint." The man laughed. "I know of you, Captain. Surely you know we've been looking for you. You have maps you've refused to share with us, and we only want but a peek of the treasure you are hiding."

The leader walked past Patty and looked towards the deck, turning to his men and pointing. "Gather the shipmates and bring them up top. Whoever we can add to our crew we will take and whoever refuses will be left on deck. Go!"

The men complied as they pulled out their pistols and cutlasses, heading below deck to where my father was.

I turned to Reuben as we remained still near the center. "Is that Bartleby? The blonde man?" I whispered.

Reuben shook his head. "I don't think so. Bartleby's hair should be darker."

"Then where is he?"

Before Reuben could answer, the sound of a pistol shot suddenly made us both jump in fright and turn to the deck. I instantly thought of my father trying to be brave, fighting the men trying to take him above deck, but after seeing Patty's crew suddenly be herded to where we were, a few of Bartleby's men shooting their pistols in the air for fright, I breathed a sigh of relief. My father, alongside Hammy, was ushered towards the railing and bade to kneel.

The leader soon encircled us, motioning for us to go on our knees like the others. We complied in silence, the man speaking afterwards. "My name is Bartholomew Severn," he projected as he put his hands behind his back and strolled around the deck. "I am first mate to Admiral Rudiger Bartleby and the captain of *Revolution's Wrath*. I will speak and you will listen."

I sat closely to Reuben, feeling him shaking as much as I was in fear, watching the first mate as he made his way past us in his address. So far we were fortunate Bartleby had not come on board. I could only hope that Severn was unfamiliar with Bartleby's hunt for the Nameless Navigator and only saw Patty as the man with the maps.

Severn stopped near the center mast as he continued. "I offer full pardon and quarter for any man who is skilled in carpentry, navigation, and medicine, if you are willing to swear loyalty to the admiral and his crew. Any who refuse will remain on this ship and be bound to its fate." He paused, looking about the deck. "Stand and approach with hands raised if you wish to join me."

I watched as a number of Patty's crew – about thirty in all - stood to their feet and raised their hands. Amongst them were many of Hammy's helpers and Red, Patty's quartermaster. Red approached with a bow of his head. "My name is Redmond Cade, sir. I'm the ship's lead carpenter and this is my help. We're experienced with galleons and would be much obliged to join your crew if it means sparing our lives and gaining us coin."

I watched with lowered brow, trying to figure out the madness before me. Hammy was the carpenter of the ship, not Red! Whatever Plan 47 was had to involve a lot of deception on the crew's part. I could only imagine what would come of it, and hoped and prayed it would work.

Severn laughed as he clasped Red on the shoulder. "Thank you," he replied. "The admiral welcomes you to his crew. We are in need of more carpenters upon the *Carolina Gust* and will transfer you there at the earliest convenience. For now, make your way to the *Wrath* and await further instruction."

Red nodded as he and the men followed two others towards the wooden plank and onto Bartleby's ship.

Severn looked to the rest of us. "Are there any other takers?"

The remainder of the crew remained silent, and the first mate nodded as he unclasped his hands and turned to his men. "Very well. Call for the admiral. He would wish to speak with Captain Peterson regarding his maps."

One of the men nodded and ran towards the ship, leaving the rest of us to await the arrival of Rudiger Bartleby.

Chapter Fourteen:
The Real Captain Patty

The ship was quiet with fear. No one dared to speak as the sounds of heavy footsteps slowly *thunk, thunk, thunked* against the floor boards, coming closer to where we were all lined up. I turned, my knees already becoming sore for sitting on them for so long, and looked at my father who was far to my left. His head remained bowed and he refused to look at me. The thought that he wouldn't even meet my gaze saddened my heart.

"He's trying to protect you," Reuben whispered next to me, noticing my eyes were turned to him. I looked to my friend, a perplexed expression on my face. "He's a British officer and anyone connected to him is in danger. If he's caught looking at you, Bartleby may suspect a connection."

But my father's uniform was thrown overboard to hide his identity. Wasn't that enough?

I turned away, too afraid to answer. Then suddenly the footsteps stopped.

I looked ahead to see two giant leather boots, worn and of a faded gray color, in front of me. I looked up, and that's when I saw him.

Rudiger Bartleby was a tall man, clean and trim with hair like a pony's mane, only thicker. It was wavy and he sported a long mustache and goatee that was perfectly kept and darkened like his hair so as to hide any shades of gray. He was an older man, that much was sure, but he dressed quite young, and his beaded eyes that were a sea-shade of blue searched every gaze that met his.

I was one who looked at such a man, and he looked back at me. His face remained expressionless as his hands remained behind his back, gently puckering out his crisp brown coat. He stared at me for only a few seconds, letting out a light scoff, before turning to Reuben and then Captain Patty.

"Taking them awfully young, aren't we, Captain?" Bartleby strode to Patty and stood before him, towering over with a smirk.

The captain looked up, not an ounce of fear in his eyes. "The boy was a stowaway, the girl rescued from a shipwreck a few weeks back."

"You are brave to bring a girl on board." Bartleby eyed me again, making me shudder. "Many say they bring misfortune on the seas." He laughed lightly, turning back to the captain. "Stand."

Patty obeyed, facing the villain nose-to-nose. I held my breath, as did Reuben, wondering what would happen next. A thousand thoughts ran through my mind during those few seconds of silence that passed between them. Would Bartleby pull out a pistol or cutlass and strike Patty down? My heart went out to poor Reuben. He already lost his mother. He couldn't lose a father, too. Or would Bartleby only take the maps, letting us live but stranding us on the sea, our fates unknown? It was a cruel way to perish, but there was a chance of being found. Or maybe we wouldn't be left to the ship at all. Maybe we would become part of his crew, bound to the *Wrath* until we passed into eternity.

Bartleby held out his hand, his palm facing upwards. It was a strange way to face Patty, and I pondered as to what it might mean. Bartleby lowered his brow and set his face sternly. "You have the maps."

"Aye," Patty agreed, giving his own glare.

"Give them to me."

Patty paused, and I could only imagine what was going through his mind at the moment. If he didn't give Bartleby the maps, we would be doomed. But then again, the same could happen if he did. And then if Bartleby had the maps, no ship could hide from his plundering wrath. And then the Nameless Navigator...

Wait. The Nameless Navigator. If Patty was him, wouldn't Bartleby had recognized him?

My thoughts were interrupted as Patty spoke. "I have but a few. They are in my quarters in a chest beside my bed. The key is in the desk drawer."

Bartleby turned to his first mate, nodding. "Go."

Severn ran off to do his captain's bidding, but as he left, the most unexpected things began to happen.

Bartleby edged closer to Patty, eyeing him up and down, but squinting his eyes as he beheld his face. I held my breath.

"You look very familiar to me," Bartleby whispered.

My heart felt like it would stop. There! Bartleby knew. Captain Patty had to be the Nameless Navigator. My eyes widened, wondering what to do. Reuben couldn't lose his father. Bartleby would have no mercy on the only man who outwitted him. I turned to my father, and to my surprise, his head remained bowed. I lowered my brow, ashamed. My once brave father now cowered like the rest of the crew!

I turned back to Patty. He said nothing, only looking ahead. Bartleby stepped back, giving a laugh that sent chills down my spine, and he started to pace back and forth in front of us. "If I remember," he began, "some years ago, we met in South Carolina, did we not?"

Captain Patty's letter to Louis suddenly sprang into my mind, and I looked at Reuben. His eyes were wide with fear, and I could tell he was thinking the same as I.

"In my journeys I have fought many men – officers, soldiers, farmers." Bartleby stopped as he faced Patty. "Map makers."

He stood in front of Patty once more, erect as an admiral should be. "We fought on the docks of Ellingsport, didn't we, Captain?"

Patty remained unfazed, not a muscle in his body moving. "Perhaps."

"And if I remember correctly..." Bartleby lifted his hand, putting a gloved finger between Patty's brows. "I shot you point-blank right there."

Patty said nothing as I gasped. Patty was shot? No one survives a shot to the head. Only by a miracle of God would anyone make it through something like that. Something wasn't right...

Bartleby grinned as he noticed sweat starting to trickle down Patty's temple. "So either you are not the Patrick Peterson I met so long ago, or you are a very hard man to kill."

Suddenly he whipped out a pistol from the right side of his belt. "Perhaps we should test which is correct?"

Reuben looked as if his world was about to come to an end. I turned to him, praying as hard as I could that somehow, someway Bartleby would put the pistol away. He only held it in front of him, waiting for the first mate to return with the maps.

He didn't have to wait long. The man ran, a satchel in his hands. "The maps are here. There seems to be some missing, but we have a good stock."

"We can work with that," Bartleby replied coolly. He turned back to Patty and grinned. "Thank you for your services, Captain. It has certainly been a pleasure."

Then he cocked the pistol, aiming it to Patty's forehead.

My mouth stood agape, tears filling my eyes. I looked to my father and he remained silent, his head still down. Coward! I burned with anger, my heart ashamed of the man I loved and wanted to be like. How could he, a protector of the innocent, not act at such a time as this?

Bartleby gripped the pistol tightly with a final grin. Patty remained silent, but his eyes drifted to Reuben.

And then a shout was heard.

"MAMA!"

I turned, my ears surely deceiving me. Reuben was on the floor, his hands pressed hard against the wood, as if he were crawling, begging for Bartleby to listen. The boy's eyes were filled with tears and he looked towards Captain Patty, who only looked back in a teary shock, shaking his head no.

"Hush, Reuben," the captain whispered, but it was too late. Bartleby lowered his pistol, stepping towards Reuben and I.

He turned to the boy, his look keen. "What did you say?"

Reuben's face paled as he quivered back next to me. He looked to Patty, then back to Bartleby. "I...I didn't say anything..."

Bartleby stopped and went back to Patty, facing him. "Now I remember you..." Then, with a quick swipe, he put his fingers to

Patty's mustache, ripping it off. I kneeled there, shocked, as Bartleby next removed Patty's hat, coat, and neck cravat.

Captain Patty wasn't a man, but a woman!

Even my father looked up in wonder. There was no denying it. Without the pomp of her coat and cravat to cover her neck and features, and without the hat and fake mustache to hide her true face, she was as womanly as a lady of Nassau.

"It makes much more sense, now." Bartleby snickered as he tossed Patty's items to the ground. "Your husband would be happy knowing you've kept his name alive, even though he isn't."

Reuben's face was full of horror. It was clear the revelation wasn't supposed to be known. The story of who Captain Patty really was slowly began to unravel - she was Reuben's mother, not his father. If she lived, that must've meant Reuben's father, the real Captain Patty, was dead, killed by Bartleby. But how Reuben's mother became the captain, how she made maps as well as her husband, and how she could fool her crew (who was just as shocked as the rest of us) for so long were questions that needed answering. And then her real name - that was a mystery, too.

But then that meant something else. Captain Patty couldn't be the Nameless Navigator. The Royal Navy or any merchant would never have allowed a woman on a ship under commission, and the real Captain Patty was killed by Bartleby, making his search for the Nameless Navigator useless if it was him.

So many questions needed answering. So many mysteries needed solving. But as I looked back to Rudiger Bartleby, triumph in his eyes as he paced circles around the woman I knew as Captain Patty, all I could think of was one thing:

What now?

It was on Bartleby's mind too, and he made it up fast. He turned to his first mate. "Take the maps and put them in my quarters. And to you, 'Captain Peterson'," he said as he glared at her, "you know well I don't like deception." He stepped beside another pirate from his ship. "Bring the boy and our fellow captain to the *Wrath* and take the craftsmen to the *Gust*. Leave the others here. It would be a waste of time and gunpowder sinking a vessel that is already on its way down."

Patty's eyes blazed with rage. "I insist you leave my son out of this! Reuben's done nothing wrong. It's me you want. *Leave him here!*"

She struggled as two men grabbed each arm, holding her at bay. Another took Reuben from beside me and he kicked and screamed to be let go. Bartleby only shook his head, merciless cruelty etched into his skin. "Oh, don't worry Mrs. Peterson. He will be well looked after. It's you I'd be more worried about."

They were being led to the *Wrath* and I struggled to think of how to help them. None of the crew dared to move an inch, the fear of a bullet or tip of the cutlass making them unable and unwilling to help. But as Bartleby started to follow his new prisoners, he stopped, pointing to something in the water.

"What is that?" he asked. "Fetch it."

A man from the ship took a pole and drew it into the water, pulling whatever the captain saw up to the surface. I held my breath as I saw it. Cursed luck! The tide returned my father's officer's coat to the ship, and now it rested in Bartleby's hand.

He returned to us in the greatest of haste, the uniform dripping with salt water onto his boot. "Whose is this?" he asked, and when none of our crew answered, he shouted it. *"Whose is this?"*

My father lowered his head once more. I prayed Bartleby wouldn't find the truth.

Chapter Fifteen:
Caught

Reuben and Patty were held in silence as Bartleby returned to our captive group. He held the smelly wet coat at arm's length, high in the air for everyone to see.

"I tire of repeating myself," he slurred. "Who does this belong to?"

We remained silent, looking away.

Bartleby lowered the coat, clutching it in his right hand as he went back to Patty. "You said the girl was shipwrecked. Was there anyone else?"

I held my breath at Bartleby's mentioning of me. He was a smart man, that one, and I prayed he wouldn't be able to figure out my father was with me.

"There was no one else," Patty lied with a sneer. "Believe me or not. Just leave the crew be!"

But Bartleby returned to us, this time tossing the coat to the floor. He pulled out his pistol and stood before me, suddenly grabbing my shoulder and pulling me up. I trembled at his grasp and began to cry. It was all I could do to keep my fear from overwhelming me. I looked to the crowd, my eyes pierced with fear and my body shaking as if dipped in ice.

As much as I tried not to, I looked to my father. His head was slightly lifted and I saw a new panic enter his face.

Bartleby pulled my collar towards him, making me gasp. "This girl was not rescued alone. There was at least one other with her, and this uniform belongs to that man. Step forward, officer, and the girl shall live. Remain silent and you shall seal her fate."

Chapter Fifteen: Caught

Nothing was said, making my heart fall to its darkest depth. Tears streamed down my face as I heard Bartleby scoff.

"No one? Very well." He lifted the pistol and I screamed, closing my eyes as tight as I could get them. But before anything else could happen, I heard my father's voice boom from the back.

"Stop! I confess!" I opened my eyes to see my father standing near the edge of the ship, one hand on the ropes and the other held high in the air. He stood on the railing, balancing himself with the rope.

I sobbed as I stood there, grateful that my father spoke up to save me and yet terrified that he was now in danger of becoming a prisoner himself.

"It is my uniform," my father answered, and Bartleby shoved me to the ground, my hands breaking my fall. "You will not harm her!" My father exclaimed in anger as he saw me look back up. "She is innocent, a fellow passenger on our ship that was bound for the mainland. Now leave her be!"

I glanced at Bartleby as I turned. He had a fiery look about him, one I had never seen. He looked terrified, yet confident; angry, yet excited.

"I've finally found you," I heard him whisper under his breath, and to me he sounded as if he was in awe. He stepped forward, his crew members backing away to let him face the officer who answered him.

My father clenched the rope with his fist. Bartleby stopped a few feet away from him and I scrambled to my feet, watching and waiting. The two looked at each other as if much past was between them - a past held on to for so long that it built up and was ready to explode at any moment. It put a fear in my heart and I suddenly had a feeling that the next few minutes were about to change my life forever.

"Two in one day..." Bartleby murmured breathlessly. "What a grand luck this is! For years I searched for the maps that would lead me to you, yet here you are, the man whom my vengeance could not quench, the man who has eluded me for over a decade."

My eyes widened. What was Bartleby talking about? There was a history between him and my father, but to me it sounded big - much bigger than what I thought before.

Bartleby smiled, making me shiver. "Tell me, Nameless Navigator. What do you really call yourself?"

My eyes, already swollen with tears, shed more. My heart raced. My breathing stopped. My knees gave way and I crashed to the ground. How? Why? I stifled a cry that was so desperate to come out. For all this time I thought Captain Patty was the Nameless Navigator!

I was wrong. It was never the captain. It was my father.

"Charles," my father answered, his brow lowered. "And I propose a truce, Admiral."

"A truce with my sworn enemy?" Bartleby laughed, the mockery in his tone making me burn with anger. "You are funny, *Charles*, but I am willing to listen. What is it?"

"You will return Captain Peterson's wife and son to *The Sally* and leave them and the crew with the ship. I will go with you, and only me. They are innocent in our feud and need not be caught up in it. Why add even more names to the list the Royal Navy wishes to hang you for? You have the maps and me. That is all you need."

"And if I don't accept these terms?"

"Then I shall throw myself overboard. You will have your maps, but your thirst for vengeance will be denied you. I have escaped you before. I can escape you again."

Bartleby frowned, knowing he wanted my father alive for himself. Either option was hateful to me, however. I didn't want my father to be captured by Bartleby only to be tortured and killed. And I didn't want my father to sacrifice himself to save us. I loved him, needed him. He was the only family I had left.

There had to be another option, another way to get out. But Bartleby only laughed some more.

"I have a response to your truce," he began, walking towards me. He grabbed my shirt, yanking me up with his cruel strength. I cried out in pain as he squeezed my arm, pushing me towards his first mate. "Take her. Now here is your choice, Mr. Charles."

The first mate drug me towards the *Wrath,* and I screamed for help. My father's face turned red in anger as Bartleby approached him a second time. "Either come aboard willingly and the girl lives, or throw yourself overboard and join the girl in the watery depths."

Severn picked me up, pushing me over the bridge yet holding me so I wouldn't fall over. I eyed the white foam that splashed beneath me, the sounds of Patty and Reuben both screaming for the first mate to stop. "Please don't!" I yelled, and my father scrambled off the ledge.

"She is innocent!" my father pleaded. "Take me instead! She was just a passenger on the ship!"

"I am not stupid," Bartleby said, nodding to two of his men to grab my father and drag him towards me. He turned to him and whispered in his ear. "She has your eyes."

Bartleby turned to Severn. "Take Mr. Charles and his daughter, along with our other guests, aboard." His men followed, their pistols and cutlasses pointed to Patty's crew so they would stay on board. "And to you, noble gentlemen." Bartleby turned to them, the last of his ship to leave, and smiled. "Good day to you."

The bridge was brought back and we were taken aboard the *Wrath*. The outside world - the clouds, the sky, the sea - suddenly faded away as we were forced below deck, the darkness of the lower prison cells surrounding us. We were pushed forward into a tiny, barred cell full of hay and mold and mud. The cell door swung shut with a loud, metallic clang, and I scrambled up, grabbing the bars.

My father remained outside, Bartleby's men holding him tight. I screamed for my father, pulling the bars back and forth as hard as I could, hoping they would break. They remained strong, and I cried all the more.

The woman I called Patty put a gentle hand on my shoulder as my father was dragged back up the stairs.

"Be strong, darling!" he called to me before he disappeared from view. "Everything will be alright. I promise!"

Then suddenly he was gone, leaving me with Patty and Reuben alone in the darkness of the cell.

Chapter Sixteen:
Le Bateau

All I could do was cry. Cry for my father, cry for being captured, cry for all the rotten luck that had suddenly come our way. We were so close to freedom, and yet it still crashed down upon us! Still we sprung a leak. Still Bartleby caught up. Still we were imprisoned against our will. Plan 47, whatever it was, was still in motion, but how it would end was anyone's guess.

Everything had suddenly changed. Patty was a woman - a female pirate captain, something even I had never heard of in all the stories on the docks - and my father was a wanted man. Not by the navy, of course, but by one of the most infamous pirates of the seven seas. My father was the Nameless Navigator. He was the one who defied Bartleby, outwitted him, nearly destroyed him all those years ago. Daddy was a legend among pirates and I never even knew it.

My thoughts lingered to my father. Where was he? What would Bartleby do to him? My heart cried out in worry. I prayed for the Lord to give him strength, wherever he was. I dared not think of what a tyrant like Bartleby would do. It was too hurtful to think about, but my mind remained fixed on thinking about it, for it was all I could do.

Those thoughts turned my cries to sobs, but soon I felt arms gather me in a close embrace.

"It's alright, Samantha," I heard the woman whisper. "You mustn't fear. We'll escape this place soon!"

I looked up, wiping as many tears away as I could so as to see who Captain Patty really was. She was a pretty lady, albeit a little grubby and dirty like any other sailor cooped up in a jail, but her brown eyes still shone with hope.

"Captain Patty?" I asked, unsure of what to call her now. "I mean, Mrs. Peterson...I mean...Reuben's mother..."

"You can still call me Patty if it's easier," Patty replied with a grin. "And I'm still a captain, am I not?"

"Oh, Captain!" I sniffled, embracing her back. "What will they do to my daddy?"

"Nothing for the moment, I should think," Patty replied, giving me a warm pat on the head. "Grown-ups always talk before they do things. At least the smart ones do, anyways. And Bartleby's pretty smart. He won't do anything too big yet."

"But how are we going to get out of here?" Reuben asked, finally speaking after his long silence. "I don't want to stay here, Mama." He stopped and put his hand over his mouth as if unsure whether to say anything, but Patty gathered him to her and kissed his cheek.

"It's alright. You can say it now."

Reuben sighed in relief, a smile coming upon his face.

Patty then turned to the bars, eyeing them and fumbling with the lock to no avail. "These bars are good," she mumbled with a frown. "Too good. Unless there's a key nearby, we won't be going anywhere soon."

"But can't we do something?" I asked, my lip quivering.

"Nothing yet," Patty replied. "We must wait until the opportunity to escape comes."

I sat in an angry huff, crossing my arms and wiggling to get comfortable in that poky pile of hay. "Oh, bless it all!" I snarled. "What good will waiting do us?"

"Patience is a virtue whose cultivation produces good fruit," Patty said softly as she and Reuben sat beside me. "We have no choice but to wait until the plan reaches its next step."

"But I can't wait!" I said as more tears started to come. "My daddy is up there! Who knows what Bartleby is doing to him. We have to help him!"

"We can pray for him, Samantha. That's the only choice we have right now."

"But he's the Nameless Navigator!" My voice neared a yell, and I could tell from the look on Reuben's face that I was already being too noisy. I didn't care. I would shout my anger and hurt from the mountain tops if I could. "Bartleby will have no mercy..."

A creak from the door leading to our cell was heard and I was instantly silenced, fear gripping me that somehow my loud voice alerted some guards. I cowered away from the bars, inching closer to Patty and Reuben for protection, and waited for Bartleby's crew to arrive and scold us.

The shuffling of feet coming down the steps were slow and rhythmic, as if the walker was weighed down with carrying a burden too heavy to lift. A lone man approached us and met our gazes with his own.

I squinted as I approached the bars, pressing my face against their cold, steel frame. The man was difficult to see at first with the darkness of the room we were in, but soon I was able to make out his features. He was an average sized man, yet strong and well-built. He was dressed in the simplest of sailor's clothing, much of which was wet and dirty, and his hair was dark and his eyes brown. It was cut short - about like my father's when he wasn't wearing a powdered wig - and he had heavy stubble as if he shaved only once a week.

But his face was different, and not just because it was the most handsome I had ever seen in a man. Pirate though he be and a servant of Bartleby, he looked like an honest individual. That much I could tell. His eyes told the tale of someone who had seen much yet said little, and his lips graced a warm smile that even the darkest of cells couldn't hide. He had an air about him that made me wonder if he was truly a pirate at heart, and it made me think of Captain Patty.

"Who are you?" I asked.

The man approached the bars and bent. He had a set of tools hanging from his belt and made a light clanging sound as he walked. "They call me *Le Bateau*," he replied, his voice more soft-spoken than I expected. "You are the new prisoners, yes?"

I nodded as Captain Patty stepped up beside me. She looked at him hard, and I wondered if she thought the same about the mysterious man. "What do you do here, Monsieur Bateau?"

The man smiled as he removed a few items from the sack on his shoulder. "I do many things, mainly taking care of the ship.

A deckhand or janitor, I suppose. But Bartleby has requested that food be brought to you. Here."

He handed us some wrapped bundles and a few skins of drink. I was surprised to see the bread and dried meats were of a fitting taste. Bartleby struck me as a man who would give his guests moldy and stale food instead of things that were actually edible.

"Your captain is being unusually kind to his prisoners," Patty replied, giving Bateau a curious brow.

Bateau shrugged, ignoring the comment.

I tapped the bar for Bateau's attention. My father remained on my mind and I longed to know of what happened to him. Bateau turned back to me.

"Yes, little one?"

"My father," I replied, my lip quivering in wanting to cry. "Admiral Bartleby took him and separated us. He is the Nameless Navigator, you see. Do you know anything of what's happened to him? Is he alright?"

Bateau let out a long sigh, and I knew that to be a bad sign. He lowered his head as if he wished I did not ask such a question. "I'm not sure," he said quietly. "Bartleby has taken him to another cell with some of his men. That is all I know."

I frowned, but nodded in thanks nonetheless. Some information was better than none, but my worry remained.

Bateau put a hand to the bars and faced me. "I will do what I can to help, only speak nothing of it. Agreed?"

I nodded, a smile coming to my face. "Agreed. Thank you, Monsieur Bateau."

"Of course," he replied, standing back up and heading towards the door. "Farewell."

I watched as he left, and I took a bundle of food and ate.

Chapter Seventeen:
Dinner with Bartleby

It had to be late. Ten, eleven, maybe even midnight. The ship was dark save a few candles that were lit in lanterns above me, and the deck gently rocked under the calm waves of evening tide. Reuben fell asleep, and though Captain Patty tried to remain alert, even she became quiet, as if slowly succumbing to rest. I suppose I did the same, at least partially. I sat on the straw, my face leaning against the cold, metal bars, watching the stairs ahead of me.

I had heard nothing of my father. Nothing from him, nothing about him, nothing completely or remotely related to a rumor. Bateau was mostly absent, busy working I suppose, and though he brought us our dinner, he said nothing to answer my questions as he was surrounded by some fellow deckhands.

That was four hours ago. Now I watched and waited, desperate for even a sound.

My thoughts swirled within me. Perhaps I was waiting for nothing. Bartleby was cruel and hated my father deeply. What would keep him from killing Daddy outright? Then again, it wouldn't be that easy, would it? Bartleby was prone to make others suffer. He would keep my father alive for as long as he could, only to make him miserable.

And then I thought of Patty, Reuben and me. What of us? What would our fates be? Were we to be enslaved or harmed like the rest of Bartleby's victims, or were we to be stranded in these cells, trapped in the dampness of the dark, to rot? It was an uncomfortable feeling, staring into the unknown. All I could do was pray for comfort and strength, hoping somehow the good Lord would deliver us out of our mess with whatever Plan 47 had left.

As my eyes slowly began to get heavy and as my mind started to dream, I heard footsteps, at first heavy and shuffling, followed by a separate pair that was fair and soft. I wondered if the first was a fellow deckhand - after all, they all sounded the same - but the second had me guessing. He had the walk of a gentleman, educated in the propriety of grace.

I could only think of my father.

I straightened up, my heart filling with excitement. Perhaps my father was alive and would join me and Patty in the cells. I even smiled a little, knowing simply resting in my father's arms would be of greater comfort than dining at the admiral's table. My hand gripped the bar of my cage and I raised my head.

The footsteps soon came into view. Sure enough, the first was a deckhand, dirty and gruff with the smell of rum on his beard. Then I saw boots emerge in the moonlight, and as I gasped in excitement, the figure finally came into view.

My heart stopped, suddenly paralyzed by fear. It wasn't my father. It was Bartleby.

By this time Patty and Reuben had awakened. The deckhand hit the bars with the butt of his cutlass, telling us to sit up and be at attention with the admiral in the room. Bartleby eyed us one by one, his cold glare piercing every one of our souls, and he nodded as he folded his hands behind his back.

His eyes turned to me. "Miss Charles?"

He still didn't know my name, letting me know my father told him nothing. Good. The fiend needn't know anything about my father or me.

I held my tongue as I met his gaze. He laughed after our mutual silence, and then crossed his arms. "I know it is you, so there is no denying it." He turned to the deckhand. "Come, open the door."

Patty stood to her feet, eyeing the admiral with her own icy glare. "What do you want, Bartleby?"

"You needn't worry about yourself or your son for now, Mrs. Peterson," Bartleby scoffed. "I'm here to see the girl."

My eyes widened, the thoughts of my father returning. He had to be alive but wasn't giving Bartleby the information he wanted. There was only one choice now: bring me in to make my father talk...or worse.

Apparently Patty had the same idea, for she grabbed me by the shoulders, pulling me behind her. "You aren't taking her anywhere!"

Bartleby laughed, making my arms chill. "I can and I will." Then he nodded to the deckhand, who began to pull Patty away from me. The brave captain fought back, as did Reuben, but as quick as lightning Bartleby came in and swooped me away, slamming the door and locking Patty and Reuben back in.

Patty scrambled up from off the floor where she had been thrown. "Keep her out of this conflict!"

Bartleby smirked. "You need not worry, Mrs. Peterson. No harm will come to the child. At this you have my word."

As Patty yelled and screamed, desperate to pull the bars apart, the deckhand grabbed me by the shoulders and pulled me up towards the deck. Patty's yells soon became an echo as I was brought out into the open, the fullness of the moon nearly blinding to me as I was faced with it. The night was a beautiful starry canvas, the wind a cool breeze, and on any other night it would have been a magical moment. But the deckhand's pull made me forget whatever good could come from nature's glory, and I found myself being escorted into a cabin much similar to Captain Patty's on the beginning of my journey.

It was a dining room, large and warm. I was sat on a chair across from a table filled with various foods. A bare plate was set before me, along with a goblet, cloth napkin, and silver. Bartleby sat across from me, a setting before him as well, and he lifted a bottle, taking it to the goblet.

"Would you like something to drink, Miss Charles, with your dinner?"

It was a little late for dinner, but the bread and water I was given earlier neither filled nor settled my stomach, and I admit the salted meats and pastries set before me seemed more than appetizing. Were my father here, he would refuse out right, fearing the food poisoned or Bartleby up to no good. But I admit seeing the admiral fill his plate and take a bite made me rule out poison, and I was hungry. So very hungry.

"What do you have?" I asked carefully, playing along.

"Mead, ale, rum…" he replied. "Perhaps you would like some wine or beer instead?"

I frowned. Clearly the man had no experience speaking with children. "I'm not allowed to drink those types of beverages, sir. I'm only twelve."

"Ah. Beer it is, then."

"Water, thank you."

He nodded and filled my glass with a rotting, stinking sort of water that could only be described as filth. "Water, if that is what you wish."

I watched him as he set some food upon my plate, seeing as I hadn't already. It was a strange sight seeing Bartleby so composed...so kind. Though I often mocked my father for his overly-cautious manner, for once I could see where it would be helpful, and I kept a wary eye on the man, wondering what game he was trying to play.

I prayed for wisdom as we both began to eat. He said little, as did I, as if we were both playing chess and trying to figure out the other's strategies. But after a few minutes, he made the first move, wiping his mouth with his napkin and sitting up for conversation.

"What is your name?"

It was folly to answer. My father only gave his first name, making it sound like his last. I had better do something similar, at least for my own protection.

"You call me Miss Charles. Is that not enough?"

"I mean your first name, little one."

Should I be honest, or should I lie? It was difficult to decide. Then again, my father was honest, and as long as the name Wellington remained hidden, he would have trouble finding me. I conceded. "Samantha," I replied.

Bartleby nodded, taking a sip of ale. "A unique name."

"My mother was a unique woman. She wasn't too fond of things traditional and loved anything different."

The admiral smiled slightly, making me feel he was acting odd. "Indeed."

I nodded in politeness, returning to my food. More silence followed, which he broke within minutes.

"I must apologize, Miss Samantha, for your earlier mistreatment. I have a reputation to keep amongst my men and could not be seen giving preferential treatment to you and not the other prisoners. I trust you will forgive me?"

The move was unexpected. He seemed genuine in his speech, but a part of me was uneasy. He was a pirate, a greatly feared one at that, and rumors of his cruelty spread fast amongst the seven seas. And yet a part of me wanted to believe him, for if I was wrong about Patty, perhaps I was wrong about him.

"It is the Lord's will that I always forgive," I replied carefully. "You are forgiven."

He smiled warmly as he looked towards the table. "That gladdens me, Miss Samantha. I wish to be on good terms with you. It has been so long since I've seen you, and I wish to make up for lost years."

I paused in the middle of chewing a pastry. What was he going on about? Was it some sort of trick? "What do you mean?" I asked.

"It has been twelve years since I saw you last, little one. You were but a newborn."

I swallowed hard, unsure of what the man might be talking about. I had never met a pirate before Captain Patty. My father would've told me.

"You look troubled, Miss Samantha."

I cleared my throat, returning to the scene as my thoughts rushed to the back of my mind. I needed a clear head, not memories. "I am troubled, Admiral," I said, not knowing what else to do but be honest. "You bring me from my cell to your dining hall where you feed me the grandest of meals and treat me as your guest of honor, blabbering on about being glad to see me and making up for lost time. What are you getting on about, and where is my father?"

The mention of my father brought a frown to his face, but he retained his composure. "Your father is in a separate room and alive. That is all you will know. As for your other question, do you not know I seek to honor your mother?"

"My mother?" I asked, confusion filling my soul. "What madness was this? My mother has been dead for nearly as long as I've been alive! Why do you insult me by bringing her up?"

My voice was loud and I didn't care, but soon I came to regret my rash arrogance. Bartleby's face hardened like it had earlier and he stood from his chair, slowly bending down so he could look at me eye to eye.

"Do you know who your mother was, girl?"

My heart sped within me, and I was suddenly afraid. Whether I lied or told the truth, I felt as if my rash words would become the undoing of me. "Her name was Sarah Jane Wellington, sir, and she was simply my mother."

"Wellington." The name brought a sneer from Bartleby's lips as his eyes beaded, and I knew I had just endangered my father and I more. "Foolish girl. You think you know so much. She was Sarah Jane Finway, but her name was to be Bartleby. We were to be married before your father stole her from me."

I shook my head, tears filling my eyes. He had to be lying. He had to be! "What? No, no! You lie through your cold heart!"

"I see your 'honorable' father did not tell you the whole story of the woman you never knew," Bartleby declared, pushing himself up and pacing around me. "Did he even mention that she knew me?"

"He never mentioned you at all," I squeaked as I lowered into my chair to hide.

"Well allow me to enlighten you," Bartleby replied. "Your mother was a poor, orphaned Irish maid begging off the streets of Dublin. Desperate for coin, she began to take on whatever jobs she could to buy bread. She eventually came to the docks, where she and I met. She was lonely, as was I, and she joined my crew as we set sail. For five years we traveled the seas, battering the Mediterranean ships that carried the most wealth, and she was as brave as any man I had aboard. But as I acquired wealth, I found something more worthy than gold and coin. I found the love of my life, and we were to be married as soon as we landed ashore.

"And then, when that day came, she left as we docked in London. At first I thought she was kidnapped or captured by the Royal Navy, so I began to search for her. I found no record of where she went or where she lived and I began to search the seas, thinking she had been taken to the Americas.

"Two years after she disappeared, I began to lose hope. I returned to piracy, but with luck I came upon a merchant ship that was crossing the Atlantic, bound for Philadelphia. I saw your mother on that ship, and so I came to rightfully claim what was mine."

His voice lowered and he stopped, looking towards the ground. "And then came your father." He turned to me, hatred in his eyes. "I learned how he took your mother away from me, keeping her hidden so she wouldn't have to live in piracy any longer. As if I forced her to sail on the seas! Bah! I captured their ship and was going to take her back, but he led the crew in a revolt against me. And so we fought to the death...or at least, I hoped we would. But then your mother stepped in."

"What...what happened?" I asked, my eyes filling with tears.

"She died because of your *wretch* of a father!" Bartleby yelled. "I loved Sarah Jane more than anyone or anything. Not a day has gone by that I haven't regretted what has happened!"

"But...my father said she died of illness..."

"Your father lied to you, little one. He is at fault for your mother's death and could not bear to tell you the truth!"

"No! You're the one who's lying!"

"Tell me, Samantha," Bartleby seethed. "When I met you first, your ship was bound for Philadelphia, yet you were sailing from England. Where did you live after that?"

"Port Royal."

"And did you stay there?"

"No...we moved to Charles Town after a year..."

"And did you stay in Charles Town?"

"No...we went to Williamsburg..."

Bartleby laughed. "And I'm sure there are other cities and colonies you lived in. Where were you sailing from this time?"

I looked away, not wanting to answer anymore but knowing I had to. "Nassau."

"And you were heading back to the mainland. Tell me – did your father give a reason for leaving Nassau?"

"He said he was being requested to command another ship."

"And my sources tell me Nassau was requesting more Royal Navy ships to come to their port because of me. I find it odd that your father leaves the one port that is desperate for sailors, don't you?"

My eyes widened. What he was saying started to make sense.

"Wake up, little girl!" Bartleby snapped. "Your father has been running from me your entire life. You know what I speak is the truth!"

I hated to admit it made sense. My father's constant transfers within the navy. His paranoia and severe distrust of pirates. His panic when he first saw Bartleby's men in Florida.

And then it hit me. His apologies to Patty before we were caught...the way he spoke as if saying good-bye. He knew Bartleby's vengeance was deeper than simply outsmarting him. It explained why my father quieted and was reminiscing about Mother when we first arrived at Louis's. Patty's mention of being wanted by Bartleby reminded him of what happened to my mother!

"So then what do you want from me?" I asked, my eyes filling with tears. "To break my heart with your 'revelation'?"

"Atonement," he replied, his face sorrowful and broken. "Sarah Jane would want it. She wanted a life on the seas and never got to live it. You, Samantha, can. Do not deny that you long for a pirate's life. I can see it in you."

"I want a sailor's life, not a pirate's," I said quietly. "But you will find no atonement from me. Only God can do that."

"I do not seek the mercies of the Almighty," Bartleby scoffed. "For I will find and ask for none."

"Then what of my father? What do you want from him?"

"Vengeance." His face lit up once more. "He is a thief who should be brought to justice, and I will bring it."

"Do you think my mother would support such treachery?" I asked. "She would turn in her grave knowing you plan on such a thing, if it were true!"

"If it *were* true?" Bartleby snarled. "You still do not believe me?"

I shook my head, lowering my brow. "I heard the legend. Reuben told it to me. He said the Nameless Navigator was the only one who ever outsmarted you, and that you were nearly defeated because of his revolt. It was because of this loss that you've been hunting him ever since, to erase the taint of your shamed name."

Bartleby laughed, and I admit that it made me feel as small as an ant. He shook his head, cackling heartily, as he approached me once more. "Is that what the rumors are these days?" he continued. "I see they haven't changed much. Before, they said he was my first mate gone rogue!"

He laughed some more, making my face turn red from embarrassment. Seeing my sorry state, he calmed, and spoke to me in a sterner voice. "Your mother was a pirate, Samantha, and your father is a liar who never told you the reality. You'd best understand that all legends are a slab of truth and fact, seasoned with lies. It makes the story better."

I said nothing in response, still unwilling to believe. He sneered as he shook his head. "Shall I bring your father to confirm what I say? Ask him yourself! Surely he would not lie to you a second time."

He turned to a guard stationed near the door of the cabin. "Bring me the prisoner. I should like to have a chat with him."

The guard obeyed, and we sat there in silence as we waited for my father to be brought to us.

A thousand thoughts raced through my mind as I waited. I ate nothing and refused any drink, for the thoughts of my mother perishing at the hands of the monster that stood before me sickened me. But even more horrific was the fact that my father could have possibly kept the truth from me. We had always vowed honesty with each other. He had said since I was a baby that if there was ever anything I needed to talk about, I could talk about it with him. Could he not see that trust went both ways? That he should trust me as much as I was supposed to trust him?

I hoped and prayed what Bartleby said was a lie, but after the look on my father's face when he arrived, I was certain the pirate's words were more truth than what I wanted to believe.

My father was held by a guard and his hands were chained behind his back. Poor man, he looked dreadful and beaten when he was brought forth. He called my name and I answered, but before we were allowed to embrace, Bartleby stood between us and turned to my father.

"It seems you've been a dishonest man, Mr. *Wellington*," he began, and after hearing his real name, my father sighed, looking to the ground. "I've been having a chat with your daughter and she tells me that she knew nothing of how her mother really perished."

I approached my father with a quivering lip. "Bartleby says Mother died because of you; that she was a pirate and you took her and she was killed while you and the admiral fought each other." I paused, watching as my father's eyes widened in horror as I spoke. I could tell by the way he looked that Bartleby spoke the truth, but I had to hear it confirmed from his own lips. I had to know.

"Samantha, whatever he told you..." my father began, but I interrupted him.

"Is it true, Daddy? Did Mother sail with Bartleby? Did she really die in battle?"

Hurt and sorrow fell upon my father's face as he watched me. He said nothing, exhaling slowly and wanting to look away. Bartleby wouldn't let him stay silent, however, and after a hit to the mouth, the pirate growled and clutched my father's collar, yanking him forward. "Tell her the truth, you wretch!"

He let go of my father roughly and pushed him to the ground. My father got back up and faced me once more. "Yes," he said quietly. "What Bartleby says is true."

"But Daddy..." Try as I could, the tears refused to be held back. "Why didn't you tell me?"

"Samantha," my father said with a plea in his voice, "do not believe everything he tells you. Yes, your mother was a pirate, but I did not take her against her will. She escaped because she feared him..."

"YOU LIE!" Bartleby yelled as he slapped my father once more.

"I swear it to you, darling. Your mother escaped and she was found by myself and my crew as we sailed." My father gasped for air as Bartleby struck him in the stomach. "I tried to protect her. I tried to keep her safe. I'm so sorry I failed you..."

"But why didn't you tell me the truth?" I cried.

"Because I was afraid of how it would affect you. I didn't want you growing up wanting vengeance. I didn't want you to become bitter and judgmental like I had." Bartleby kicked him, making my father fall over in pain, and my father rushed his words before Bartleby could silence him. "I only...tried to protect you...I didn't want...a pirate's life for you..." He paused, swallowing hard after another hit from the admiral.

"Your mother wanted us to have a normal life. We left England and I was going to leave the navy once we reached the colonies. But then Bartleby's ship attacked. We tried to fight back and escape, but your mother tried to protect me. Bartleby killed her..."

"LIES! It was you who killed her, you who turned her against me!"

My father turned to Bartleby and yelled back. "She tried to save us both, but your rage blinded you! You couldn't see that she only wanted to end the fighting, but you couldn't handle that she didn't want to return to you!"

Before my father could finish, Bartleby picked him up and shoved him towards the guard. "GET HIM OUT OF MY SIGHT!" he shouted, and the guard immediately obeyed, dragging my injured father away.

I cried and held out my hands to grab hold of him, to pull him back towards me, but Bartleby held me back. My father reached out for me and struggled, but all he could say was "I'm sorry" before being dragged out of the room and leaving me with Bartleby.

"Now you know the truth," he heaved as he sat me back down in my chair. "Does it not anger you?"

I sat there pondering on whether it really did. I felt confused, disoriented. I loved my father and always had. And yet there was suddenly a doubt entering my heart, clouding my feelings. Why did he not tell me? Why had he not been honest? We promised to always be truthful to each other, and I was always honest with him. I knew he trusted few, but I was his daughter. Did he not trust me as well?

I couldn't answer Bartleby on my feelings. Maybe I was angry. Maybe I wasn't. The truth was I didn't know, and that terrified me.

I turned back to the admiral, my eyes suddenly dry as I was bound and determined to be brave. My father was a naval officer and my mother was a pirate. Surely courage was a family trait that I had deep down within me, confused feelings or not. "You have proven your word, sir, that it is true. I cannot deny that. Whatever else my opinions may be remain irrelevant."

"And what of my atonement?" Bartleby asked, crossing his arms. "Do you not care for that, as well?"

"I cannot help you with that, sir," I replied.

He stood erectly, returning to where his seat sat empty. He rested his hands on the edge, looking back at me. "Indeed you can. I give you an opportunity, Miss Samantha, and I swear it upon your mother's soul that I shall give you anything you want, up to becoming my first mate, if you would but stay and sail the seas. It shall be my only act of kindness before I depart this earth, and I do it in honor of your mother."

The offer was eerily tempting, but I knew what I wanted more than adventure and glory. I wanted a good name, something Bartleby could never give me. "And if I refuse?"

"There is no refusal."

Of course there was a refusal. He just couldn't live up to himself having to put me in with the others. But then the thought hit me, and whether it was Providence or my own sense of desperation, I began to remember Plan 47. Patty told my father to trust her, but now it was my turn. I had to trust she had created an opportunity to escape when the time came.

But I didn't know what the plan was, nor was it guaranteed to work. *The Sally* was stranded and slowly sinking in the ocean and Patty's other crewman were on a separate ship in Bartleby's fleet. Even if everything did go according to plan (whatever it was), we had no chance of escaping. A handful of pirates could not commandeer an entire fleet no matter how clever Patty was.

I felt my heart sink within me. No matter what, Patty nor my father could save us. And now that I held the sway of Bartleby's mercy, luck was on my side. I had a chance to guarantee everyone's survival.

It was a chance I would take without a second thought, if not to buy Patty more time for her plan, but to save them in case it didn't work.

"Admiral," I began, calm and confident as I could make myself. "You say you shall give me anything I ask, in honor of my mother?"

He nodded. "I swear it."

"If I agree to stay with you and sail under your command, will you release Captain Patty and Reuben?"

Bartleby thought for a moment, and though I could tell he wasn't entirely pleased with my request, he was, at the same time, happy that I was a clever bargainer. "If you wish it, I shall release them."

"And not just to some abandoned island or out in the middle of the ocean," I cleared, knowing full well the pirate would find a loophole in my request. "You must bring them to another ship - either Royal Navy or merchant or someone they trust - and safely allow them to cross. Or maybe an island or port, where they can find food and shelter. Like Tortuga."

Bartleby nodded. "It would be difficult, but it could be arranged. Very well."

"Thank you," I replied. "And may I make one last request?"

"And what is that?" he asked, his brow going up.

I looked at him straight in the eye, giving a quick pause. "Release my father."

He looked away, clearly unhappy, and I could see his lip curl down in a growl. "I cannot do that," he replied under his breath.

"You want vengeance, but you know in your heart my mother would not wish it," I answered. "And if you truly want to honor her by honoring me, you will do as I request. This man raised the only child of the love of your life and did everything he could to protect her. You owe him his freedom for keeping his promise to a dying woman."

Bartleby looked at me and nodded, though his lips were still frowned. "You are clever and brave, girl, for making such a request. Were it not for my word I should maroon you for it. But I will honor it, as much as it pains me, for the sake of your mother. I will release the others once we near Tortuga."

I was shocked, and a part of it showed on my face. Quickly regaining my composure, I forced a smile. "Thank you, sir."

He pulled out the chair and sat on it. "Do not be so quick to thank me, little one. My heart is still angry with your father, and it forever will be."

It was another truth the pirate admiral gave me, one I feared him for. I had to be smart and cunning from that moment forward. I took another bite of my pastry as Bartleby continued with his meal, eating in silence, feigning loyalty to bide my time.

Chapter Eighteen:
Part of the Crew

After dinner, I was led to a small room towards the end of the ship. I think it used to be a small storage room or a place for some of the deckhands to sleep, but now that my arrangement with Bartleby was complete, it was to be my own personal quarters. Bartleby wasted no time in having it prepared for my stay. By the time I had arrived, a hammock was strung (until a bed could be stolen from a port) and a lantern was set at the corner so I could see inside. There was a small port hole, but other than that there was little comfort about it. As my eyes gazed around what would be my new home for probably the rest of my life, I sighed with sadness.

It was no *Sally*, nor was it a cozy guest bedroom at Louis's trading post. And more than anything, it was not the grand bedroom full of greens and blues and pillows that I loved back in Nassau.

"Thank you," was all I could mutter before the deckhands left me alone so I could get some sleep.

They left and I was met with the silence of the room. I should have probably been more thankful for my new lodging, but Bartleby's words about my father...and what really happened to my mother...ruined whatever thankfulness I could have.

Thoughts raced through my mind as I paced the floor, looking at my new surroundings. Why had my father kept quiet? Why had he lied over what happened to my mother? Doubtless he wanted to keep from hurting me, but his lies proved to be anything but protecting. I was angry. I was hurt. I was worried. I was confused. A month ago I was learning my lessons from my governess on the beach, and now I stood, a pirate under the command of the most notorious man on the sea!

No. No, I was no pirate. I loved and respected my father enough to know I should never join their vile ranks in thievery and sin. Maybe the words Bartleby spoke were of a game he sought to play to confuse me, or maybe "his truth" about my mother wasn't the entire story. If I could ask my father, he would know. Surely he would tell me.

But then again, he was silent before. And I wasn't sure I was ready to talk just yet.

I sighed, scuttling up to the hammock, swinging my legs over and rocking myself in it like a chair. I felt a little jiggle in my pocket, and to my surprise a very sleepy Franky peeped his head out for a look.

"Oh Franky!" I said aloud, picking up my furry friend and kissing his nose. "I'd forgotten about you! Were you in my pocket this entire time?"

Franky only looked at me with a pout, clearly offended that I had not pulled him out of the deep crevice of my pocket sooner. I shrugged, setting him down atop a crate and putting some straw from the floor beside him.

"There's a nice bed for you," I said, patting down the straw. "Hopefully there's some hamster food around here somewhere."

A knock was heard at the door, and I turned my head. A part of me wanted to jump in fear, wondering if Bartleby would go back on his word and throw me off the ship along with Patty and the others. But then I heard a familiar voice quietly calling me from behind. "Miss?"

I recognized the voice of Bateau quickly, and my heart leapt within me. Out of all the people on Bartleby's ship, Le Bateau was the only one I deemed decent. "Come in," I said, and Bateau quickly entered, leaving the door open.

"I see your accommodations have improved," he replied, giving my quarters a quick glance. "Nice room."

"It's not as comforting as the old one," I said with a shrug.

Bateau turned to the crate, seeing Franky snuggle into the hay. "Ah...pardon me, little one, but I recommend not befriending the rats. If it's a pet you want, I'm sure we can find a parrot or rabbit..."

I laughed, wondering if Bateau was being serious. The little smirk he gave made me question him. "It's not a rat. It's a hamster. And his name is Franky."

He gave a slight bow to Franky. "Forgive me, Sir Franky. I see I should have paid attention more in school when learning about the animals."

I giggled, making him smile. Bateau reached into the sack slung across his shoulders and pulled out some items, handing them to me. "The admiral has requested I give these to you," he said, putting the bundle in my hands. In the bundle was a dress, some undergarments, and a few more changes of clothes. Bateau also reached into his sack and pulled out a warm blanket, and even though it looked as if it were old and used, I gladly accepted it.

"And this," Bateau whispered after glancing to the door, "is courtesy of myself. I am sorry it isn't in better condition. There are very few of these aboard, but I figured you would need it. Sometimes the ship gets cold at night."

I held the blanket close to my chest, giving a slight smile. I wondered if the blanket had belonged to him. "Thank you, Monsieur Bateau. I appreciate it very much."

"Now the admiral..." Bateau began rather loudly, glancing back towards the door, "has requested you be ready in the morning for breakfast. He expects you to dine with him and the rest of the crew. After that, he will give you further instruction on your duties for the day."

Bateau paused for a moment, leaning in and whispering. "I must be quick. They are listening for me. Now say something about agreeing to see Bartleby."

I nodded. "Thank you, Monsieur," I said, trying to be loud at Bateau's prompt. "I will be much obliged to meet the admiral and crew for breakfast."

"Good," Bateau continued, rummaging through his sack and pulling out a hammer. "Oh my, let me take a look at the hammock for you. I don't think it's strung properly."

He got up beside the crate, blocking my view of the door. "Here, let me fix that," he continued loudly. But instead of working on the hammock, he turned to my ear. "I have learned where your father is being held," he whispered. "He is in a cell near the admiral's quarters and is alive."

I nodded at the mention of my father. "I know. I just saw him during my dinner with Bartleby."

Bateau gave me a confused glance, but quickly pretended to hammer the nail near the hammock. He glanced back out to the door, noticing no one was looking in, and turned back to me. "It seems I'm out of the loop, then. I am a bit confused to find you here. As happy as I am to see you out of prison, I'm wondering as to why Bartleby gave you a new room."

I frowned, not wanting to reveal the truth, unsure of whether Bateau was trustworthy enough to know or not. "I guess the admiral has a soft spot," I whispered quickly. "I think he felt sorry for me."

Bateau lowered the hammer and looked at me with doubt. Somehow I knew my father would look the same, wondering how on earth I could expect a monster like Bartleby to have compassion. "What of the little boy? He isn't in a room like this. Why would Bartleby have compassion on you and not him?"

I looked away, not knowing how to answer. Bateau seemed to understand that I wasn't being completely honest with him.

"You needn't worry. Whatever his reasons for favoring you, I won't pry. I only wanted to let you know I'm here to help if you need it," Bateau said, putting his hammer back to his sack. A noise was heard and in walked a guard.

"Bateau? What's taking ye so long?"

"Fixing the hammock," Bateau replied, pointing to it. "It was loose. I didn't think the admiral would want the girl to have an accident while she slept."

The guard nodded with a sneer as he walked out the door. It was Bateau's cue to exit as well. "I'm sorry I can't stay longer," Bateau continued with a frown. "Remember there is breakfast in the morning. For now, have a pleasant rest." Before leaving, he whispered to me one last time. "And if you can help it, try not to talk to Bartleby. Be wary of what he wants to give you. Don't trust him - everything he does is for a reason, and he will seek to gain your favor only to betray you in the end. For now, sleep and pray. I will see what I can do to make things easier for you."

With that, he turned. I clutched the blanket to me, holding it like a doll as I watched Bateau walk out. What did he mean that Bartleby did everything for a reason? Was it possible Bateau knew of my deal? No, no…he would've said something. But maybe he suspected a deal. Or maybe he just didn't trust Bartleby. The thoughts of what he could mean ran through my mind as I laid down on the hammock, and no matter how hard I tried, I could not sleep a wink.

The morning arrived quickly, and I was greeted with a hard pound on the door, telling me to dress and be ready for breakfast in the mess cabin. I rubbed my tired eyes, sore and dry after a long and sleepless night, and yawned. I was terribly weak, either from lack of sleep or sadness from the last day or both.

But I made myself get up. After all, a deal was a deal, and I had best get used to waking every morning on this ship under Bartleby's command. A pain hit my stomach at the thought of the *Wrath* being my home from now on. Never would I see Boston (unless it was to be raided). Never again would I see the beautiful cobblestone road that led up to my home above the docks in Nassau. Never again would I have my father tuck me in before bed, reading from my school primer or the Bible.

Never again would I have a normal life. No. It was a pirate's life I would be living now.

I sighed, feeling nothing but dread.

As I fixed myself up as best I could, I tried to think of the positives. I loved life on the sea, and perhaps being on Bartleby's ship would bring me some adventures. No one would doubt I'd live a life most girls could only dream of, and after all the fun I had on Patty's ship, maybe the *Wrath* wouldn't be so bad.

But in my heart I knew my sadness would outweigh any adventure I would have here. I pushed the thoughts from my mind as I walked out the door, waiting for someone to show me where the mess cabin was. I couldn't, after all, be seen walking in all blubbering and sniffling about like a scared town girl. If I was going to face these pirates, it was going to be with bravery.

Within seconds Bartleby's first mate walked up to me. He was a tall man, lean and thin, but had a harsh and wrinkled face that made me wonder if he didn't sleep well at night, either. Or maybe he was just grumpy all the time.

"Where's the mess cabin, sir?" I squeaked, his beady eyes staring me down.

Severn huffed with a snarl, twitching his head forward. "This way," he muttered, and I followed him from behind.

The mess cabin was at the center of the ship, down one flight of stairs that led to the second level. It was a large room filled with plain walls, wooden benches, tables, and pirates. Not the tame, happy, friendly pirates of Captain Patty's ship. No, these men were different. Snarling, raging, loud - anything and everything that made me want to turn around and run back to my quarters. As I followed Severn into the room, huddling as close to the man's backside as I could, I was greeted with howls and stares that made the hair on my arms stand on end.

Severn stopped in his tracks and faced me with his own icy glare. "Find your seat."

I gulped, not knowing where to sit for fear of becoming a main course of the meal. These pirates not only looked mean, but hungry too. My hands curled up to my chin and all thoughts of being brave suddenly left. All I wanted to do was cry, knowing there was no escape.

Suddenly I felt a light hand, warm and gentle, touch my shoulder. "Here, sit with me." I recognized Bateau's soft voice, so easily distinguished from the other growls I heard, and latched onto his arm. He led me towards a table that was empty save for a few others who were old and haggard. I wondered if they were even healthy enough to sail.

They ignored me as I sat down, Bateau plopping right beside of me. I remained quiet as well, afraid to send a greeting to my fellow crewmen, knowing they would love nothing better than to make me jump overboard or swab the decks or do something else horrid. I bowed my head, praying for strength and wishing more than ever that I was with my father or back in the cell with Patty and Reuben.

"Sleep good last night?" I heard Bateau ask, breaking my thoughts.

"Not really," I replied, pulling Franky out of my pocket. The poor hamster was still sleepy after a restless night as well.

Chapter Eighteen: Part of the Crew

Bateau eyed my furry friend as he wobbled about on the table, sniffing around. "You brought your pet rat?"

"A hamster."

"A what?"

"A hamster, silly."

Bateau's brow went up and he shook his head. "It still looks like an orange rat to me."

"Rat?" One of the men at our table suddenly turned towards us, his eyes having a greedy look about them. They went to Franky and he grinned wildly, licking his lips. "Just had me one yesterday. Fresh meat. Best dinner I've had in months!"

I widened my eyes. Did the man just say he ate a rat?

Bateau turned to the man and leaned forward. "It is a child's pet, Mr. Wayson. Nothing more. And if it is a rat, it has to be diseased. Look at its color! You want to get the smallpox?"

Wayson lowered his brow. "I can survive the smallpox, Bateau. Starvation is a whole 'nother story."

"Wait..." I interrupted. "Are you saying you want to eat Franky?"

"Tell you what, little girl," Wayson repeated, edging closer as I scooped up Franky towards my chest. "You give me the rat, and I'll give you my only coin. Deal?"

"No deal." Bateau stood and slammed his fist on the table, facing Wayson head on. "Unless you want me to talk to the admiral as to why you're stealing the ship's best supply of meat."

Wayson's harsh look suddenly turned to fear. I admit my own heart was racing as I watched him and Bateau argue over such a trivial thing as a hamster. There was a stare between the two, and I wondered if Wayson was debating whether to chance Bateau talking to Bartleby, but then he got up and headed to another table.

"Watch your back, Bateau. Just because the admiral wants you alive doesn't mean the others do," Wayson muttered with a sneer, getting up to go to another seat. "I hunt other things besides rats."

Bateau ignored him, sitting back down next to me. "You know," he began as he smirked, "he hunts roaches, too."

All I could do was stare back at Bateau blankly. Was he trying to be funny or was he serious?

Bateau sighed, seeing as I didn't get it. "True story."

I nodded slowly, grossed out.

Bateau shook his head. "If you think that's bad, I've got plenty more. I could write a novel about this place."

"A novel?" I asked, making sure I put Franky back into my pocket so no one else would want to eat him. "What would you write about?"

"About being the clean-up boy on a pirate ship," Bateau replied. "You'd be shocked with what goes on here."

"If it's the story of you, I'd think it'd be very interesting," I said. "Although, I'm not sure about the ending."

Footsteps were heard from the stairs and I noticed the first few men brought large platters for the admiral and his first mate. These trays were filled with dried meats, sliced vegetables and fruits (undoubtedly taken from a raid in Florida), and bread. Behind the men with the platters came about five others carrying large, steaming pots and small bowls and mugs. They sat the pots next to a few kegs and began to disperse the morning meal.

"You know what I think?" Bateau continued as I watched every man and boy aboard get a bowl and a mug. "I think that I'll have a happy ending for my story. How about you? Will your story be happy in the end?"

"I don't know," I replied, thinking of my sorry state in being Bartleby's prisoner. "What do you think?"

"I think it'll be happy if you want it to be."

Bateau's hope made me smile, and then I looked at the bowl and mug set in front of me.

Inside the bowl was a watery mess. I wasn't sure what was in it. It smelled like seaweed and fish, but it looked like water mixed with soured milk. In the mug was a smelly brownish liquid.

I sniffed my breakfast and made a face. Even Franky didn't want to come out of the pocket from the bad smelling mess before me. I turned to Bateau, who was gobbling it down like he had never eaten before.

"What's this?" I asked.

He paused in the middle of his feast. "Breakfast."

"Well I know that," I replied. "What's it made of, though?"

"If I knew," Bateau replied as he finished his bowl, "I probably wouldn't want to eat it anymore."

I frowned as I swished the smelly gruel in my bowl, eyeing Bartleby and his first mate as they feasted on their food fit for kings. They laughed as they ate with the politeness of gentlemen, while the others in the room gorged on their gruel, refilling their mugs with the strong smelling brown liquid that came from the kegs.

It was foul how Bartleby treated his men. Captain Patty would have never done such a thing, and neither would my father. I won't pretend that life on a ship is easy by any means, but the crew should at least be fed something sustaining.

"Why does Bartleby get the good food and the others get this stuff?" I asked Bateau.

Bateau's face became serious as he whispered. "He's the leader. He does what he wants, plus it's his way of showing he's in charge. Only the officers on the ship get something edible."

I thought back to the evening before when Bartleby gave me a decent meal. The fact that I had anything showed his favoritism. I couldn't help but wonder if he gave me the gruel for breakfast in retaliation for asking for my father's release. "It doesn't make it right, though."

"No, but that's how it is. If anyone questions, they get shot. Besides, it's better to eat this than to starve."

I took a sip from my gruel, abhorring the sour taste it gave. I pushed it forward, not wanting another bite. I'd rather go hungry. "I think I liked the food you gave us in the prison better."

"Sh!" he hushed with a wink. "No one's supposed to know about that."

"Oh Bateau, did you steal it?" I shook my head.

"The admiral told me to bring you food." Bateau smiled. "He didn't say where from."

A yell was heard and soon three men at the front of the room were up and hitting each other. I recognized one of them as Wayson. The other two were young Spaniards shouting about "thievery and treachery". Instantly the room's attention settled on the three men, their empty bowls spilling to the floor with a crash as they stood and cheered.

"Gut 'im, Leo!" shouted one.

"Rip his eyes out!" shouted another.

Yells in English, Spanish, German, and French could be heard all around. As the men continued to brawl, their fight going to the top of the entire table, Bartleby waived his pistol in the air and laughed, his feet remaining propped onto his own table.

Within seconds of the fight, I felt Bateau tug my arm. "Time to go," he whispered, pulling me to my feet.

"Go where?" I asked, my eyes glued to the fight.

"Three men full of rum and gruel are fighting," Bateau began as he led me to the steps that went to the deck. "It won't be long before everyone's involved."

"What do you mean?" I asked, but then I understood as we made it to the top of the steps. More shouts were heard, men arguing about being hungry and wanting more food and then accusing each other of stealing the other's breakfast. Crashes of wood and pewter and glass could be heard smashing against the walls and floors. Language that was fouler than the abyss was spoken, and I could only imagine the anger my father would feel knowing such things were said near my presence. As we made it to the deck, I heard a shot, and suddenly all went quiet save a lone thunk on the ground.

I jumped at the sound, wondering what had happened. Sounds of cheers came from below and I could only imagine the revelry that was happening there. I froze, not knowing whether to cry or scream or do nothing. Bateau continued to lead me away, all the while muttering, "Lesson one on a pirate boat: always sit near the stairs. Lesson two: go easy on the rum."

Bartleby's ship was nothing like Patty's. It was dreadful, it was cruel, and it was frightening. It was then my eyes began to tear up. Now, more than ever, I wanted to be back home. I wanted off of Bartleby's dreadful pirate ship and I wanted off the seas. I wanted no more adventure. I didn't want to be a pirate!

But as I stood upon the deck, standing with Bateau, I realized that was all I was: a pirate bound to the service of Rudiger Bartleby.

Chapter Nineteen:
A Gift of Understanding

The captain returned to his work and I was bade to follow the other cabin boys in their chores for the day. The last thing I felt like doing was work, especially after the ordeal I had witnessed, but after a look from Severn and a desire to not test Bartleby's temper, I scurried away below deck to join the other cabin boys in scrubbing the mess cabin after breakfast.

The room was a disaster to be sure. Even Louis's office was tidy compared to the wreck we were forced to clean up. Food (or at least I think it was food) was splattered all about the floor. Chairs and stools were turned over. Rum was spilt. Cutlery somehow got stuck on the tables and dishes were broken. Even a toddler would be better behaved than these men!

I made my way into the mess as best I could, picking up a cloth handed to me by one of the older boys and taking a bucket of sudsy water to a spot in the corner.

I began my work quietly, not feeling very social. After witnessing the foolishness of Rudiger Bartleby's crew, all I could do was think about how much I wanted to be back on Patty's ship and have things be back to how they once were.

But fate must have had a funny way of reminding me that isolation wasn't always the best answer to feeling down, for a familiar voice suddenly caught my attention.

"Golly! I didn't expect to see you here! I was wondering what Bartleby did with you."

I turned to see Reuben, busy trying to pull a spoon that somehow got wedged in a chair.

I ran to embrace him, happy to finally see a familiar face that I knew I could trust.

"I thought you were in the prison with your mother," I said.

Reuben shrugged. "Bartleby thought me more useful as a cabin boy, I suppose. No sense in wasting the talents of a young man and all of that."

He smirked at me, attempting a joke, and I admit it lightened my mood a little.

"I only wish Bartleby wasn't such a neat freak," Reuben continued as he pulled the spoon out of the chair and took his bucket of suds along with me back to my corner. "Bless it, the man goes nutty over a spot that isn't shining or a crumb that's on the floor."

I smiled as I listened, washing the table as Reuben talked.

"But I guess I shouldn't complain," Reuben said with a sigh. "I mean, after this I should finally get some breakfast. Did you eat yet?"

I tilted my head from side to side. Technically I *did* go to breakfast, but then again, my food wasn't particularly appetizing and I had no desire to eat after the morning's events.

"You know, you're not talking much."

I looked up to Reuben, wanting to tell him he was talking *too* much. The poor boy was a chattering child when he was nervous, but I couldn't blame him for it. He had went through a lot in the past few days, too.

"I guess I don't feel like talking," I said as I continued to work.

Reuben stopped. "Why not?"

"Because it's been a bad day."

"Been a bad week, more like it."

I gave a chuckle. He was right on that one.

"Is it because you miss your dad?"

I sighed, not sure in how to answer. Yes? No? A little of both? "I guess."

"Well something's wrong, because you look like you've just seen the saddest thing in the world."

I looked up, pouting my lower lip in a frown. I guess I wasn't as good in hiding my emotions after all. I shrugged, knowing Reuben wouldn't give me a rest until I talked. "Can I ask you something? And be honest with me."

Reuben paused from his cleaning. "Sure."

"Did your mother tell you the truth about what happened to your father?"

Reuben rubbed the back of his neck and didn't say anything first as he looked away. "She didn't say much," he began. "She still hasn't told me all of it. Said it was too much for me to understand just yet. All I knew was that my dad died getting us out of South Carolina and that he was killed by Bartleby."

"And when did she tell you?"

"A few years ago. I asked her one day why she wanted to be a pirate. She told me it wasn't about wanting to be one, but having to be one."

Reuben's answer surprised me. "So before that, you never knew he was killed by Bartleby?"

"Not a clue. All I knew was that he died when I was a baby." He paused, giving me a quizzical look. "Why are you asking, anyways? Is it because your dad didn't tell you he was the Nameless Navigator?"

"Not so much that," I said quietly. "It was more what Bartleby told me."

"And what did he tell you?"

"That he knew my mother and that he killed her."

"Who? Your father?"

"No. Bartleby. Bartleby killed my mother."

Reuben gave a low whistle, getting closer to me and providing a look of pity. "Must be hard hearing that. I know it was hard for me."

"I just don't understand why Daddy didn't tell me!" I huffed as quietly as I could, hoping the other cabin boys wouldn't hear me. "Doesn't he trust me? Doesn't he know he should've been honest?"

Reuben bit his lip, and I think I made the poor boy even more nervous with my ramblings. Feeling the way I did, however, I didn't care. "I think he trusts you, Samantha. I wouldn't question that."

"So why didn't he tell me the truth?"

"Maybe he thought it'd hurt you."

"But your mother told you the truth!"

"Mama told me the truth a few years ago. Before that, I was in the dark, too."

I rubbed my brow, not caring that I got soap suds in my hair. "So what did you do?"

"Nothing. I went on with my life knowing a little more than what I did."

"But didn't it hurt you that she didn't tell you before?"

"Well...yeah. I mean, I wished she would've told me sooner. But after a while, and a few talks with her, I learned some things that helped me see it all differently."

"Like what?"

"Well, for starters, our parents aren't perfect. They make mistakes."

I gave a scoff. That was a lesson I'd figured out already.

"And," Reuben continued, "I think they were hurt themselves. My mama won't admit this, but some nights, when she sleeps...she has nightmares. Dreams about when my dad died. She'll wake up in the middle of the night and cry quietly to herself. She'll pretend it's nothing, but I know it hurts her. And I almost wonder if that's why it took so long for her to tell me. Maybe she was scared I'd be like her, you know? Having nightmares and feeling sad and trying to hide it from everyone."

Reuben paused as I listened intently. How many times had I witnessed my father not sleep at all, busying himself with work when he didn't need to? I remembered our first night in Florida at Louis's, watching my father as he stared into a void, lost in a memory he was never to find his way out of. Louis had mentioned Bartleby that day. Had the conversation been a reminder of the hurt my father experienced witnessing his wife, my mother, die in front of him?

"Look," Reuben continued, crossing his arms. "I'm not going to pretend they were right in keeping the truth from us. Your dad should've been honest with you and you shouldn't have found out through Bartleby. And I know you're hurt. And I know you're probably mad. That's understandable. Just don't stay mad for long, alright? Your dad's a good guy. I mean, yeah, he has his issues. He worries all the time and he's the most judgmental person I know, but he loves you. You're his world, you know? And he's the type of guy that'll do anything to keep you from hurt or pain. If that means lying to you and making you think your mother had a fair death instead of a horrible one, then he'd do it if it kept you from being hurt and angry."

I listened, my lip quivering from holding back tears. I'd only known Reuben for a little while, but I think that was the moment I saw him as the best friend I ever had. And we weren't friends because we never argued or agreed on everything. We were friends simply because we understood one another. We both had no siblings at a time when everyone did. We both lost a parent (to the same man, ironically). We both had parents who were captains and navigators.

I rushed forward, not caring that I knocked over my bucket of suds onto our feet and covered the floor. I embraced him tightly, and at first he was taken aback by either the hug or the soapy mess that soaked his shoes, but after the initial shock, he embraced me back.

"Thank you, Reuben," I said through my tears.

He only patted my back as he told the staring cabin boys to mind their own business and get back to work.

When the evening meal came, Reuben and I decided to meet up in the mess cabin. It did no good for us to remain separated, and with Reuben reminding me that his mother still had Plan 47 (whatever it was) going on, he suggested we stick together as much as possible when Plan 47 provided an escape.

"Do you know how we'll escape?" I whispered to him as we sat near a corner, waiting for our gruel.

"Not a clue. Mama didn't tell me anything except to keep my eyes open and wait for her."

I snickered. "Well that doesn't give us much to go on."

"Tell me about it."

"Are you nervous about it, though? Whether all of this will work out?"

Reuben shrugged as he leaned forward in his seat. "A little, I suppose. I mean, I don't want to be stuck on this ship cleaning up Bartleby's messes for the rest of my life. But Mama's been in worse spots before. At least she says she has."

"It's quite fascinating, at any rate."

Reuben looked up. "What is?"

"You're mother commanding a pirate ship." I grinned, thinking it very intriguing. "I've never heard of a female captain before. How on earth did that happen? Was she really kidnapped and separated from her sister like she said she was?"

"Nope," Reuben replied. "That was what happened with my dad. But she had to tell his story, pretending to be him and all. Her story is a little different. For starters, she doesn't have any sisters and she wasn't really kidnapped."

I rested my chin on my palms, eager to hear what really happened to "Patty" (if that was her name). "Well, do tell me her story, Reuben! I'm awfully curious."

"Well, it all started when she and my uncle were living in Cardiff, and..."

"Miss?"

It was imperfect timing as I *really* wanted to know what happened to Patty, but after seeing Bateau approach, Reuben instantly quieted, unsure of whether to say any more.

"Good evening, Bateau," I said, trying to hide my frustration at the interruption.

He sat down beside us and lifted a brow in confusion. "I'm not interrupting anything, am I?"

"No," Reuben said, looking away.

Bateau gave a look that showed he didn't believe us, but shrugged as I'm sure he knew we wouldn't tell him what we were talking about. "I have news on your father, Miss, if you want to hear it."

My eyes lit up with excitement. "What is it?"

"Your father has been recently moved to the same cell that the lady pirate is in."

My eyes widened. It was a grand stroke of luck to have my father and Patty in the same prison. The more of us that were together, the easier our escape would be.

"At least he'll have company now," I said with a smile. "Thank you, Bateau. I'm glad you've been so much help to me."

Reuben remained quiet, giving Bateau a glare. I couldn't help but be reminded of my father.

Bateau ignored Reuben's look as he turned back to me. "Has the food been served yet?"

Chapter Nineteen: A Gift of Understanding

"No. Though I'm not particularly looking forward to it, if it's like how breakfast was."

"It should be a little better this time," Bateau said, trying to sound cheerful. "I heard they found some bilge rats. We should be getting protein with our dinner."

Even Reuben made a face at that remark, and I made sure Franky stayed nice and safe with me.

"The food's not appetizing, but it's better than starving, I suppose." Reuben made a gulp and I could've sworn his face was starting to turn green. "What about that food you gave us in the prison, Bateau? That wasn't made of rat. Where'd you get it again?"

Bateau put his finger to his lips, urging Reuben to be quiet. "I got it straight from the captain when he wasn't looking. It's best not to go on about that, if you don't mind."

"And why is that?"

"I'd rather not be on Bartleby's bad side."

"Understandable. So why risk it?"

"Because I'm not heartless like the rest of the crew on this ship."

"Well I'm not heartless, and I wouldn't risk it."

Bateau shrugged.

"You know, you're awfully keen on helping us," Reuben continued. "If you're spying on us for Bartleby, it won't work. We don't have any important information, anyways. We're just kids. It's not like our parents tell us things or anything like that."

Bateau shook his head, rubbing his brow with a sigh. "Little boy, if I was a spy for Bartleby, rest assured you would've just proven to me that you *do* know something by suggesting you've got nothing to hide — especially when all I talked about was dinner."

Reuben gulped as he sank a little lower in his seat, looking away.

"I'm not a spy for Bartleby, if that's what you're worried over," Bateau replied, taking a mug of beer and drinking out of it. "I'm a prisoner on this ship just like you. At least for the moment. And going by the calmness of the lady pirate and how well you both seem to be handling being prisoners aboard a pirate ship, I'm willing to bet you have a way out of this mess. Or you're planning one."

Reuben looked to me as his eyes widened. How did we answer that?

"I never said...I mean, I don't know what you're talking about..." Reuben's stuttering only made things worse, and I wanted to smack myself in the forehead. If only he'd keep his mouth shut...

"So there is a plan, then." Bateau chuckled. "No worries, my friend. Your secret is safe with me. I only ask that you be careful when being around the crew. Try not to bring attention to yourselves and especially stay away from Bartleby. If I can tell you're hiding something after five minutes of conversation, you can be sure he'll figure it out, too."

He set the mug down as Reuben's face blushed in embarrassment. Bateau turned back to me with a grin. "Delightful lad. I can see why you like him."

"He does know how to keep a conversation interesting." I laughed.

Reuben huffed, crossing his arms. "Don't tell me you two were in league with each other this whole time, now."

"Don't worry, Reuben. Bateau's been quite nice and helpful. He even saved Franky from being eaten at breakfast!"

Franky peeped his head out from my pocket and I gently rubbed his ears.

Reuben could only roll his eyes.

I decided to change the subject, to prevent Reuben from further embarrassing himself and to find out more on what I hoped Bateau had information on: my father. "Bateau," I asked, getting his attention. "How is my father doing? Bartleby hasn't hurt him or anything, has he?"

"I don't know," Bateau replied. "I haven't seen him. I'm only going by what I overheard from the crew."

"What all are they saying?"

Bateau exhaled lowly as he swished the liquid in his mug of beer. "Not much. All I know is Bartleby is in a good mood and that worries me."

"How so?"

"Bartleby is never in a good mood."

I frowned. It wasn't a good sign, indeed.

"Don't worry about it for now," Bateau said, standing to his feet. "Be content knowing he is alive and well. Bartleby typically does not treat his prisoners like this, so something must be up." He took the mug of beer in his hands. "I'm going to check on the food and bring you some. I'll be back." He turned to Reuben. "Wait here. And try not to talk too loudly about your...ponderings...next time."

Reuben and I watched as Bateau went and stood in line near the cook.

"I don't like this," I said quietly.

"I don't either," Reuben muttered. "That Bateau fellow is being awfully nice to us. I don't trust him."

I smirked. "You sound like my father now."

Reuben's eyes widened and he frowned. "Ouch. Thanks a lot. If I were really like him, I would've stood to my feet, slapped the man in the face, and challenged him to a duel!"

I giggled, but soon straightened my face. "Do you think our parents are alright being in that cell?"

"I don't know," Reuben said. "I admit I don't like not knowing what's going on. If Bartleby hurts Mama in any way, he'll have to deal with me!"

"Do you think we could check on them? To see if they're doing well?"

Reuben paused as if in thought, but then nodded. "I don't see why not. It'll only be a few minutes, right? To put our minds at ease."

"Maybe we should leave now, while everyone's at dinner," I suggested.

"And then hurry back so we can at least get some food."

"Bateau will be in line anyways. It'll be like we were never gone."

"Let's go, then."

We hurried out of the mess cabin and made our way towards the prison cell.

Chapter Twenty:
Keelhauling

Sneaking into a prison sounds difficult, but when the majority of the crew is busy eating their dinner, or busy thinking about it, finding your way below deck is easier than what it sounds like. There were a few times Reuben and I were nearly caught by a few crewmen walking by, but otherwise we found ourselves having a clear view into the bilge prisons. We passed quietly behind the guards when they weren't looking and tiptoed down the steps into the cell area, careful not to make too much of a splash on the damp and puddle-filled floor.

Patty and my father were a funny sight sitting in their prison. They both sat down, legs stretched out on some hay, backs against the bars and talking to each other as if they hadn't anything better to do (which, when I think about it, they didn't.)

"So...how long have you been a woman?"

Patty looked up at my father with widened eyes. "What sort of question is that?"

"I mean...I know you've always been a woman, but how long have you been a man?"

"Are you serious?"

My father could only rub his brow in frustration. "I'm sorry. I know I'm not making much sense. I'm just worried..."

"About Samantha?" I paused from my tiptoeing, pulling Reuben to a stop. They were talking of me.

"I don't know what Bartleby's done to her. He's told her everything, and the look on her face when she heard about her mother..."

Doubtless my father told Patty what had happened. "It's alright. Reuben's out there, too. I'm sure they're looking out for one another."

"But the things that Bartleby told her..." I saw my father lower his head in shame. Was he crying? I couldn't tell, but the hoarseness in his voice proved to me how sorry he was for what happened. It made me feel wretched I was ever angry with him.

"She knows how bad Bartleby is, Charlie. She'll believe you over him and besides – she's a smart girl. She knows who'll be there for her in the long run."

"I feel terrible, Captain. I'm so worried, and..."

I could bear it no longer. I rushed to the cells, splashing or not, and grabbed hold of the cell bars in front of my father. "It's alright, Daddy! I'm here!"

My father scrambled to his feet and approached me, looking shocked. Patty followed, facing Reuben, and after getting a clear look at them both, I could see just how much my father suffered under Bartleby's hand within a day.

There were bruises upon his face and hands. His lip was busted and swollen. His right eye was starting to blacken. Patty looked better, but even she was starting to look pale. I wondered if she hadn't eaten since I was in the prison with her.

"Sam, you shouldn't be here. They'll find you," my father began, but after stroking my cheek with his hand and seeing the tears swell up in my eyes, he stopped speaking and embraced me as best he could through the bars.

I embraced him back, holding him tight. "Daddy, I'm sorry. I didn't mean..."

"No, darling. It was me. I should've been honest with you. I should've told you the truth before you heard it from Bartleby. I just didn't want you to be hurt."

"I know," I replied, facing him. "I know you didn't mean it. I just want you to be honest with me, alright? I can handle it. I promise. You can trust me."

"I trust you, Samantha. I always have. And you're right; I should've told you the truth."

He leaned back as he rested on his knees, holding my hand with his. "What Bartleby told you is true. Your mother joined his crew and left Ireland because she couldn't afford to make a living. Bartleby offered her money and protection and she took it. But after sailing with him, she realized how dangerous he really was. She didn't want to hurt anyone. She didn't want to steal. And when they made port one day, she escaped.

"I found her at the docks while working as a navigator under Captain Avis Wilmar. She was hungry and tired, and after I took her to the physician for medical treatment, she began to tell me of where she had been. I told my captain and we arranged to keep her protected while Wilmar used the information she had in taking down Bartleby's piracy schemes.

"I was in charge of getting the coordinates to the places Bartleby frequented. Your mother and I worked together a lot, and it wasn't long before we fell in love and got married. After you were born, however, we received word that Bartleby had left the Americas and had set his sights on plundering the ships near England. Captain Wilmar was afraid that Bartleby would find us and so transferred me to the colonies where Bartleby would be absent.

"We had only been gone from London a week before Bartleby's ship attacked. We fought him off as best we could, but Bartleby was able to board. I tried to hide you and your mother, and Mr. Lewisham kept watch over you both. I coordinated the counterattack against Bartleby to get him off the ship, and then a battle ensued.

"Bartleby and I fought each other that night. It was dreadful business, and I daresay the battle would've been lost had not another Royal Navy ship been in the waters and saw us that night. But your mother was worried, and she feared you and I would be killed out of Bartleby's jealous rage, and so she left you with Mr. Lewisham and joined the battle.

"She came between Bartleby and I, urging us to put down our weapons. I listened, but Bartleby didn't, and he demanded to know why she had left. She told him the truth, how she was afraid of how terrible he was and how she didn't want a life with him. He became angry and demanded to know where she went. I stepped forward, trying to protect her, and told him I was taking care of her and would defend her until death."

My father paused, looking down as he gave a squeeze to my hand. "Had I stayed silent, your mother may have survived, Samantha. But when Bartleby realized she was my wife, his fury rose to its greatest heights. He aimed the pistol to shoot me, but then turned it to her and..." His voice choked and he looked back up at me. "It was so fast that I couldn't step in to save her. I charged at Bartleby and we fought. The other vessel came to our defense and Bartleby was forced to retreat after being wounded. Had he not been shot and then pulled away by his first mate, he would've surely stayed and fought to the death. We survived, but it was a terrible loss seeing your mother killed. We had to bury her at sea."

I watched as my father took in a deep breath. It was as if a great burden had lifted off his shoulders and he sat up just a little straighter. Telling me everything was difficult (I could see it on him), but it was also freeing...for both of us.

"Thank you for telling me, Daddy."

He faced me with honest eyes. "I'm sorry I didn't tell you sooner."

"It's alright." I smiled. "Now I know."

"See," Captain Patty said as she nudged my father in the arm and grinned. "Told you she'd be fine."

My father nodded and gave a chuckle. "I admit you were right."

"Wouldn't be the first time."

My father could only shake his head in amusement.

"As much as I'd like you two to stay," Patty began, her face suddenly frowning, "you both need to return to your posts. If Bartleby catches you, it could make things difficult."

"Everyone's eating dinner, so we shouldn't be caught," Reuben added. "Besides, he's working us as cabin boys." He paused, looking at me. "I mean, cabin girls...uhm...cabin kids..."

"Don't worry," I interrupted. "We'll stay together. And we'll go back up and eat dinner. Bateau's probably wondering where we're at anyways, and..."

Before I could continue, however, I heard the heavy stomping of boots rush down the stairs. I turned, my voice suddenly silenced, and looked at the man who now stood before me.

It was Rudiger Bartleby, and he looked livid. "I was going to invite you to my table this evening. Why do you not eat, Samantha? Are you not happy with dinner?" he asked, though his voice hinted of a demand.

I could see now why my mother left the man for my father. Bartleby was ill-tempered and easily brought to anger if things did not go his way. It frightened me, and I knew I had to tread carefully with my words, especially given my surroundings. "I'm sorry, Admiral. I just got scared and started missing my father and..."

"She meant no harm by it," my father interrupted, standing to his feet. "If you are to blame anyone, blame me. The shock of her mother's death has been too much on her and..."

"Shut up!" Bartleby gave a glare to my father before turning back to me. "Were you upset about what happened to your mother?"

"Yes, sir," I answered.

"Then why did you go to your father and not to me?"

He leaned forward and eyed me with a glare that made my heart pound in fear. "I just wanted to see him, sir. I only wanted to see him and make sure he was alright."

"And why would you do that? After all that he'd done to your mother?" Bartleby asked.

I shuddered, but swallowed my fear as best I could. "I forgave him, sir, for not telling me what really happened. And that's what my mother would want. So if I want to spend time with my father, then I shall!"

I stood my ground, stepping in front of my father, feeling the most brave I had ever been.

"Is that what you want, Samantha? Time with your father?" Bartleby asked.

"Yes, Admiral. And you will grant me my request in honor of my mother."

There was a pause, almost as if he was hurt by my words, but then a flash came before his eyes that showed something strange. "Very well, then." Bartleby grinned. "I shall grant it."

The mercy was almost too good to be true. "Thank you, Admiral."

"Of course, little one," Bartleby replied as he turned to Severn, who had just come down the stairs and stood beside him. "I'm not a rude man, after all."

He smiled as he looked at me, and it was then I knew that the worst was yet to come.

Chapter Twenty: Keelhauling

The admiral ordered his first mate to bring my father, Patty, and Reuben onto the deck. Severn nodded and hurried to fetch some more guards, and as the joy in seeing my family and friends began to fall in my heart, the look on my father's face suddenly crushed it. He looked scared, terrified...suspended in disbelief.

He knew what was coming, and I realized I was the cause of it.

Bartleby only laughed as he pulled me back up to the deck and began shouting to the rest of the crew. "Everyone gather! We're going to have a keelhaul!"

My heart nearly stopped as the crew began to cheer.

When I was little, my father once told me a story of a privateer he had worked with when hunting pirates off the coast near Williamsburg. The privateer was a harsh man, only doing the work for money and protection from the hangman's noose, and he had a reputation for having a completely obedient crew. They never questioned him no matter how crazy the order. My father, curious as to how the man could command such obedience, asked him what was the secret to his success.

The man could only laugh as he picked up a rope and swung it on his side. "Keelhauling, m' friend! No one wants t' go under like that!"

My father had been mortified and never worked with the privateer again.

When I asked my father what keelhauling was, he only shook his head and said, "Something that no sailor ever wants to experience."

"Why?" I had asked.

"Because it almost always guarantees death."

I was left to myself as my begs for mercy were ignored by Bartleby and Severn. They began to instruct the crew to prepare the punishment with ropes and materials. Bateau found me as he came out of the mess cabin with a crowd, and I could only burst into tears as he faced me.

"What happened? Where's Reuben? I thought you two were at the table..."

I could only mutter through stifled sobs what had happened during the last few minutes – why we left, the story my father told, and how I tried to be brave only to make others suffer.

As I stood there on the deck, clinging to Bateau as he was my only support, the sounds of cheering from the crew became deafening and I wanted to do nothing but scream and tell them all to be silent. Though I was unfamiliar with keelhauling, I knew it had to be bad, and as my father was being held away from me, I turned back to Bateau in tears.

"What are they going to do? What's keelhauling? *What are they going to do?*"

He refused to answer me as he stepped up to the admiral, his face hardened in fury. "Bartleby, your cruelty is as vile as the devil himself. I beg of you, *please*, have mercy for the sake of this poor girl! She shouldn't bear witness to such an ordeal!"

"I was younger than she when I witnessed hangings and floggings, Bateau," Bartleby said without a care. "She is old enough to understand and handle it. Besides, this is justice."

"Justice for whom?"

Bartleby beaded his eyes and lowered his voice. "For the woman I love."

He turned to leave, perturbed by Bateau's insistence, but the man grabbed the admiral's arm and pulled him back. "Sir," Bateau pleaded, "leave justice to the Almighty. If you take it into your own hands, you will never be rid of it and it will consume you!"

Bartleby flung his arm back and grabbed Bateau by the collar, pulling him forward. "*God has done nothing!*" he spat. "*I've waited long enough!*"

"Then maybe it isn't justice that needs to be served," Bateau answered calmly. "Maybe it's mercy."

Bartleby snarled. "He will receive *none*." He pushed Bateau away and turned to leave towards the first mate who was bringing my father to him.

"At least let the girl not see this!" Bateau called.

"*She stays,*" was all that the admiral would say.

I watched as Bateau returned to my side. I could hear the men continue to jeer as my father was brought forward and prepped for whatever danger beheld him. Reuben and Patty were brought up from below deck and tied to the mast to watch. Reuben was quiet, but Patty was alert. She looked around and I could tell she knew what was about to happen because she looked at me with an apologetic glance.

"What's going to happen, Bateau?" I asked as my eyes went to my father. They began to tie his hands together with rope and men took positions on each side of the ship. I tried to make eye contact with him, but Bateau gently led my face away. I think he and my father saw each other and understood something unspoken, for he held my gaze and turned me to face him and him alone.

"Samantha, I need you to stay calm."

"What do you mean?" The tears couldn't be held back.

"They're going to pull your father under the boat and pull him back up," he replied. "It's a form of punishment sailors do. Whatever happens, I don't want you to be afraid, alright?"

"I don't understand," I replied, sniffling. "How will they pull him under the boat? He can't stay under that long or he'll drown!"

"I know," Bateau said with a sigh. "I just need you to stay calm and not be afraid. Can you be brave for your father?"

I nodded, hoping and praying I could.

"Good girl," Bateau replied. "I promise, he'll be fine."

I turned to my father as the ropes were secured. At first, he begged Bartleby with the same request Bateau had. "Please don't let her watch this, Rudiger..." he said, but Bartleby responded with a smack to the jaw. My father lifted his head, his busted lip now bleeding again, and watched me with pity. He mouthed a quick "I love you" before Severn and a few others began to drag him towards the edge of the boat.

Bartleby walked by Captain Patty and Reuben as he made his way forward. Patty struggled to free herself from the ropes but they were too tight, and she tried to kick Bartleby as he passed her by. The admiral stopped, giving her an icy glare, and she swung to kick him again before he stepped back.

"If your aim is to torture us, then you are a sick man indeed!" Patty spat, and Bartleby only laughed.

"You and your son are not here for punishment, Mrs. Peterson," Bartleby said. "I made a promise that I would leave you both untouched. You are only here to watch and warn others of my justice. When you are released at port, I expect you to spread the word of my integrity."

"I'll spread the word, alright," Patty replied with a sneer. "I'll tell every privateer and shipman in the navy that you're a sadist who belongs in prison!"

Bartleby turned to her and smiled. "And I'm sure you're the one to put me there. Justice for your husband, hmm?"

"I'm not a judge," Patty replied bravely. "But God is. And do not think your evil will go unnoticed."

"It has gone unnoticed for decades, Mrs. Peterson, and I am sure it will continue that way."

Patty smirked. "Don't be so sure."

"Then I await your punishment. For now, however, I am content to deal out my own!" He walked towards my father, all the while meeting my gaze. He soon stopped and grabbed the ropes at my father's hands and held them up for the crew to see.

I pleaded for mercy from Bartleby. Surely the thought of my mother would stay his hand. "Please, sir. Please don't do this. You know Mother wouldn't want you to."

"Perhaps not," Bartleby replied, his eyes fiery. "But I want to. She deserves justice, Samantha. Your wretched father killed her!"

"He didn't kill her, Admiral," I said, my voice shaking. "You did!"

At first he looked as if he was going to stagger, and he looked at me with sorrowful eyes. But whatever moment of mercy he had suddenly was gone, replaced with the fury of a bitter and cruel man, and he forced my father onto the railing, turning to the crew.

"Behold the Nameless Navigator, he who thought he could hide in the seven seas!" The crowd jeered at my father as he said nothing, turning back to me. Never before had I beheld my father with such bravery and love as I did then. "For the death of my dear Sarah Jane," Bartleby continued, letting go of the ropes and leaning my father towards the sea, "I sentence you to be keelhauled!"

My father struggled to get away but Bartleby overpowered him and pushed him overboard.

Chapter Twenty: Keelhauling

A great splash was heard and I gave a gasp, rushing to the railing of the ship while being followed closely by Bateau. I heard a yelling by Patty and Reuben, but I couldn't figure what they said as the pirates around me began to cheer. Some of the men began to pull the ropes, and I could hear the scraping against the ship's outer edges.

"Away from the railing," Bateau said gently as he led me away, but I pulled back, searching the water for a sign of my father. There was none.

If ever there was a moment I cried out to the Almighty, it was then. I knew not the outcome of keelhauling save it was dangerous and risked a man drowning. My father was an excellent swimmer and was trained in holding his breath, but I knew every man, no matter how strong his lungs were, had a limit. I prayed and prayed that the Lord would somehow keep my father safe…that my daddy would come back onto the deck alive and well.

I never prayed so hard in my life.

The ship fell silent save the sounds of the ropes pulling. Bateau led me away from the rails, never leaving my side as I stood there watching, waiting for my father to return. Seconds seemed like minutes. Minutes seemed like hours. And every moment that passed by, with each heavy scrape of the rope against the wood of the ship, my heart filled with worry.

Too much time had passed. Even panic began to settle on Patty's face as she yelled, "Pull him up now, Bartleby! *NOW!*"

The admiral only stood still with arms crossed, watching the other side of the ship.

Another minute passed before one of the sailors announced that they were pulling my father back up. My heart leapt within me and I rushed forward, watching as my father was lifted out of the water and pulled back onto the deck.

But before I could reach him, I was stopped by Bateau.

He tried to pull me away, to not look at my father, but I had already seen too much. His clothes were torn. Cuts, many of them deep, covered his body. But worst of all he was silent.

My father wasn't breathing. In fact, he did nothing at all.

All I could do was scream as a few of the men checked him, announcing he had drowned while under the ship. Reuben gave a yell and began to cry, looking away, and even Patty was shocked as she stood there, watching with teary eyes and begging for someone with any ounce of mercy to help my father breathe.

My fury was unquenchable as I rushed to Bartleby, flinging my fists and shouting so loudly my voice turned hoarse. *"You monster! You wretched, horrible beast! You promised you'd release my father once we reached port!"*

Bartleby looked back at me with unapologetic eyes, his cruelty nearly blinding me. "And I will keep my word, Miss Wellington. I never promised I'd deliver him alive."

Those were words I didn't want to hear, and my fury engulfed me as I lunged at him.

Hands pulled me away from the admiral, and I fully expected it to be Bateau. But as I looked at my captors, I realized I didn't recognize them. They were simple crewmen, lads I hadn't even met yet. Bateau, however, had rushed to my father and was busy doing something to his face.

He pushed his head back, elevating my father's feet as best he could with his boot. He was pressing against my father's abdomen and chest and soon began breathing into his mouth. Whatever Bateau was doing was completely foreign to me, and soon Bartleby noticed.

The admiral approached the Frenchman with fury. "The man is dead! Leave him be!"

"He's not dead," Bateau replied as he gave my father another breath.

Bartleby pulled out his pistol and aimed it at Bateau. "I said *leave him be.*"

Bateau looked up as his hands continued to work. "No."

Bartleby cocked the pistol.

Bateau kept his gaze upon the admiral. "You and I both know you're not allowed to pull that trigger, Admiral. Now stand down and let me save this man."

There was a pause, and I wondered how on earth the ship's janitor (of all people) had enough bravery to stand up to the admiral. Did the man have no fear? Or was he mad?

But then the miraculous must have happened because soon Bartleby put his pistol away and gave a loud curse.

Whatever power Bateau held on the ship, it must've been grand, indeed, for the admiral to abstain his hand.

But Bateau's influence became the least of my concerns as I soon heard the greatest sound in my entire life.

A cough, full of water and sounding like a mixture of choking and vomit, but it was the most wonderful sound as I watched my father lift his head and open his eyes.

He was breathing once more.

Bateau helped him lean on his side as he coughed up more water, and my father groaned in pain as he was gently laid on his back once the coughing stopped. My father called my name and I rushed to him, and when I saw his face and he saw mine, I daresay both of us were never happier than what we were during that moment.

He painfully lifted his scraped hand, brushing a strand of hair away from my forehead. "Samantha," he whispered lovingly, before he was interrupted by Bartleby's men, lifting him to his feet and away from me.

"Take him with the others back to the cell!" Bartleby barked. My father was led away from me and the admiral glared at Bateau. "And *you*, Frenchman!" He struck Bateau on the mouth, nearly knocking him over. "Do not think the brotherhood will have mercy on you when I tell them of what you've done in disobeying me!"

"Do your worst, Bartleby," Bateau replied as he wiped his mouth. "I have faced every fear I've ever had. You can do nothing to me."

"We'll see about that," Bartleby replied. He turned to Severn. "Put him in the cells with the others. He's not even worthy enough to work on my ship."

Severn nodded and took Bateau, dragging him below deck. Before I could say anything, the admiral ordered I be put near the cells for the night. Hands grabbed my arms and began to pull me behind Bateau. "Say your good-byes to your father now, Samantha," Bartleby said with a sneer. "For soon he hangs!"

I only glared at him as I was taken back into the darkness of my former cell.

Chapter Twenty-One:
Faith

Sunlight turned to darkness as the brightness of the sea was taken away. I was back in my earlier abode of humid, smelly bilge water and hay, surrounded by metal bars and a few flickers of light from candles. My father, Patty, Reuben, and Bateau were all stuck inside a cell while I was left outside. I was told to have my time with Daddy and that I was expected to go back to the crew when they called.

I looked around and saw my father be placed on his back to be treated by Bateau, Patty gently assisting as best she could.

Bateau gave me a glance and then turned to my captors. "I need more alcohol, bandages, and a fresh set of clothes. Some more thread, too, if you have it."

The sailor scoffed and shook his head. "The prisoner gets nothing. Admiral's orders."

I could barely hear Bateau mutter under his breath, but I understood what he said. "He might not survive until morning."

My heart nearly stopped at the thought. The sailor ignored Bateau as another sailor quickly approached, nudging the man in the arm. "Gunpowder mishap on the *Carolina Gust*. Admiral says he wants us on board there to help clean up the mess before the navy sees the smoke." The guard scoffed, nodding, and he trudged up back onto the deck with the other crewmen, leaving us alone.

Patty watched them leave, a smirk coming upon her face as she turned. "Welcome back," Patty said warmly as she looked at me. I could tell she knew I was upset, but her confident gaze gave me hope. "We're keeping your father comfortable. He'll be better in no time."

"Because they're sewing me back up," my father said quietly with a chuckle that pained him. "Out of all the men you could've befriended here, Sam, I'm glad it was the ship's surgeon."

I looked to Bateau with a quizzical brow. "I thought you said you were Bartleby's janitor."

"I am." Bateau grinned. "But I'm a doctor, too. At least back in France, I was."

I gave a smile. For once, something good happened amidst all the bad. Perhaps the Almighty was watching out for us after all. "Is there anything you can't do, Bateau?"

He shrugged as he finished stitching the deep gashes on my father's neck. "I'm a terrible cook."

I shook my head. I'd believe it when I saw it.

"How are you feeling? I'm sorry you had to see all of that," my father said as I approached him as best I could. Poor man, he looked dreadfully pale. I could tell he was in a lot of pain, but he grinned and tried to keep his breathing steady.

"I'm fine," I replied. "And you?"

He gave a weak smile for an answer, but I could tell he wasn't well enough to talk much. He whispered, "I'm doing better," before shutting his eyes and resting.

"He's very lucky to be alive," Patty chimed in as she dabbed his right shoulder with a makeshift cloth made from Bateau's cravat. "To survive a keelhaul that long is a miracle. The Almighty was certainly looking out for you." She looked up at Bateau. "And I still don't know what you did to bring him back. How did you know he was alive?"

"He had a pulse," Bateau replied as he worked.

Patty nodded. "I take it you've saved drowning victims before."

"Not really," Bateau said, making Patty's brows rise. "I didn't know if it'd work, to be honest. I'd only heard about the technique from a friend I practiced medicine with."

"I'm glad it worked, then."

"Me too," Reuben added.

My father gave a stifled cry, interrupting the conversation, as Bateau began feeling around the gash on his stomach. He paused studying the area of the wound a little more. He looked to Patty with a frown and then to me. I knew something had to be wrong.

"Reuben, why don't you and Samantha have a chat over there?" Patty said, motioning for us to go to the corner. Reuben nodded, obeying, as he led me to look away.

I began to protest, but Reuben nudged me along anyways. "Trust me," he said. "It's better you not watch."

"Why?" I asked. "What are they going to do?"

"My best guess is surgery."

My eyes widened. "*What?*"

"I know, I know," Reuben replied with an attempt at comfort. It didn't work. "Just try not to be alarmed. This happens sometimes on a ship."

A yell from my father made me want to turn again, but Reuben faced me away to look at the wall.

"The keelhauling probably hurt some of his insides. Bateau's going to fix it so he'll get better."

It was rare for my father to groan in pain, so whatever Bateau was doing, I hoped it was worth it.

"Have you ever seen a surgery?" I asked.

"Sure. A few months ago we had a poor chap who was cleaning his pistol and accidentally shot himself in the leg. We had to get the bullet out and clean the wound so it wouldn't get infected. He's fine and dandy now."

"It probably doesn't matter what Bateau does, though," I said sadly, remembering Bartleby's words. "The admiral said that he's going to hang my father."

Reuben blinked. "Try not to think about it. I'm sure there's something we can do to delay it."

"That Bartleby is a monster, I tell you!" I seethed as my father's yells began to lessen. Whatever Bateau was doing must've been over with...or my father passed out. "Torturing us, telling me I have to stay here!"

"What do you mean he's having you stay here?" Patty asked as she approached us, wiping her hands on a cloth. "What did he tell you?"

As Bateau continued to work on my father, I relayed everything Bartleby told me to Patty and Reuben. About the dinner, the promise, Bartleby's behavior...everything.

Chapter Twenty-One: Faith

By the end of the tale, Patty could only whistle and rub her brow. "No wonder Bartleby was so obsessed. He only wanted the maps to find your father and avenge what happened to her."

"I don't know how he can 'avenge' her when he's the madman who pulled the trigger!" My anger was still boiling. I wanted nothing more than to see Rudiger Bartleby be shackled to the stocks for eternity! "That evil man already took away my mother and nearly took away my father! He's nothing but an evil pirate who deserves what's coming to him! I hope the Royal Navy comes and blows him out of the water!"

"I just hope we're not on the boat when it happens," Reuben chimed in.

Patty sighed. "I understand you're upset, Samantha…"

"I'm not upset!" I yelled. "I'm furious! Look at what he's done!"

Patty frowned. "No one understands you better than me, Samantha. But if we want to make it off of this ship, we need clear heads and noble hearts. Not anger and revenge."

"But aren't you mad?" I asked, tears threatening me again. "Bartleby took away your husband, too!"

"He did," Patty replied, crossing her arms. I couldn't help but be reminded of my own mother, had she been alive and able to scold me. "And I watched it happen. But anger and vengeance isn't going to bring him back, nor will it protect your father from further harm."

"But Bartleby said he's going to hang him!"

Patty offered a confident smile. "Or so he thinks." She bent forward and lowered herself to my level, putting her hand on my shoulder. "Just remember, Samantha – have faith."

"But what good has it done me? As soon as a good thing happens, an even worse thing comes and replaces it!"

"Having faith is keeping hope even during the worst of times. Faith is easy when things are good, but we really find out how strong we can be when times get tough," Patty replied. "I promise – things will get better."

"But Bartleby said he was going to hang my daddy soon!"

I'd thought Patty would be mortified and match the look of terror and hurt upon my face. Surprisingly, however, she smiled. "Then you definitely have nothing to worry about."

"Of course I have plenty to worry about!" I added.

"Remember, Samantha. Have faith. You never know what tomorrow – or even tonight – might bring."

I sighed, conceding defeat. Patty was right. Anger was only making me miserable, and vengeance was something I knew my father wouldn't approve of. I couldn't help but wonder if that's what my father meant when he explained why he didn't tell me what really happened to my mother. Perhaps he knew the worry and anguish would consume me just like it did him.

"Alright," I said, lowering my head. "I'll have faith then. So what do I do now?"

"Get ready." Patty smirked. "Because by this time tomorrow, we'll be off of this ship."

My heart lifted as I suddenly remembered Plan 47.

It had been hours since Bateau finished whatever patching up he had to do on my father. Stitches were sewn to the best of his ability and whatever extra fabric he had was used for dressing. Patty had been given a mug of beer earlier, and instead of drinking it, she helped Bateau clean my father's cuts. Eventually Patty told us to get as much rest as we could. I could only think it was because whatever she had planned was going to happen soon and we'd need as much strength as we could during our escape.

Of course resting was difficult as my father laid injured on the hay. I stayed near him, and though Patty encouraged me to sleep early on, she eventually saw that I wasn't going to budge and left me with my father. He didn't say much as I sat with him – simple small talk or telling me how proud he was of my bravery. Eventually the talking ceased, and all he could do was shut his eyes and sleep, the pain from his injuries too much to bear.

He held my hand through the bars, keeping it close to his heart, and I treasured the sight of it. I had not the courage to tell him Bartleby had sentenced him to hang, and I was bound and determined to hold onto that tiny bit of hope Patty had given earlier. Had I any faith? I wasn't sure, but whatever I had, I was going to hold on to it and never give up for my father's sake.

Night came and my father started to groan as if not feeling well. When he opened his eyes, they were glassy, and his skin had turned quite pale. He was shivering, too, and I covered him up as best I could with some straw to keep him warm. He went back to sleep, but I could tell it wasn't a healing rest. All he did was moan and try to move.

Patty seemed to notice it as she got up from her spot and put a hand on my shoulder. "Get some rest. Plan 47 begins at any moment. You'll need your strength helping your father escape."

I nodded, finally obeying. "Will we be able to get my daddy out safely?"

"Of course."

"And what of Bartleby? He says I have to stay here."

"You needn't worry. I made a promise to your father that I'd take care of you, and I intend to keep that promise."

I smiled, hugging Patty as I made my way to a spot near the stairs where it was dry.

I snuggled to the hay as comfortably as I could, shutting my eyes and longing for rest; but like all tense moments and anxious nights, my thoughts bested me and kept me awake. I shut my eyes closed, hoping to trick myself into sleeping, but eventually I gave up, knowing until I was safe back on *The Sally*, there was no rest for me.

I laid there, listening to my father's shallow breathing or the gentle snores Reuben gave. And then, as I *finally* started to doze off myself, footsteps were heard.

My eyes shot open. Was it morning already?

I looked to Patty and she had a look of concern upon her face as she glanced towards the stairs. Heavy *thunks* there were, and soon six men were visible in the moonlight that trickled down from the deck.

Bartleby, Severn, and some guards stood before us.

"*Wake up.*" Bartleby's voice was firm as he motioned for the guards to open the cells doors. I was shoved aside as they went in, dragging Patty away from my father and pulling Bateau and Reuben to their feet. Bartleby stepped inside the cell, approaching my father as he laid there, slapping him in the face hard. "I said *wake up*, you worm!"

My father rolled painfully on his side as he tried to find his bearings. His eyes danced about the room, searching for anyone familiar, and he called my name. We locked eyes before Bartleby picked him up by his shirt and threw him to the ground and into a pile of hay and bilge water.

Bateau and Patty both gave a shout and I tried to reach my father before being held back by Severn. It was clear my father had started to fight a fever, infection undoubtedly beginning, and being thrown in bilge water that was rank and fouler than the abyss only made my father's propensity towards illness grow. He struggled to get back up, the pain and dizziness nearly overwhelming, but he pulled himself to stand, facing Bartleby like a man.

"Ready to hang, Mr. Wellington?" Bartleby asked with a grin.

My fury rose as I tried to rush towards him, Severn tightening his grip on my arms. "You promised to keep him alive 'til I said good-bye!"

Bartleby sneered at me as he pushed my father towards another guard. "I'm impatient, girl! Justice has waited long enough!"

"But - "

"Take him on deck!"

My cries were all in vain as we were pushed up the stairs and onto the deck where the crew began to gather. The moon stood still in the sky as clouds began to cover it, and Bartleby ordered some torches to be lit so we could see in the darkness.

As the light shone in front of me, I could see the noose being prepared.

My heart raced within me as I tried my best to get to my father. He was barely able to stand, but he held it together for my sake. His words became begs as Bartleby led him towards the rope. "Bartleby...please," my father began, his voice barely above a whisper. "I beg of you! Kill me if...you wish, but...spare my daughter...the sight of it. It will...only bring her...pain and anger."

"It will bring her joy, Charles, in seeing you pay for what you did to Sarah Jane!"

"It will bring her grief..." His voice was silenced as Bartleby struck him again, shoving him into the arms of the guard.

My eyes never left my father as he stood there, looking back at me. It was then that I could see he was saying good-bye, that he loved me and was proud and that every day he was out at sea, he wished he could have those days back so he would've been home to see me more than he did. I watched him, my eyes filling with tears, as Bartleby began to address his crew.

"Tonight, my brothers, we gather in honor of a woman who was once one of us!"

Thoughts entered my mind and I began to remember the most wonderful moments I had been given with my father. *Christmas Day in Williamsburg, sitting by the fire as the snow fell outside and Mrs. Lewisham burnt the holiday ham. He was holding my mother's picture and telling me stories of her.*

Bartleby's voice boomed louder. "Tonight justice is served! This coward, this wretch, will pay for his crimes!"

It was summer in Port Royal and my father was being honored by his captain. "Not a passenger lost!" they said as they recounted the tale of a poor passenger ship attacked by pirates that was rescued by my father and his crew. "Never has the kingdom seen such bravery!"

"You knew him as the Nameless Navigator," Bartleby said with a sneer as he faced my father. "But I say he is simply a man who has been beaten! Charles Wellington, the forgotten failure!"

It was evening in Nassau and he was to leave in the morning for a patrol of the island. His bag of maps and instruments were hidden under my pillow, and as he searched for them and found them in my room, he didn't scold me for trying to keep him home a day longer. Instead he hugged me tight and kissed the top of my head, saying no matter how far away we were from each other, we'd always be together in our hearts.

"I sentence you to die by hanging!"

Bartleby's words cut the memories like scissors to string, and the world seemed to slow as I realized the next moments were to be the last I'd ever have with him.

My heart whispered *faith*, but how could I have it when it was failing me right before my eyes? I prayed desperately for the Lord to give me and my father strength. Now, more than ever, we needed a miracle.

A drummer began to roll a beat on his snare and the guard took the rope, handing it to Bartleby. As the last note was played, Bartleby held the rope up, but before he could do anything a strange sound was heard.

It was the sound of laughter. Pure, somewhat stifled, laughter.

Where it came from, I didn't know, but Bartleby became perturbed as he lowered the rope and turned around to see who it was that was disturbing his "justice". I looked around too, curious as to who would laugh at such a hideous event, and to my surprise it came from a fellow prisoner: Patty.

Even Reuben looked at his mother with a quizzical brow. Had she gone mad? Surely laughing at a hanging was not part of Plan 47. If it was, then we were doomed.

"Do you find something amusing, Mrs. Peterson?" Bartleby asked as he approached her, the rope still in his hands.

At first she shook her head no, but after a snort and a purse of her lips, she suddenly burst into giggles again. It was a strange sight to see, and I overheard one of the sailors mutter behind me, "See? This is why women don't make good pirates. Can't take anything seriously, can they?"

Bartleby lifted Patty's chin up to face him and she continued to snort and stifle her laughs as she stared at him. "What's so funny?"

"Well..." she began, going into another fit of laughter. "If you really want me to be honest, I think you're not the brightest candle in the chandelier."

Bartleby lowered his brow. "I don't follow."

"Exactly!" Patty burst into laughter once more.

Bartleby gave a growl as he threw the rope onto the floor and grabbed her by the shirt, pulling her forward. "Is this madness, Mrs. Peterson, or are you playing at something?"

"Neither," Patty answered as she gave a quick glance to the sea before turning back to the admiral. Her grin widened even further. "I just can't believe how well this is all going. Really, Rudiger – you could have done everything I wanted you to do, and it still wouldn't have gone this well!"

By now Bartleby's anger turned to fury, and his face reddened. "Shut up with your fancies, woman, and tell me what it is you're going on about!"

Patty's laughing stopped and she grinned. "You're about to lose your fleet."

"And why is that?"

"Because I'm a clever girl." She pressed her lips together and leaned forward, nearly whispering in his ear. "If you listen carefully, you can hear the destruction coming."

Bartleby beaded his eyes as Patty backed away. "I suggest you be working on a surrender, Admiral. I'd be much more merciful than the Royal Navy after they're alerted to your position when your ships burn."

The sailors began to mutter about, asking, "What's she saying? She makes no sense, that one!" until Bartleby held up his hand, demanding absolute quiet.

No one made a sound, but if you listened closely, the faint splashes of waves could be heard. But these weren't just any waves that were crashing onto Bartleby's anchored fleet. This was of something moving, and it was moving *fast*.

My eyes widened as Bartleby suddenly turned towards the railing of the deck, shouting at the top of his voice. "Lighting! Give me..."

Before he could finish, however, a giant ball of fire suddenly lit up the seas.

I strained to get a glimpse of it, but after a few pushes and shoves from a now panicked crew, I finally managed to see what had happened. The *Carolina Gust* was engulfed in flame, torn in the middle by another ship that had apparently rammed into it and exploded on impact. After beading my eyes, I managed to read what wording was left upon the other ship's hull. It said *The Smooching Sally*.

My eyes widened as I realized what had just happened. Patty's ship had returned to attack. Looking closely, I could see a few rowboats empty in the water as if they had been used, which I found odd, but that became the least of my concerns as I realized Patty had taken out one of Bartleby's ships! At first I was ecstatic, thinking it a brilliant move on Patty's part, but then I suddenly realized we were now left without a ride home and were truly stuck on Bartleby's fleet no matter what.

I don't know what madness Patty had in mind for Plan 47, but it was unique to say the least.

I watched as Bartleby began ordering his men to get on boats to rescue the crew from the *Gust* now hanging on debris in the water, calling out for pickup. Bartleby was about to turn to Patty, ready to demand what on earth was going on, but he had no time as canon fire was suddenly heard.

Revolution's Wrath was hit multiple times and the jolt from the impact threw me to the floor. I scrambled towards my father, who grabbed on to me, and I looked up as I watched the *Malina Serus* suddenly fire upon her commanding ship again.

It was then that I remembered Red and the others had been put on the *Gust* when they "surrendered" to Bartleby. They must've triggered some sort of signal to Hammy to ram the ship, and once they saw Hammy coming, they probably made their way to the *Serus*. Hammy and the crew that had been left behind on *The Sally* must have jumped ship before it ran into the *Gust*, rowing on the rowboats to the *Serus* and helping Red take over the ship!

"What devilry is this?" Bartleby demanded as he pulled out his cutlass. "Man the cannons! Cut the anchor if you can't get it up in time! Get us moving, *now!* Our own ship has betrayed us!"

In the midst of the commotion, I saw Patty, Reuben, and Bateau run towards us. "Time to go!" Patty hurried as she and Bateau helped my father stand. "We don't want to be on this ship when it sinks!"

I could only nod in agreement as I followed them towards the nearest rowing boat.

Chapter Twenty-Two:
Escape

The commotion around us was nearly overwhelming. Men ran here and there, some of the younger ones panicking and hurrying below deck to try and stop the leaks that now plagued the ship. Some of the sailors had seen that we were running away and they chased after us, but after a punch and a few kicks from Patty and a shove from Bateau, our chasers were forced to the ground. Patty took three pistols from them and my father took two. Reuben picked up a few stinkpots to throw (though Patty begged him not to use it unless he had to) while Bateau picked up a long knife, two pistols, and a cutlass.

"What's the plan, Captain?" Bateau asked, looking around.

"We get off this ship," Patty replied.

Reuben's eyes widened. "What about our maps?"

Patty let out a pained sigh. "There's no time to get them."

"But...all that hard work..."

I looked at Patty sadly, as did my father, and she shrugged. "It's not worth risking our lives. I don't know where Bartleby has them and we don't have the time to look. It's more important to survive."

"But..."

"No time, Reuben," Patty said, giving him a nudge forward. "I'll remake them later. For now, we need to move!"

Off we ran into the madness of the ship, Patty leading the charge as Reuben and I were left to help my father follow. By now the excitement of the battle kicked in and my father no longer needed to lean on anyone, and before Reuben and I could do anything further, we saw Bateau run on ahead and save Patty from being cut down by a blade from one of Bartleby's men.

Patty turned, surprised she had missed an attacker, and thanked him with a grin.

"Such a gentleman, Bateau!" She laughed as she turned back to the battle and parried a cutlass with her pistol. She knocked her attacker down with a swift kick and moved on. "It's nice to see one amidst all these crude and uncivilized men!"

"Well, you know how it is these days," Bateau chimed in as he swung his cutlass swiftly, disarming his opponent of a pistol. "Somebody has to keep chivalry alive."

"A knight in pirate armor if I've ever seen one."

The comment made Bateau give a smirk, but I could've sworn I heard my father grumble under his breath as he raised his pistol, taking aim and firing.

To all of our surprise, one of Bartleby's men had gotten back up and nearly struck Patty with a knife, but thanks to my father, the man would be back on the floor again.

Patty and Bateau both looked to my father and blinked.

"You missed one," my father muttered with a weak chuckle.

Patty could only shake her head and smile back.

We fought our way through the deck, our aim being the back end of the ship where a small rowboat stood perched and ready to be taken. "It was designated as an escape craft for the admiral," Bateau had said as he led us through a mess of railings and ropes that gave us a shortcut to the rowboat. "We can get on it and escape in the darkness."

"Sounds like a plan," Patty replied.

"But where will we go then?" Reuben asked. "I'd rather not be stranded in the ocean, thank you very much."

"We'll board the *Serus*."

"I thought the point was to *escape* Bartleby, Mama."

"We are," Patty said with a grin. "On his ship."

Before Reuben could answer, we heard the rush of more men coming towards us. Though the crew was busy manning the canons to fight off the *Gust's* attacks, Bartleby was not one to let us get away. Bateau turned around, brandishing his knife and cutlass, and called out to us. "Go on ahead! I'll cover the rear and catch up!"

I turned for a moment to watch Bateau run towards the group of men, and I thought for certain that would be the end of him.

He was a doctor and a deckhand, but not a soldier. What overcame him to risk his life for us?

But after seeing the skill he had with the sword, I began to doubt Bateau was in danger. Rather, it was the opposite – Bateau was dangerous!

I stopped in my tracks for a moment, as did Patty, as we watched Bateau face his enemies. I'd seen enough pirate fights over the last few days to know how brutal and dirty it could be. Typically there were lots of grunts, curses, bashes, and heavy hitting. But what Bateau did made it seem almost like a dance. He made no sound as he parried and poked and slashed, his feet moving in such a precise rhythm that it was like he'd practiced the fight before entering it. Even my father, who had been trained since he was younger, was not that graceful in his stance.

I wanted to watch more, but I felt my father's tug on my hand, pulling me away. Patty got a longer glimpse, but soon she followed as we rushed towards the boat.

A few of Bartleby's men in front charged towards us, and with Bateau covering behind, Patty rushed forward to clear our path with her pistols. She took out her men, but two others followed behind, and before anyone could blink, we heard a shout.

"Watch out, Mama!"

I soon saw a round stinkpot go flying through the air, and Patty was lucky to catch sight of it to get out of its way. It landed with a great and smelly *thud*, and soon the deck was full of the vilest smelling…whatever it was…that was inside of it. I won't deny my eyes were watering and even my father started to gag, but the thing must've done its job because our path was soon cleared as no one wanted to go near the smelly thing.

"And I thought Daddy's coat was bad!" I whined to Reuben as I pinched my nose. *"What was in that?"*

"I don't know, but whatever it was – I want to learn how to make it!" Reuben exclaimed happily.

Patty and my father could only shake their heads in horror as we hurried ahead.

The rowboat, high and perched by the back railing and just waiting for us to enter it, was in our sights. We ran as fast as we could towards it, and my father and Patty both took out the guards that were standing near. Before any of us could touch the edge to climb in, two shots were heard from behind.

Time seemed to slow in that instant as I saw my father suddenly crumple to the ground, clutching his left side. It was a grazed wound, that was for certain, but whatever energy he had from battle seemed to suddenly wane as he struggled to get back up, cringing in pain.

Patty was just about to turn and fight off the shooter when the second shot reached its target. The rope that held the rowboat in place suddenly broke, and our escape went crashing down towards the ocean.

I turned to see Bartleby lowering two of his pistols, the smoke still coming from them.

His eyes matched the fires that burned around us as canon fire continued to rock our surroundings. "Did you really think you'd escape me?" Bartleby asked, pulling out his cutlass. A group of men was behind him and they stepped forward to aid their admiral, but he held his hand out, ordering them to be still.

Patty scrambled to help my father to his feet, keeping her pistol aimed at our enemy. "And did you really think I wouldn't try?"

Bartleby laughed as he stopped in his tracks, Patty cocking the pistol and readying to fire. "Not another step," she said as she motioned for us all towards the edge of the railing. I got a peek of the ocean and saw that the rowboat was still in one piece, gently floating alongside us.

"There's no need for further violence," Bartleby said. "Leave the girl and her father here with me and you're free to go. You have my word."

"I know how much you honor your word, sir," Patty said as she beaded her eyes. "You promised to spare my husband and the town if he gave you the maps."

"Those were fake maps, Mrs. Peterson."

"And yet even when you thought they were real, that didn't stop you from attacking the town...from attacking Patrick."

I watched as my father turned pale, looking as if he was going to faint. The pain from his side and the wounds from the keelhaul were finally starting to be felt. Reuben looked pale as well, frightened over not being able to escape, and he inched closer to Patty for comfort. Bateau...

And that's when I blinked in confusion. Where was Bateau? Had we lost him in our flight to the rowboat?

I hadn't the time to think of it as I suddenly saw a change in Patty's face. She looked...angry...as if the self-control she had mastered was starting to weaken.

"Ah, so it still bothers you after all these years." Bartleby grinned, making Patty's face red in fury. "Is that what this little escapade has been? Taking out my fleet in order to avenge your husband's death?"

Patty's hand began to tremble as Bartleby took a step forward. "I'm not like you. I don't take vengeance."

Bartleby took another step. "Are you sure? Because I think you do. I mean, how else did you get Willy Whalebone's ship?"

Patty only frowned as she tightened her grip on the pistol. Bartleby stepped forward again, this time lifting his cutlass. "I said stay back!"

Bartleby smiled as he stood face to face with Patty. "No."

But before he could do anything else, something grabbed him from behind.

Bateau had taken out Bartleby's guards faster than I could blink and swiftly kicked the admiral off of his feet, swiping his pistol from his hand and throwing it off the ship. As Bartleby scrambled back up, cutlass in hand, Bateau parried with quick movements that mimicked something I had once imagined from reading a book on knights. Cutlass in his right hand and a long knife in his left, it was in no time at all before Bartleby's cutlass was on the ground and Bateau's knife was pointed at the admiral's throat.

Bartleby was held back as Bateau kept him close, the knife never leaving his neck.

"Sorry I'm late, Captain," Bateau said as he panted, not letting go of Bartleby as he squirmed. "There were a lot of pirates to take care of."

Patty breathed a sigh of relief as she lowered her pistol. She smiled and gave an out of breath laugh. "Thank you, Bateau. I'm glad you made it!"

"Of course," Bateau replied. "Now, if you don't mind, I recommend you not tarry as your escape craft is starting to float away."

Bartleby struggled, cursing Bateau's name, but after a point of his knife and a whisper that he should be silent, Bateau convinced the ornery admiral to remain quiet.

"Down the rope we go, Reuben," Patty began as Reuben climbed over the railing and dangled down. "We'll have to go into the water and swim to the boat. Do you think you can manage?"

"It's not like I have much of a choice," Reuben said with a sigh. "Bless it, I hate being a pirate. Why can't I be like other boys and have my biggest worry be school and impressing girls?"

"I'm a girl," I said as I followed him. "You can try to impress me."

"Yeah, but you don't count."

"And why not?"

"Because I've already impressed you!"

"And how do you know that?"

"Because I'm just that amazing, by golly."

I wanted to push him off the rope with my foot for that remark, but Bateau cleared his throat, urging us forward. "It won't be long before reinforcements arrive. I suggest you save your banter for when you're in the rowboat."

"Oh, fine!" I muttered, making my way down.

I could barely hear what my father and Patty were saying near the edge. "Can you make it down there, Charlie?"

Sweat beaded from my father's brow as he swallowed hard. "I...I think I can." He tried to stand but quickly fell back down.

"Here, hold on to me," Patty said as she put his arm around her shoulder. "We'll go down together."

"But...Captain, I can...cover for us..."

"That cover won't last long in the shape you're in."

My father said nothing as he held onto her.

"Come on, Bateau!" I heard Patty say as she lifted her pistol once more. "I'll cover for you. Make your way to the rowboat."

"With all due respect to you, Captain," Bateau began, his knife still to Bartleby, "I'm not coming with you."

Patty's brow rose. "Why not? Aren't you wanting to escape?"

Chapter Twenty-Two: Escape

"I'm a prisoner of Bartleby," Bateau replied. "And I'm bound for capture by the pirate brotherhood. My presence will only endanger you."

"Then why did you help us?"

"Because I wanted to."

"Then let me help you by bringing you aboard my ship!"

"There's no time to argue, Captain," Bateau said, his voice firm. My father began to moan and Patty held him up, still unwilling to leave without our aid.

"Bartleby will not spare you, Bateau."

"Oh, he will," Bateau said as he pulled Bartleby's head back, making him cringe. "He's not allowed to harm me until I reach Tortuga. I promise you, Captain, that I am in safer hands than what you would be."

He stepped forward, taking Bartleby with him. "Now go! Severn and his men are on their way! Leave while you can!"

I could hear shouts from the distance, and doubtless Bateau told the truth of Severn coming to Bartleby's rescue. Reuben dropped into the sea, scrambling towards the rowboat and dragging it back towards us and getting into it. Patty hesitated for a moment, but after another yell from Bateau, she complied, helping my father down the rope.

After getting on the boat, I watched as Patty and my father dropped onto it. "I'll come back and get you out, Bateau!" Patty's voice echoed in the night as we began to drift away, Reuben and Patty both rowing towards the *Malina Serus*.

"You have your priorities, Captain, and I have mine! Godspeed to you." It was the last words of Bateau I thought I'd ever hear, and as we rowed away into the darkness, holding on to my father as he fought with fainting, I saw Bateau lower his knife and cutlass away from Bartleby. Bartleby gave a swing of his fist, knocking our rescuer to the ground and ordering his men to disarm him. The admiral then turned to us, shouting into the air, "You will not escape me, Charles Wellington! I will find you again if I have to search for you all eternity!"

I held onto my father tightly as we rowed away in the darkness.

We soon approached our new ship, careful to stay clear of the canon fire and entering through the back. We were fortunate it was evening and dark out, for if it was daylight we would've been spotted and fired upon while in the water. I'll admit once we reached the *Serus*, however, we had to tread carefully as fires from both ships soon began to light up the sea. Shots were fired and Reuben and I had to finish rowing as Patty shot back. Even my father, barely conscious, lifted his pistol to shoot and defend us, though most of his shots missed.

When we made it to the ship, ladders were lowered and we were helped up onto the deck by Red and a dozen new crew members who figured helping Patty's men fight Bartleby was a better option than being a prisoner aboard their own ship.

"We haven't much time for an escape," Patty said as she saw Hammy approach, water dripping from him like he'd been taking a swim, too. "Continue firing the canons until we're out of range. We should be able to outrun Bartleby if the damage to his ship is adequate. Make towards the mainland." Red nodded and hurried away as Patty faced Hammy, embracing him.

"I admit this is a surprise," Hammy said with a grin.

"Because the plan of you repairing my ship and then crashing it into Bartleby's fleet actually worked?"

"No," Hammy said with a laugh. "Because my captain is a woman and I never knew it."

Patty's brow went up. "That won't be a problem now, will it Mr. Pye?"

"It'll take some getting used to, and I'm not sure all the men aboard are willing to go along with it after all of this," Hammy replied. "But if the pay is still good and the adventure continues, you could be a pink and purple zebra for all I care."

"Good to hear it, then!" Patty said as she turned to the crew. "Now let's get out of here, men! Hoist the sails and man the guns to make clear our escape!" She turned to my father. "And you, Charlie, need a doctor." She tugged Reuben towards her. "Take Mr. Wellington to the surgeon. You and Samantha stay together, alright?"

"Yes, Mama," Reuben replied, and he began to lead my father and I across the deck.

Explosions continued to rock the boat, and before we could take ten steps, my father collapsed onto the deck, too weak to move. I followed him down and noticed he had passed out, and I turned to Reuben in a panic.

"We need a surgeon or a doctor! Where are they?"

"I don't know," Reuben said as he helped me sit my father up. "It's so chaotic here and everyone's manning the cannons...besides, I've never been on this ship. I don't even know how to get below deck!"

"Well this is just brilliant! Now what do we do?"

"Panic?"

"What good would that do?"

"It was the only thing that came to mind!"

I moved my father's shoulder to rouse him. Surely he would help us while Patty commanded the ship. "Wake up, Daddy! Oh don't be unconscious just yet!"

The rousing must've worked because my father batted his eyes and squinted. "What happened?"

"We're on Bartleby's other ship," Reuben replied. "We need to get you to a surgeon. You don't by chance have the ability to stand and walk, do you? That'd make finding one a whole lot easier."

My father nodded, though I could tell he was struggling to hold onto consciousness. "Help me up," he muttered as he struggled to his feet, leaning on us both.

I looked out and noticed we were moving, but to my shock *Revolution's Wrath* was moving, too. Had the anchor been lifted by Bartleby? Even with his ship damaged, could he still move as fast?

But then I remembered our ship was damaged, too. Maybe our escape wasn't over yet, after all.

I looked to the sails and noticed there were holes in them. Patty was busy scurrying about, trying to get solid ones hoisted to catch the wind and make us go faster, but we wouldn't have time.

"Bartleby's going to catch us," I whispered as my eyes widened.

"What?" Reuben asked.

"We're not going fast enough. Bartleby's going to catch us!"

A canon shot came and we all ducked to miss being hit by it. A loud crash was heard, and I watched as the main mast holding our sails came crashing to the deck.

Whatever wind we could catch had suddenly been taken from us, and our speed nearly became a stop.

"Oh no...oh no..." I held onto my father tightly as the sudden realization hit me. We were going to be caught. We were going to be prisoners of Bartleby again!

But when *Revolution's Wrath* faced us, Bartleby's canons aimed and ready, I realized we weren't going to be taken prisoner again.

This was to be our final battle, and I never dreaded adventure more.

The next moments were like something from a dream. Time seemed to stand still as everything happened around us, and in the midst of the chaos, all I could do was watch.

Canons fired at a steady rhythm and lit up the night sky with flame. Sometimes the rushing of water against the ship echoed in our ears, but for the most part it was the constant *booms* that thundered in the darkness. It was like watching a storm over the sea – the clap of thunder, the flash of lightning – and each time it struck, it was followed by noise of a different kind. Yells. Shouts. Screams. Curses. What the voices said, I didn't know, but the cry of battle is one that is both haunting and life-changing at the same time.

I stayed with my father as I watched the action unfold. To the corner was a fight between Patty's men and a few of Bartleby's that had come up from deck, missed by Red and Hammy when the ship was first taken over. To the left were deckhands busy trying to keep the ship steady and in one piece as it battled one of the biggest ships in the Atlantic. To my front was Patty, giving out orders and firing pistols to Bartleby's ship as we desperately tried to get away. But despite our speed, our ship had taken damage, and when facing a giant like *Revolution's Wrath*, speed can only be so much of an advantage after most of the sails and ship have been torn apart.

I don't know how long Patty fought, but dawn began to approach and it seemed like an age before a huge chunk of the *Serus'* side had been blown off, putting the battle at a pause. Hammy said something about "nearly sinking", and after the

Wrath faced us side to side, it finally dawned on Patty that we were outgunned.

Rather than risk being sunk and losing everyone, Patty ordered a cease-fire and the white flag of surrender raised. Bartleby's ship was too big, his cannons too many for us to have a chance in defeating him head on. Our ship was too damaged to take any more, and whatever hits it could take had been absorbed during our initial escape.

I stood on the deck, holding onto my father as we faced Bartleby and his crew. The pirate admiral gave us a glare before turning to Patty, who came near us and grabbed hold of Reuben.

"You, Samantha, and Mr. Wellington make for the boats. Row away to safety. The Royal Navy should be here soon after seeing the fires," Patty ordered.

"But Mama," Reuben whispered back. "Bartleby'll shoot us before we can get off the ship!"

Patty gave a gulp, realizing he was right. Bartleby cackled as she turned back to face him, and he yelled out to her. "Any last minute escape is reckless, Mrs. Peterson. I'll shoot anything that tries to move away."

Patty took Reuben's hand in hers and faced Bartleby. "What do you want, then, Rudiger? You have us."

"I only want the girl back on board. The rest can stay and await the end."

My fury and courage surfaced as I stepped forward, still holding onto my father. "I'll never join your crew, Bartleby! I'm staying here with my daddy where I belong!"

Bartleby sneered as he shook his head. "I do not wish to harm you, girl."

My father squeezed my hand gently. "Samantha, maybe you should..."

"*No.*" My voice was firm and I frowned. "I'm not going anywhere, Daddy, and you can't make me!"

Normally my father would have scolded me for not obeying, but either he was too tired and weak to object or he was certain Bartleby wouldn't keep me safe like he promised.

"Do your worst, you wretched beast! I don't fear you anymore!" My shouts only angered Bartleby further, and he clenched his fists.

"You want to join them in the depths? So be it!" He turned to Severn. "Aim the cannons!"

Patty stepped forward, holding her hand out. "Let us talk terms! There is no need for..."

"There are no terms with me, Mrs. Peterson!" Bartleby shouted. I looked and saw that Bateau was sitting on the deck, being guarded by two other men. He watched us with pity and a sorrowful look as if he wished he could do more to help us.

"Ready the cannons!"

The cannons were aimed and I could hear the fires aching to be released.

"Rudiger, please, no!" Patty's yells were to no avail as Bartleby lifted his cutlass.

"Take your aim!"

My father took hold of me and held me close. I could feel him shiver and he turned me to face him. "Don't look, darling."

"Mama..." Reuben's voice startled me and my heart started to race as I heard Patty respond. "Oh Reuben..."

But before the cannons could fire a great rumbling...a moaning from the depths of the sea...interrupted any battle that was to arrive.

Bartleby held his cutlass still as a crash was heard. We all turned to the east where the remains of *The Sally* and the *Carolina Gust* burned into the night. Whatever was left of *The Sally* was suddenly slammed into the sea, and the pieces of it rained back onto the water.

The great bellowing voice that followed it suddenly became louder, and my heart lifted up in hope.

I knew that sound, and never had I been happier to hear it.

"Jonah's whale..." Reuben whispered in awe.

I could hear a few of Bartleby's men begin to panic. "What is that thing?"

"It's a monster!"

"Shoot it! It's heading right for us!"

Bartleby ordered a few of the cannons to be aimed at the creature, to destroy it before it reached us. The weapons were fired and the night sky lit up once more, and after some great splashes and crashes upon the water, the bellowing of Jonah's whale suddenly went quiet.

Chapter Twenty-Two: Escape

We all watched in silence, the only sound we could hear being the thumping of our hearts beat against our chests. At first I wondered if the whale had been destroyed by Bartleby, but after a few seconds of utter silence the most terrible roar I'd ever heard suddenly came from the depths.

That was when I saw it. Gray and terrible with teeth like a shark's, springing from the water and ramming itself to the middle of Bartleby's ship. All the men were knocked over, many of them into the sea, and Bartleby ordered all cannons to fire upon the creature.

The area was lit up as if it were day, the roars of the sea creature and the battle cries of the men drowning out any other noise that came our way. All we could do was watch the chaos at first, and after a moment, Patty ordered us to slowly back away from the creature lest it attack us as well.

Bartleby saw that we started to move away and he shouted as loud as he could amidst the battle. "No! You won't escape me! You can't! I WILL HAVE MY VENGEANCE!"

Patty never left his gaze, nor did my father as he wobbled to her side. "Continue our course," Patty ordered. "Put a perimeter around us and do not antagonize the creature!"

I stood by my father and the others, watching as Bartleby's ship was rammed once more. The ship overturned and whoever was left on deck was suddenly thrown into the sea. I watched as I saw Bateau get hurled amongst some of the debris into the water, and I screamed his name, pointing to Patty where he was. I searched for him but the darkness blinded me, and as I looked, I noticed Bartleby clinging upon the rail of his ship.

The ship was rammed one final time, and whatever was left of it suddenly fell to pieces and crumbled into the sea. I couldn't tell what happened to Bartleby, but where he and others fell, the whale followed, and I never saw them again.

It was a minute before we realized the whale had finally gone. We looked over the railing and saw many of Bartleby's crew swimming amongst the debris, and Patty ordered an immediate rescue.

"Get them out of the water! If they give you a fight, put them in the prison cells. If they're injured, treat them as best you can! Once everyone's aboard, we embark for the mainland!"

I watched as Patty went to work, hoping and praying she would find Bateau, but all thoughts disappeared when my father collapsed once more.

Chapter Twenty-Three:
A Commission from a Fellow
Captain

The sunlight shined into the room and I watched as my father stirred from sleep. He turned his head, giving a soft groan as if wanting to rest a few minutes more, but after the light from the window hit his eyes, he lifted his hand and rubbed them open, taking a moment to look about the room.

"Where am I?" he asked weakly. He tried to lift himself out of the bed only to find dizziness overwhelm him and send him crashing back down onto the pillow.

I leaned forward as I remained by his side, watching as Ralph the parrot flew overhead and landed on the headboard of the bed.

The parrot leaned forward and faced my father. "Don't follow the light! Don't follow the light!"

"Bother it all…" my father muttered as he closed his eyes again. "I've died, haven't I?"

Ralph leaned closer, giving a flap of his wings. *"Bienvenue à Louis's Trading Post!"*

My father opened his eyes, squinting. "Lord help me, I've gone to the other place…"

"Not quite," I answered with a giggle as I shooed Ralph away. Franky wobbled onto the bed as I stood to my feet, facing my father. His eyes met mine and we both smiled. "You are at Louis's, though, and Patty was able to talk him into letting you sleep on a bed instead of the couch this time!"

My father rubbed his brow and made a second attempt at sitting up. He was successful that time as he rested his head against the wall. "I don't understand. Last I remember, we were on the ship and that whale showed up."

"You sort of fainted after that. You've been in and out of consciousness since then."

"And how long has that been?"

"About three days."

My father let out a slow exhale as he shut his eyes once more. "I feel terrible I've missed so much," he began, but suddenly he opened his eyes and looked at me with fear. "But wait! Bartleby...he'll know we're here. We should leave...we need to..."

"You can't go anywhere yet," I added, calming him. "Captain Patty says the ship's not repaired yet. Besides, she's still got to rename it and all. And Bateau will not be happy knowing his patient isn't following the doctor's orders!"

My father blinked in confusion. "I don't understand."

I gave a grin as I sat beside him on the bed, recounting the tale. "Well, after you blacked out, there wasn't much else to do but get you some help. I stayed with you as Reuben went to find the surgeon, but after a while we learned the poor surgeon got hurt during the battle, too, so he couldn't help. We thought for sure you weren't going to make it, but then a miracle happened!"

"And what was it?"

"Bateau."

"I thought he went down with Bartleby's ship."

"Oh he did," I added. "But he survived it, along with a few others of his crew. And would you believe we found Franky floating on a crate? Apparently the poor thing got out of my pocket while we were escaping and I didn't know it. I swear, that little hamster is the biggest survivor I know! Anyways, Patty picked Bateau up from the water and as soon as he was aboard, he went to work getting that bullet out of your leg and patching you back up."

"But what of Severn? Bartleby? Did Patty find them?"

I shrugged. "Yes and no. We fished Severn out towards the end of our search, and he went straight to the prison cells. Louis and Ines turned him and a few others to the local authorities, claiming they were the pirates who raided the town a week ago.

I'm not sure where Severn is now. As for Bartleby, we never did find him. Either he's lost at sea or the whale got him for good."

My father breathed a sigh of relief as he put his hand upon mine. "So…we're safe, I take it?"

"Very," I said. "Well…we are. Poor Patty's been in trouble ever since we arrived."

"What for?" My father lowered his brow in concern. "If the navy has arrested her for piracy, then let me out of this bed! I will not waste a moment in getting her freed!"

I couldn't help but smile at my father's sudden chivalrous manner towards her. A few weeks ago, he thought her the scum of the seas, and now he was willing to fight his own livelihood to make sure she was safe. It was funny how an adventure changed things. "Relax. She's not in trouble with them. She's in trouble with Louis."

"She left that terrible parrot when Bartleby arrived!" I turned to find Louis at the door, his arms crossed and mustache flaring. "Never have I lost so much sleep in my life!"

The parrot squawked as Patty walked in, smirking. "*Él es muy guapo! Él es muy guapo!*"

"You're going to be *ma nourriture* if you don't shut your beak, you pestering animal!" Louis muttered.

Patty snickered under her hand as Louis rolled his eyes. "When you leave, you take that terrible thing with you. I hated it before and I hate it even more now! Ines won't quiet about wanting one!" Louis turned to my father and pointed his finger at him. "And you, Englishman! Now that you're alert, I can have my bed back! You get the couch tonight."

My father shrugged in agreement, watching Louis storm out of the room.

His eyes met Patty's as she approached the bed. "Glad to see you better. You had us worried for a bit, you know."

"I hear you found a doctor at sea," my father answered.

"I did, and he's now running a mini hospital right at the post. We had some other injuries, but I think they'll all recover."

My father smiled. "I'm glad to hear it."

"Me, too." Patty grinned back. "How are you feeling now, though?"

"Dizzy, hungry, and more than a little sore," my father replied. "But I think that will remedy itself in time."

"The dizziness and pain will ease up soon and I can get you some lunch to help with the hunger. The only thing I can't help you with, though, are some of the scars you're going to get from the bullet removal and those cuts from the keelhaul. Nothing I can do about that."

My father chuckled. "Those don't matter. They'll just make me look tough and impress the ladies."

He gave her a look that she matched, and I saw her snicker as she looked away. "Well, you'll certainly have enough to impress them with. For now, though, stay in bed and rest. I'll have Bateau come in and check the stitches and make sure the infection stays away. I'll have Ines make you some lunch, too."

"Thank you," my father said, and as Patty turned to leave, he called out once more. "And Captain?"

She nodded, facing him.

"Thank you for keeping your promise."

She smiled as she stood at the doorway. "Any time, Charlie. You know I always will."

We stayed at Louis's for a few more weeks as my father recovered and the ship was repaired. We heard no news of Bartleby ever being found, and we assumed him taken by the whale. We were now free to live our lives in peace, and we celebrated our victory with a great feast given by Ines and Louis on the beach.

As we readied to sail once more, Patty gathered all of her crew (along with Bartleby's former crew who had been helpful to her) and offered them all a choice – continue to sail with her aboard the newly christened *Belching Bertha* (formerly the *Malina Serus*), or make a new life for themselves in whichever way they chose. Many of Bartleby's men chose freedom as they wanted to leave their life at sea, and the two Spaniards we had witnessed be kidnapped at Francisco's Tavern went happily back home where they hoped to never see another boat again.

Some of Bartleby's new crew decided to stay with Patty and help her with remaking the maps that had been lost at sea with

Chapter Twenty-Three: A Commission from a Fellow Captain

Bartleby. I was happy to see that one of the men who stayed was Bateau, and he offered his services of medical expertise to Patty and volunteered to be a surgeon aboard the ship. She accepted without protest, and Bateau took his medical belongings aboard immediately.

Patty then turned to her own crew, a crew she had known and sailed with for years but had also deceived into thinking she was a man. Though she hoped all would stay, some thought it unheard of to sail with a woman as their captain, and they left Patty's service, seeking employment on other ships. I was sad to see that Red was among them, and though he admitted Patty was a smart woman and could certainly hold her own in battle, he didn't think she was as good as a man could be, so he left.

She didn't say anything in protest, but I could tell it bothered her. When she was a man, people thought her invincible, but when she was a woman, people questioned her simply because of being a girl. And though she was the first to admit it was the grace of Almighty God and the arrival of the whale that saved us from Bartleby, it was her cunning, and because she trained her crew so well, that two of Bartleby's three ships were taken out.

Some had left, yet many refused to leave, including Hammy, who was happy to volunteer himself again as the ship's head carpenter. Though some of the men found it awkward serving under a woman (whom many had become smitten with), they realized it was leadership and loyalty that mattered in a captain, and whether it be a man or woman, if he or she could get the job done, they would follow.

Of course, Reuben didn't have a say in the matter. Though he admitted he wasn't fond of life at sea, he loved his mother and was determined to make sure she "stayed safe, because someone had to see that order remained and no other blasted pirate would ever be mean to her again."

And so that left my father and I. As much as I hoped my father would forsake his duty with the Royal Navy and sail with Patty, I knew he couldn't. Boston was expecting us and I had to let Mr. and Mrs. Lewisham know that I hadn't perished when I fell overboard during the storm.

We boarded the *Bertha* and set sail for Boston, our adventure finally coming to an end.

"Look at the water, Sam."

I stepped over the railing and peeked overboard, my father keeping his hand around me and making sure I didn't fall. I frowned as I looked upon it and let out a sigh. "It's not as clear as it was back in Nassau," I said quietly.

A breeze blew by and I shivered. My father removed his coat (*not* his Royal Navy one, which was probably floating somewhere in the Atlantic and still smelling like seaweed and fish), and put it upon my shoulders. "The weather is cooler in Boston and it'll take some getting used to, but I think you'll like it here. It's a very lively city and there'll be much to do."

"Aye, there will be." I pouted as my eyes looked out into the distance, the buildings of the city and its port coming into view.

Patty had lowered the pirate flag and rose the British one to make sure no one thought we were docking on the bay to raid. I admit my spirit had sunk within me because I knew Boston was the end of my adventure. The end of my sailing with pirates, the end of my seeing new places and experiencing new things.

But most importantly, it felt like I was losing a part of my family all over again. Though my father was still with me, he would return to his duties with the navy and be put on patrol. I would have to go back to my governess, back to lessons and embroidery and all kinds of boring things. But worst of all, I wouldn't see Patty or Reuben anymore. They would return to the Caribbean to remake the maps they had lost, and I couldn't go back with them and help.

My father left to help lower the anchor and dock. Reuben approached me, wringing his hands together and looking towards the ground.

"We're here," he said quietly.

"I know," I answered.

"Sorry we got you here late." He made an attempt at a laugh, but it quickly turned to a frown and he cleared his throat.

I watched as the dock workers busied themselves at the port. The city was so busy, so full of life. All I could think of was how much I wanted to explore it with Reuben and Patty!

"So…there's something I wanted you to have." I looked to Reuben as he held out his hand, setting something furry and familiar into mine.

"Franky?" I asked, surprised. The little hamster nuzzled his nose warmly against my palm. "Oh Reuben, I can't take your hamster! He'll miss you too much!"

"It's alright," Reuben said. "You're the only one he doesn't bite, and besides…Mama said she wanted you to have him, too."

I gathered Franky to my lips and kissed his furry little head. "Oh thank you, Reuben! I'll make sure he doesn't get into any trouble."

Reuben grinned sheepishly, looking away towards the city.

A moment of silence passed as we stood there, watching and waiting for the ship to dock. "I have to admit," Reuben said with a sigh, "that things'll be awfully boring here without you."

"If I had my choice, I'd stay with you instead of leaving," I admitted.

"I know," Reuben replied. "It figures your father would have to be employed by the crown. Bless it, the king's already got enough people under his employment. You think it wouldn't be a big deal letting a sailor go."

"With him being an officer, it's easier said than done."

"Well, promote someone to take his place so you two can stay, you know? It's not like the solution isn't simple."

I smiled as I rubbed Franky's ears. "You know, you and Patty could stay here. Map the Boston Harbor and Massachusetts Bay. Maybe parts of New York and Maine, too."

"With winter coming, it'll be difficult to get around. Mama likes to stay south so the ship doesn't get stuck in ice," Reuben said. "Besides, we're still *technically* pirates. The Royal Navy might get suspicious with a ship like ours sailing around the ports and taking notes."

I conceded defeat, knowing Reuben to be right. No matter what, we had to be separated. No matter what, we'd probably never see each other again after today.

We stood there in silence, unsure of how to comfort one another, before my father approached us both. "Time to get off," he told me sadly. "We're docked."

I nodded, following him away from the railing.

I thought that my father would lead me around the ship to say good-bye to the crew before we left. After all, I wanted to give Reuben and Patty one last hug and thank Bateau and Hammy for saving our lives. But as we approached the dock, my father ushered me off, turning to Patty before he followed me.

"You're sure you'll still be here when I get back?" he asked.

Patty nodded, perplexed as I was. "I'm not going to go back out to sea without restocking my supplies, Charlie."

"Good," he said, and he hurried off the boat.

I looked back to Patty and Reuben, giving a wave before I was ushered down the docks. "Oh Daddy, how can you be so cruel?" I asked, tears filling my eyes. "After all Patty's done for us...we can't just leave without saying good-bye."

"We're not saying good-bye yet, Sam."

"But..."

"Hugs and handshakes are all fine ways of saying thank you, but I have an idea that Patty might enjoy more."

I blinked, confused as to what he was getting at. "I don't understand. Are you saying you're going to get Patty a surprise?"

He smirked. "Something like that." And off he went to the nearest Royal Navy officer.

The rest of the day was filled with oddities and strange reunions. My father met with Admiral Wilmar, his commanding officer who had transferred him to Boston, and told him the tale of how he and I were rescued from the sea by a Captain Patty, who eventually was captured by Rudiger Bartleby, and how we escaped and defeated one of the most wanted pirates in America. Wilmar was taken aback, I could tell, and at first he didn't believe Bartleby was truly gone until my father swore it was the truth.

"This Captain Patty should be commended, whoever he is," Wilmar replied with his typical gruff voice. "Anyone with the bravery to face Rudiger Bartleby should at least get a dinner in his honor! Tell me - how does a simple merchant know so much of battle and strategy? Was he once in the navy?"

My father glanced at me, giving me a look that told me he wasn't willing to reveal who Patty really was quite yet. "The captain is a cartographer in the creating of seafaring maps.

Though the majority of the captain's work was destroyed when it was captured by Bartleby and went down with the ship, I can vouch first hand that the work is brilliant and would be a great asset to the Royal Navy."

Wilmar crossed his arms. "So what are you suggesting?"

"I'd like to request a commission to employ Captain Patty by the crown for the mapping and exploration of the American coastlines and the Caribbean." My father paused, giving a nervous grin. "And I'd like to receive it today, if possible, as the captain is readying to leave Boston for the south to escape the coming winter."

Wilmar sighed as he rubbed his brow. "You ask a miracle of me, but anyone who has rescued my greatest sailor and his daughter deserves such a reward. And to take out Rudiger Bartleby!" He shook his head, unwilling to believe it. "I'm astounded to say the least. I should like to meet this hero of yours, Charles, and offer him a commission as a captain in my fleet!"

My father gave a nervous grin as he wrung his hands. "Let us offer a commission for exploration first, and then we can present it to the captain together."

"Very well, Charles," Wilmar replied. "I shall get the paperwork and meet you at the governor's office. Bring the captain with you so we can all have a chat."

"Thank you, Admiral," my father replied, and we left the docks to return to Captain Patty.

"That was fast...whatever it was you did." Patty welcomed us back aboard and I grinned. What my father had asked the admiral for really was the best gift he could give Patty. Freedom to sail the seas not as a pirate, but as an explorer and privateer under the protection of the government. There would be no more hiding or constantly running to avoid the hangman's noose.

I couldn't help but let my excitement show and Patty gave a smirk as she looked at me and back at my father. "What are you two up to?" she asked.

My father could only grin back and shrug. "You'll see. First, though, I was wondering if you'd like to take a walk through town. Reuben can come along, of course, to keep Samantha company."

"If it gets me off this boat, I'm up for it," Reuben replied as he headed towards the dock. "I've got a hankering for real food, anyways."

Patty relented and followed us off the boat and onto the docks.

"So where are we going?" she asked as we walked, a few of the townspeople staring, either at the sight of a woman and girl wearing pants or because two inhabitants thought to be dead were suddenly walking about the streets alive and well.

"The governor's office."

My father's words made Patty stop, her eyes widening. Even Reuben looked at him, almost scared. "We're going *where*?"

"Relax; it's not what you think," my father reassured. "They know nothing of your connections to Whalebone and they only know you are a cartographer and explorer. As long as you don't say anything, it should be fine."

Patty pursed her lips and gave him an unbelieving look. "So what's the point of going to the governor's office?"

My father smirked. "It's a surprise."

Patty frowned as she slowly began to follow him again. "It's not made of rope, is it?"

"Oh please, Captain. Don't you trust me?"

She could only give a huff as she answered with, "Very funny, Charlie."

I could only snicker as I tugged Reuben by the arm and followed them.

We arrived at the office and there on the corner stood Admiral Wilmar, a sealed paper in his hands, looking about to see where we were at. When my father waved at him, he waved back and hurried to where we were. We were greeted and my father took the letter from the admiral's hands, and as Wilmar greeted us one by one, he stopped and gave a gasp as he saw Patty.

"Wait...you're a..." He paused, his face blushing as he continued to stutter. "Pardon me, Madam, but I thought I was meeting a captain out here and...if you don't mind me asking, why are you wearing pants?"

"This is Captain Patty, Admiral," my father said, holding tight to the commission letter.

"But…" He cleared his throat, leaning closer to my father's ear. "You never mentioned Patty was a woman!"

"Should it make a difference?"

"It always makes a difference!" Wilmar gave a fake smile to Patty as she smirked at him.

"She's the best out there. If you won't employ her, then I'll employ her myself. I take full responsibility for this decision, Admiral." My father gave a firm look to Wilmar, and I cheered inwardly for my father standing up for Patty. Wilmar gave a scowl and turned away, crossing his arms and pouting like a little child not getting his way.

My father ignored the admiral's tantrum and handed the paper to Patty. "Here. It's not much, but…it's something. And it should help you in your work."

Patty eyed the paper carefully and opened it, reading the contents as Reuben tried to peek across her arm. At first her eyes were beaded and she read it with a critical eye, but after a few moments her eyes widened and her mouth fell open in a gasp. She looked at my father and I with the biggest look of joy on her face that I'd ever seen.

"This is…this is…"

"A blasted piece of paper!" Reuben muttered. "But where's the food?"

Patty put her hand over her mouth, stifling a cry. My father could only grin widely as he said, "Welcome to the Royal Navy, Captain. Although I promise, we won't make you wear the uniform."

Instead of answering, she jumped up and wrapped her arms around him, hugging him tight.

I couldn't help but giggle as my father was taken aback, and now we were getting plenty of more stares as the townspeople were wondering why two people were displaying such affection in public. My father must have not minded, though, because after a few seconds of shock, he hugged her back, much to the dismay of the admiral who continuously cleared his throat.

"I've tried so hard to get one of these, Charlie..." Patty's voice was muffled against his shirt. "Even in South Carolina, I couldn't get one..."

"You...needn't worry...about it...now."

"I don't even know what to say! How can I ever thank you?"

"Some air...would be...nice..." My father patted Patty's shoulder, motioning for her to loosen her grip. She apologized and let him go, and they both nervously laughed.

"I hope you don't mind that you occasionally report here to Boston," my father said, breaking the awkward silence. "Though you are employed with the oversight of myself, technically you are also employed by Massachusetts Bay Colony. They may request you survey the northeastern coastal lines."

Patty gave him a playful smirk. "Trying to get me to visit, I see?"

"Well, Samantha and Reuben get along so well and..." I nudged my father, laughing. He was just as happy to have Patty come back as I was, if he was willing to admit it. "And I suppose I could...tolerate your company if you could tolerate mine."

He gave her a grin and she grinned back. "I suppose I can deal with you again," Patty said as she looked to me. "After all, Samantha needs some sanity in her life."

I could only laugh as the future never looked so bright.

It didn't take long for Patty's crew to resupply her ship, and after receiving her commission papers and orders, we followed her back to say our (temporary) good-bye. The sun was starting to set and I'll admit there were very many unhappy faces, and even though I knew Patty would eventually be back to turn in her maps, the thought of being away from her and Reuben over the winter still made me sad. I think my father was down as well, for he didn't smile, and as we said our good-byes to the crew, there were some tears shed and a few hugs given.

When we came to Bateau, my father shook the man's hand for a long time. "I owe you my life, Monsieur; not once, but twice. If there is ever a way I can repay you, please...let me know."

Bateau nodded in thanks. "Staying healthy and away from pirate prisons is a good way to start." He gave a laugh and my father smirked.

"I'll remember that. Farewell."

I gave Reuben a hug and he hugged me back, not wanting to let go. We had our differences, surely, but if there was one thing I could say about Reuben Gayle Peterson, it was that he was the best friend I ever had.

"I'll write you every day. Promise!" he said as we let each other go. "And I'll make sure Mama stays out of trouble. And I'll keep your cabin clean just in case you want to stay on the boat again. And I'll see if I can make Franky a coat so he'll stay warm during the winter. I hear Boston is dreadfully cold!"

"Thank you, Reuben," I said. "And I'll think of you every day and teach Franky some new tricks he can show you when we see each other again."

Reuben frowned as he crossed his arms. "That's it? Here I've been all heroic and protective of you and all I get are some thoughts and hamster tricks?"

I rolled my eyes and gave a chuckle. "Well what do you want me to do?"

"I don't know…something from you and not the hamster, at least." He gave a pout and I sighed, giving him a quick kiss on the cheek.

He was taken aback at first and stared at me with a dazed look as I faced him once more. I could hear Patty snicker beside me, and I waited for Reuben to say something…or at least blink. After complete silence and what I thought was a permanent daze on his face, however, I waved my hand in front of him and asked, "Reuben? Are you alright?"

"I…uhm…I'm quite fine, thank you…" he stuttered as his dazed look continued. "Yeah, that's something definitely better than hamster tricks…"

I could only roll my eyes as I made my way to Patty and my father went to Reuben, shaking his hand. Reuben could only stutter some more. "I promise, sir. She kissed me and I didn't kiss her, because I want to be a gentleman about it and all. I'll make sure I get your permission before I ask her to marry me."

My father and I both looked at him with surprise on our faces. Reuben gulped, rubbing the back of his neck as his face turned red. "I mean...uhm...I...uh...hope you enjoy Boston."

My father gave me a chuckle as I hugged Patty and she hugged me back tightly, saying she was awfully proud of my bravery and that I'd make a fine sailor just like my daddy.

"Or like you," I said with a smile. "I want to be just like you when I grow up! I want to sail around and make maps and help people."

"I think you'd do rather well at it," Patty replied as she let me go.

"I hope so," I said, my face suddenly becoming serious. "Will you come back soon, Patty? I'm going to miss you very much."

"Of course I'll be back." Patty smiled. "I promise. And you know I always keep my promises."

I smiled, giving her one last hug.

When my father made his way to Patty, I daresay there was some awkwardness at first. When they met, they were enemies. My father trusted her as much as he trusted Bartleby. But through time...and friendship...I think my father gained a kindred spirit. A girl version of himself, I suppose. And I could see Patty felt the same.

She first handed him a chocolate pie, which I happily held onto, and he thanked her for the kindness as we both knew that it was difficult for her to part with any chocolate.

"And I promise I'll do my job well," she continued as they faced each other.

"I don't doubt you will," he answered.

"You'll take care of yourself out here, alright? There's still pirates out there. And with what happened to Bartleby, I wouldn't be surprised if some of them become angry."

My father shrugged. "I'm sure if I need rescuing, you'll be there."

She smirked. "You can count on it."

He smiled back, putting out his hand for her to shake. "Safe travels, Captain. Until we meet again."

I expected her to shake his hand, but in her typical fashion, she ignored it and hugged him instead. There was no surprise this time, and he hugged her back, the sight of it warming my heart.

We left the ship and returned to the docks, watching as Patty sailed into the sunset. I admit I cried as I watched them leave, and my father held me close and remained quiet. When Patty's ship was out of sight, we found it best to return to the city and find the home my father had purchased before we left Nassau. We had a long day, and I admit I was wanting a warm dinner and a soft bed to sleep on.

We received a carriage from the admiral and made our way to the outskirts of the city where the home my father had purchased lay perched comfortably amidst the trees and plain. We were let off in the gardens so my father and I could stretch our legs and get used to being on land again, and as we walked up the walkway, I noticed a small monument in the front yard.

I squinted as I took a closer look at it, and to my surprise, our names were upon it!

IN MEMORIAM

CAPTAIN CHARLES FILLIMORE WELLINGTON
OF HIS MAJESTY'S ROYAL NAVY
B. November 23, 1717

AND

SAMANTHA JANE WELLINGTON,
HIS BELOVED DAUGHTER
B. April 22, 1739

PERISHED AT SEA
AUGUST 29, 1751

"Good heavens, Daddy! Look at this!" I said, pointing to the stone marker. "I think we missed our own funeral."

My father approached it and gave a chuckle. "It seems we have."

"And is your middle name really Fillimore?" I tried to not laugh, but I couldn't help it. It really was a name I wasn't expecting of him.

"It is," my father said, looking away. "It was my mother's maiden name. But forget about that. Let's get to the house and at least settle in for the night."

I agreed, still snickering as we approached the door.

"I wonder if it's locked? Should we knock?" I asked.

My father shrugged. "It shouldn't be inhabited. It's newly built and furnished, so it should be alright."

My father turned the doorknob and in we walked, the smell of dinner lingering through the hallway and making both of our tummies growl. "I wonder if the admiral had dinner ready for us?" I asked.

"I'm not sure," my father replied. We continued to walk further until we suddenly heard footsteps coming. We stopped, looking up as the figure faced us.

It was my governess, Mrs. Lewisham! And she apparently had her baby as she cradled it in her arms.

"Mrs. Lewisham!" I cried, opening my arms to run to her, but as I started, she gave a scream, running back into the dining room.

"GHOSTS! GEORGE, THERE'S GHOSTS IN HERE!"

My father and I stood there, somewhat frustrated, and we looked upon each other and huffed.

"Welcome home," he muttered with a roll of his eyes.

I could only shake my head and laugh.

Epilogue:
The Fugitive

P atty took a deep breath of the fresh sea air, exhaling it out slowly as she looked upon the open waters. Boston Harbor was out of sight and the Atlantic lay before her, the call of the Caribbean speaking her name. The crew busied themselves with keeping the sails going and things had returned to normal after the adventure that was the last few months. She couldn't help but admit she enjoyed the sailing more when her passengers were aboard, though. Captain Wellington could certainly be a pain, but she felt a connection with him she hadn't felt in a long time since Patrick died. And Samantha, well...she saw so much of herself in the little girl, and her cheerfulness was enough to make any bland day at sea fun.

But things had to go back to the way they were, and she had a job to do.

She gathered her new paper and quill and began the initial designs of what was to be a route down the coast of North America. She remembered much of it from memory, but she was going to retrace the route to check herself just in case. She began the initial designs at her desk, careful to make sure the rocking of the boat wouldn't squiggle her carefully measured lines. The door opened, however, interrupting her concentration, and she put the quill back into the ink bottle before a mistake could be made.

"I finished the inventory of herbs and medicines, Captain," Bateau said quietly as he remained near the door. Patty nodded, lifting her head and facing him. He'd been all business since the evening Bartleby's ship sunk, and for the most part she let him work. There were many injured, after all, including her own surgeon. Now that everyone was better and on the mend, though, Bateau had little to do but wait until someone needed him.

"Thank you, Bateau," Patty said. "If you could let me know when we run low on supplies, I'll make sure we get them restocked. I'd like to keep my crew nice and healthy."

"I will, Captain." Bateau gave a bow of his head. "If you don't need anything else, I'll be in my quarters."

He turned to leave, but Patty wasn't willing to let him go just yet. She knew there was more to Bateau than met the eye, and if there was anyone who could catch a secret, it was her. She had enough practice keeping her own to notice someone who was wanting to hide.

"Stay a moment, Bateau, and shut the door."

Bateau complied hesitantly as he looked to her in concern. "Is something wrong?"

"No. I just want to chat." She motioned for him to sit in the chair across from her. "Have a seat."

He obeyed, sitting down and facing her.

"Tell me what you're hiding, Bateau." Her request was blunt and to the point. If he was going to endanger her crew with whatever he was hiding, she wanted to be prepared to face it.

"I don't know what you mean, Captain."

"Many may think I'm a fool, Bateau, but I haven't survived this long being stupid. On Bartleby's ship you were a prisoner, yet he never truly beat you or tried to harm you. In fact, Bartleby spared you like he knew if he hurt you, it would come back to hurt him. That tells me you were an important prisoner, one that even Bartleby was afraid to touch."

Bateau looked away, frowning.

Patty wouldn't let up. "Where did Bartleby catch you from?"

"Another pirate ship where I worked."

"And what did he do with the other crew members?"

"I'm sure you could guess."

Guess, she could. She knew if a pirate could not use their captives, they were given to the sea. "Were you a surgeon on that ship, too?"

"No. I was a deckhand."

"So why did Bartleby spare you? A surgeon is useful, as they are very rare, but a deckhand can be acquired anywhere."

Bateau exhaled slowly, his face looking perturbed. Good. Let him get nervous around her. Maybe he would talk more. "Captain, I was taken by Bartleby because he knew I was strong and healthy. If you're implying..."

"I'm not implying anything," she interrupted, folding her hands and watching him. "The brotherhood was mentioned about you. Why was Bartleby taking you to them?"

"He thought they'd have a better use for me when he learned I was skilled in medicine."

"The brotherhood has many doctors, Bateau. Give me a different excuse."

He lowered his brow, becoming defensive. "It's not an excuse..."

"Here. Let me give you one that's a little better." Patty stood and walked towards him, eyeing him from above as she clasped her hands behind her back. "You're skilled with medicine and were able to save a man who not only was keelhauled but shot and suffered from the beginning stages of infection. Such knowledge shows you've gone to university and received an expensive education. But you also speak perfect English without the hint of an accent. This shows tutoring since childhood, a gift only rewarded to a select few. You're also quite skilled with the sword, and your forms show not that you are a man who's learned his fighting skills on the go like many pirates do. No, your form is precise and perfect, which shows many years of practice. Either your lessons were for ceremonial purposes or you once considered the military. Not the eldest son in the family, I take it?"

Bateau looked away, his face starting to sweat.

"I see we're getting somewhere," Patty continued, circling him. She lifted his chin and looked him up and down. "Not a scar or blemish on you, yet you claim you were a pirate. You mustn't have been one long with a lack of battle on you. A year, perhaps? Maybe even less?" She stopped as she noticed a necklace hiding down into his shirt. She bent forward and lifted it up, feeling the weight of pure gold in her hands. It was a locket, and she opened it as he watched her with sad eyes.

Two pictures painted on ivory were before her. On the left were seated three boys, clearly brothers, dressed in fanciful

French attire. On the right sat two young girls, sisters if she could guess, poised as mini queens.

"You wear a locket around your neck of five children. Clearly yours." He gently took the locket out of her hand and closed it back, returning it to his shirt. "And they are dear to you," she said quietly as she crossed her arms, leaning against her desk. "Tell me, Bateau. Why would a man such as yourself leave his five children in France to become a pirate? Did something happen to all of them?"

"No," he answered.

"Then why leave? Were you needing money?"

"No."

"Then you give me a strange puzzle, Bateau," Patty continued. "I would guess you were a man of adventure, and that is why you left, but your willingness to remain Bartleby's prisoner proves that theory wrong. You wanted to be delivered to the brotherhood, otherwise you wouldn't have risked your life to remain a prisoner aboard Bartleby's ship."

Bateau looked up with weak eyes, his face sunken and full of despair. "I promise you, Captain, that I mean your crew no harm..."

"You're harming them by keeping me in the dark, Bateau. If the brotherhood is going to be looking for you, I need to know why *now*."

She glared him down like a mother scolding a child, though he was her senior by at least five years. He gave a sigh, rubbing his brow. "I'm not a pirate, Captain. If you were in my place, you would do the same."

"Then tell me who you really are, Bateau," Patty replied. "And tell me why the brotherhood wants you prisoner."

Bateau gave a sigh as he lowered his head, beginning his story.

He could see her in his dreams.

Surrounded by light, illuminated by the beauty in her grace. Light brown hair, green eyes, and a fair complexion. Lips that were sweet to the touch and a voice that compared to Heaven itself.

Epilogue: The Fugitive

He could see her as the waters closed around him, death beckoning for him to succumb. And as the air was stifled and his body tensed for one final struggle before giving up, her name echoed in his mind.

Sarah Jane...my...Sarah Jane...

But as life inched away, he remembered the last time he saw her.

Sweat beading from her brow. Hair a mess and chest panting for air. Eyes widened in fear and voice pleading for something. Peace? A listening ear? Help? A shot was fired and suddenly the fear left her eyes and she crumbled to the ground.

The next thing he knew was that officer...that *beast*...catching her, clinging to her and crying out. His eyes were full of anger and fury, and he trembled as he put his hand to her face.

Her eyes stared ahead into nothing, life leaving her body and leaving *him* alone in this wretched, cruel world.

Sarah Jane...my...Sarah Jane...

All he could see was that officer holding the woman he loved and staring back at him with rage.

Anger surged within him as he remembered the past, remembered the reason that gave him a will to live and wake every morning with purpose. Charles Wellington, the man who stole Sarah Jane, the man who turned her against him.

Darkness surrounded Rudiger Bartleby as the hands of death pulled him down, but he refused to give up just yet. Justice had not been served. Sarah Jane had not been avenged.

He forced his eyes open and swore he would not pass into eternity without fulfilling his duty to her.

But as he looked around, he found he was no longer in the water. Instead he was in a bed, covered with fresh linen and bathed in sunlight from a window to the right. He blinked, the light too bright on his heavy eyes, and began to focus on the blur that was in front of him.

It wasn't long until he noticed the young man standing near the edge of the bed. He was dressed finely, but without the military uniform of an officer. Clearly a merchant...perhaps local...and easily swayed.

Bartleby swallowed before speaking. "What...happened?"

"I found you drifting in the water, my friend," the man began. "There was a great shipwreck and you were fortunate to survive! It looks as if you were in a great battle."

"We were attacked by pirates," Bartleby lied. "A great host of them. Were there any survivors besides me?"

"None that I know of, I'm sorry to say."

"That is a shame. I had hoped my first mate at least survived. He was very brave and loyal."

"I'm sorry," the man replied with a frown. "But thank the heavens you are alive, at least."

"Death will not claim me while I still have purpose," Bartleby said as he sat up. "Tell me...friend...where is this ship headed?"

"Nevis," the man replied. "But I can drop you off anywhere in the area if you'd like. It's the least I can do to help you get back on your feet."

"That would be good," Bartleby said, a smile coming upon his face. "I need to get to Tortuga."

To be continued in

"Captain Patty

and the

Boston Buccaneer"

About the Author

Erin Cruey first got the idea for the Captain Patty stories after dreaming of having dinner with a pirate who kept chocolate pies in his closet. She thought the dream was so entertaining that she put it into a book.

For the latest blog posts, news, and book releases, visit http://erincruey.com.